PRAISE FOR THE NOVEL OF B
MARJORIE

"This is a heart warming and a heart wrenching book. It deals with great insight into family dynamics. But more especially for me it deals wonderfully with the problems that have to be faced by the children of parents with inherited neurological diseases. It is in the "must read" category for everyone interested in neurological problems."

-Walter G. Bradley, DM, FRCP
Professor & Chairman, Department of Neurology,
University of Miami School of Medicine

"A Heartbreaking tale, When It Rains...captures the intense and incredible journey that only real life can deliver."
-The Key West Citizen

"When It Rains…is one of those rare books that is, at the same time, heart-wrenching and uplifting. Marjorie Spoto is a name you will hear a lot in the future."

-David Sloan, Author

"An Emotionally gripping story about confronting your biggest fears, and surviving against all odds. Three sisters, who haven't been a family since their mother passed away from Lou Gehrig's disease six years before, are together for Charlie's wedding. When Charlie leaves her fiancé at the altar, her two sisters think that they need to save her, but they all have their dysfunction. A couple unexpected twists tie the story together with a surprising ending. Absolutely loved this story!"
-Tuesday Night Book club

"Anyone who has ever dealt with a terminal illness and especially Lou Gehrig's disease can appreciate this emotional story. The sisters each deal with the death of their mother and the fear that they too will die from the disease in different ways. There were some surprising twists in the plot which I did not expect. Great story!"
-A Reader in Baltimore, Maryland

"When It Rains is a story about sisters and how a tragedy in life can mess up a relationship. This novel from first-time writer, Marjorie Spoto, not only told the story as if it was happening first hand, but she delved right into the minds of all the characters, telling a wonderful story about relationships and life. The novel reminds me of Steel Magnolias and Stepmom. The characters are real and the conclusion is rewarding. This is a feel-good story that will make you think."
-A Reader in Montreal, Canada

When It Rains...

A Novel

Marjorie Spoto

Published and printed in the United States of America by Weaver Books.

Weaver Books, Inc.

All rights reserved, including the right to reproduce this book or portions thereof in any form whatsoever. For information address Weaver Books, PO Box 6255, Key West, FL 33040.

ATTENTION SCHOOLS AND CORPORATIONS

This book is available at quantity discounts with bulk purchase for educational, business, or sales promotional use. For information write to: Weaver Productions - Special Sales, PO Box 6255, Key West, FL 33040 or email: info@whenitrains.com

For my sister, Candace, who selflessly put her life on hold to do the right thing.

For my husband, Bob, who had faith in me even when I lost mine.

For Kristen and Reno who both have twice the talent I do - I love you.

And for my mother, Christine, who saw her diamond in the rough and believed that it could shine.

ACKNOWLEDGEMENT

Without the love and support from the following people, this book would never have made it to completion. I thank you from the bottom of my heart.

My brother, Steven Weaver, for reading and editing the first draft of my novel and for listening to my dreams and never making me feel stupid for having them.

My sister, Candace Fedonczak, for giving me my hero.

Christiana Nelson for your guidance in keeping my story going in the right direction.

Dr. Walter Bradley DM, FRCP, Professor & Chairman, Department of Neurology, University of Miami School of Medicine, for guiding and editing my ALS storyline and keeping it real and current with modern technology. Also thank you for supporting my story.

David Sloan, for all your advice, Pam Montgomery, for pushing me to completion, and Ron Spoto for adding your caring touch to my project.

Arlene Spoto and Lucille Schror for reading the unedited final version. Andrea Quirk, for reading my book and making me complete it when I was about to give up. My editing team, Amanda Balasick, Jessica Wenzel, Robbie Hopcraft, Jennifer White, Julia Kenny and Mandy Bolen.

Reno, my son, for the times I said "uh huh" and "yes" when you asked me questions while I was writing. I know it was your big joke to come up with the most outlandish questions for me to say "yes" to. It was fun.

Kristen, my daughter and relentless teenager, for always asking me real questions while I was writing because you hoped I would say "yes".

And last, but never least, my husband, Bob, who would go to any room I was writing in just to be near me and fall asleep. Your snoring was music to my ears. If you had not been my rock, one (or both) of us would be crazy by now. I love you for holding me up when I was weak with exhaustion. Thank you for watching my back when my guard was down, but mostly thank you for being my biggest fan.

When It Rains…

Chapter 1

∧

A bride could not ask for a better wedding day. It was a typical New England June, pleasant and bright. The birds were chirping. The sky was clear and the ocean breeze was perfect. This day had the makings for the fairytale wedding every American girl dreams about.

A shiny stretch limousine glided down a shady tree-lined street heading away from the small beach house. It had just picked up a bride, her two sisters and the flower girl.

Inside the limousine the bridal party sat in silence. The only sound was the quiet hum of the tires on the pavement - the stillness contrary to what it should have been.

The bride, Charlie, dressed in a strapless Christian Dior, had her eyes affixed out the tinted window, staring at nothing as her thoughts ran rampant. Her long brown hair was swept up into a classic bun with wispy curls accentuating her heart-shaped face. Even without the shining face of a bride, Charlie was uniquely pretty.

Charlie tried desperately to blink away her thoughts. She glanced quickly at her sisters, making brief contact. They were watching her, waiting for her to say something. Her somber expression was infectious and the gloominess seemed overwhelming.

Charlie bit her thumbnail, but Catherine, her older sister and matron of honor, reached over and pulled her hand away.

"Your nervous habit is going to ruin a fresh nail job."

Charlie gave her a disapproving look. Both of her sisters were getting on her nerves, especially Catherine. If she wanted to bite her nails or dance a jig on top of the limousine naked, she would. The day had begun disastrously. What had she been thinking, suggesting that she and her sisters get ready together at her house before the wedding? The three of them had not been together since they were kids. Time had erased the memory of how they reacted to one another. Catherine with her rigorous schedule barking orders like a drill sergeant and Iris with a smart comeback for her every demand, Charlie was about to drop them both off at the next corner. Let them bicker without her as a witness.

Catherine smiled at her, "As soon as it's all over, you can chew away all your nails."

Charlie sighed and looked back out the window. She had forgotten about her nails.

"You look pale," Catherine determined after close examination. She reached for her purse and began rummaging for her blusher, found it and began swiping Charlie's cheeks.

"Please don't make me look like a hooker," Charlie leaned away from her.

"Why would I do that? You need to take a deep breath," Catherine said lunging toward her sister with the make up brush.

"Not too much," Charlie instructed with resignation. She knew it was useless to fight her.

"Trust me," Catherine said as she swept the brush across Charlie's face in a big artist's sweep, sucking in her own cheeks as if she were putting the make-up on herself.

Catherine leaned back to assess, squinting her eyes. She felt like something was amiss. "Are you feeling all right?"

Charlie nodded like an innocent child, although she was not really sure. She placed the palm of her hand to her forehead, but she felt cool and clammy, even though inside she felt like she was on fire.

"I feel a little chilly. Maybe we could turn off the air?"

Just then, a champagne cork popped, and ricocheted off the partition window causing them all to scream. The limo swerved and the driver lowered the window, "What was that?"

Iris, the youngest of the three sisters and the one holding the over-flowing bottle, answered, "Ooops! Sorry!" She shrugged, crinkling her nose at him. She began drinking from the bottle, the overflow bubbling down her face, some splashing onto her lavender bridesmaid dress.

"Iris, you're getting it on your dress!" Catherine balked, "Oh My God! You're drunk! I knew it!"

Iris blew air through her lips at Catherine and then reached for a champagne flute and poured herself a glass. "Anyone?" Catherine glared at her, but Iris paid no attention and continued helping herself.

Sitting perfectly still, just like her mother had instructed, was eight year old Christina, the spitting image of her mother, Catherine; long wavy blond hair, light complexion, big green eyes with long fluttering lashes. She began to giggle hysterically.

"She's not funny, Tina," Catherine scolded, but this only made Christina laugh harder. Iris joined in, making matters worse. Catherine glanced at Charlie, who seemed impervious and turned back to her daughter, "I'm going to tell your father."

Christina stopped laughing and sat upright. Her father would ground her - no computer and no television. Her life would be miserable. Her best friend went to her dad's house in California for the summer, so she would not be able to send her emails. Christina bit her cheeks until her mother looked away.

"Aunt Iris?" Christina leaned over and whispered. "What's wrong with Aunt Charlie? She doesn't seem too excited to be getting married."

"Oh, she's loony toons today. Watch this." Iris took her champagne glass and put it in Charlie's face. "Here, Chuck, this is what you really need. Loosen you right up!" Charlie took the glass and Iris grabbed the full bottle of champagne to toast Charlie's glass. "I propose that we just get wrecked!" Iris took a swig from the bottle and it fizzled down her chin and she wiped it off.

Catherine swiped the glass from Charlie, "No more for the bride," she said, looking for a place to set to set the glass, "and you..." pointing at Iris, "You've already had way too many."

Iris whispered to Christina, "Your mommy always could spoil a good time. You're gonna have a sorry teenage life, let me warn you now."

Christina frowned. "Shhhhh! She'll hear you."

"Honey, she's not the boss of me."

"Iris, if you ruin this day...," Catherine nagged, but stopped mid-sentence. Something was wrong. "Why are we stopping?" She questioned aloud, her eyes darting from window to window. She rapped on the limousine's partition window until it lowered.

"Why are we stopping?"

"Funeral procession," the driver said.

"Shit!" Catherine cringed, "We are going to be late. Tom's going to think we're standing him up."

"Why would Tom think that?" Iris asked and then belched loudly. "All grooms know the brides are late."

Catherine flared her nostrils and Iris took her cue to be quiet.

Charlie hit the automatic window. As it glided down she caught a glimpse of a black hearse pulling out from the funeral parlor across the street. A procession of sleek black limos, all with their headlights on, followed. All at once she felt the sorrow of all those people on her shoulders. It was an odd sensation, but somehow she could relate to how they must feel. It had been five years since her mother's death, but she could still feel the sadness as if had happened that morning. A pit formed in her stomach and she found herself swallowing the acrid taste of bile that crept up her throat.

It was her mother. Why did fate take her away so early in life? Why was she not here for her, as she had been at Catherine's wedding? It was not fair! Since her mom's death, she did not have any one. She had not seen her father since he walked out on them when she was ten years old, nor did she want to. He had hurt her mama and she did not want anything to do with him. She wondered if he even knew she had died.

Charlie grew hot with anger. Her mother should have been here. She remembered her mother at Catherine's wedding, sitting in the front pew, her head cocked sideways like she always did when she was happy; her crooked smile, her eyes filled with tears. She should be here to bless her marriage to Tom as well. Instead, there was Catherine. Catherine the Great. Catherine, who thought she was mom's replacement. Nobody could fill her mother's shoes.

Suddenly Charlie could not breathe. Everything inside the limo began to swirl. Sticking her head out the window was not working and it was becoming hard for her to hold consciousness. The air coming through the open window was not enough. She tried to shake away the black splotch that enveloped in her vision. She knew she had to get out. Flinging the door open, she practically fell out, struggling clumsily over her bulky dress. Once outside and doubled over, Charlie gulped mouthfuls of air. Passing out was not an option.

Catherine tumbled out of the limo after her sister. "Cup your hands over your mouth. You're hyperventilating!"

Charlie took her sisters advice and quickly the color came back to her vision. She stood upright, still breathing through cupped hands, her eyes darting from Catherine to the procession of cars from the funeral passing. She felt humiliated because they were all staring at her, so she forced herself to look away. Her mouth became thick, as if she tasted the tang of melancholy and it was almost too much for her to endure. It was her wedding day. Why could she not feel the bliss she was entitled to? Instead, she felt heartache like she had never felt.

"Mommy," Christina poked her head out of the limo. "Are we going to the church?"

"Get back inside, honey. Stay with Aunt Iris," Catherine nudged her daughter back inside then poked her head inside. "Iris, do you think you can stay sober? I could really use some help here."

Iris saluted, mocking her sisterly duties. Christina obediently returned to her seat next to Iris, but climbed on her knees so she could watch the action through the window.

The driver's window rolled down, "Everything alright?" he asked, too lazy to get out of the limousine.

Catherine snapped at him, her voice tight, on the verge of tears. "No, it's not alright! Does it look like everything's alright?" Catherine put her hands to her face, ashamed for her outburst, "I'm sorry. I didn't mean to take it out on you."

Catherine rubbed Charlie's back. Something was bothering Charlie and Catherine wondered if it had anything to do with the package her sister had gotten the night before. That would explain her bizarre behavior. Charlie had been acting strange all morning, and she knew it went deeper than pre-wedding jitters. Maybe it had something to do with Tom. Did he do something? Had he cheated on her at his bachelor party? She doubted that. She knew he was in love with Charlie. She wondered if her sister was having her own doubts. It was normal to have second thoughts. She had experienced doubts of her own when she and Steve had gotten married and she knew from the moment that had met that they were soul mates. Regardless, she knew Charlie would never tell her what was wrong. Charlie never divulged her feelings about anything. She vacuum-packed her emotions deep inside and only allowed people to see what she wanted them to see. Charlie was like a man when it came to her emotions.

As soon as her breathing was back to normal, Charlie dropped Catherine's hand. "I think I'm okay now."

Catherine stepped in closely, putting a loosened curl behind her ear. "You look beautiful," she smiled, "I know you're nervous, but it's natural."

Charlie smiled back at her older sister, hoping it did not look as forced as it felt. A pang of guilt shamed her. Her sister loved her and was only trying to help.

"It's gonna be alright," Charlie added, consolingly. "I'm fine."

Catherine helped Charlie back into the limousine. Before she stepped in, Charlie stopped and glanced back down the street, looking at the last few cars from the funeral procession.

"Charlie! Forget the funeral!" Catherine threw her hands in the air, and spoke to no one in particular. "This is ridiculous! Who schedules these things anyway?"

Charlie murmured, her voice whisper-soft and sad, "God does."

Chapter 2

Λ

Tom, the groom, dressed in a classic black tux, stood on the sidewalk in front of the Victorian church next to his brother and best man, Denny. Tom's curly black hair was cut short and his face was smooth. It was his day and he waved proudly as guests pulled into the church parking lot.

Denny pulled out a cigarette and lit it. He looked like a model, tall and slender, with disheveled yet stylish dark brown hair that was a little too long.

Tom fidgeted with his tie. He was nervous.

"You need a ciggy?" Denny asked, offering his lit one to his brother. Tom waved it away and then changed his mind. Unlike his brother he did not smoke, but for some reason he felt like he needed a jolt of nicotine.

"Where are they?" Tom finally asked, glancing at his watch then down the street. "Is that their limo?" He handed back the cigarette.

"Aren't you wearing your contacts?"

"Are you my mother?"

"I am when you keep asking to borrow my eyes."

"That coming from someone who doesn't wear a watch! Just tell me if that's their limo down the street. All I see is a white dot."

"It looks like a limo, but it can't be. That one's just sitting there."

"What?" Tom scrunched his eyes trying desperately to make them focus. "Then where are they?"

Steve, Catherine's husband, who resembled Clark Gable without the mustache, gave Tom a healthy wallop on the back. "Welcome to the family, Tom!"

"Yeah, if they get here."

Steve chuckled light-heartedly and then turned to Denny. "Lookin' sharp, Denny. You clean up well."

"Everyone keeps telling me that! Maybe I should dress up more often," Denny said as he playfully modeled his tuxedo.

A dumpy green Chevy van pulled up to the curb, windows down, music blaring over a grumbling tailpipe. The music suddenly muted, "Where should I park?" asked Ethan, the long-haired twenty-something who was also wearing a black tux.

"How 'bout four blocks that way," Denny pointed in the opposite direction.

"Funny!" Ethan exclaimed, deciding to find his own parking spot across the street. He climbed out and joined the group.

"Do you know Ethan?" Tom asked Steve. "He's the lead guitarist in Charlie's band."

"Yeah, I've seen you around. How's it going, Ethan?" They shook hands.

Tom looked at his watch again. "The wedding starts in fifteen minutes," Steve said, waving his hand, "There's plenty of time."

"Yeah, but Charlie's never late."

"Don't worry about it. These things never start on time," Steve said trying to sound confident although he was beginning to worry himself. His wife's biggest asset was promptness, and the delay made him wonder what was really going on.

The sound of high heels clicking on cement brought their attention to Leona as she headed toward them. All they could see was her sporty, jet-black hair bouncing behind the camera that was hiding her face. Leona was not only the wedding photographer, but Charlie's neighbor and best friend. What had started out as neighborly courtesy had evolved into a genuine friendship.

"Smile," she sang and the group pulled together for a shot.

"Leona, you look gorgeous as usual," Tom said, admiring her powder blue Jackie O suit.

"Thank you," she said, again lifting the camera to her eye. "A close up of the nervous groom." He smiled for her, and as she turned to Denny, he was already posing. "What a ham!" she chided as they took the role of model and fashion photographer. She and Denny had this *thing* between them. It was harmless. Nothing ever went past the flirtatious stage, but they had loved taunting each other. Neither one ever took it to the next level because they both got the same reward from their bond. His flirtation made her feel young and vivacious and she made him feel like a real man.

"Den-man! You should have become a model," Leona said to him and it was true. Denny had the look of a GQ model. Only thing with Denny, he never really had much ambition to do anything in life except chase women and he did that well.

Tom rolled his eyes. "Give me a friggin' break." He put his hand between the camera and Denny. "Enough shots of the egomaniac!"

Leona laughed and turned her camera on Tom. "No need to be jealous of your baby brother. You're a hot-ticket, too, but I'm afraid you're already taken." Leona patted his cheek when she put the camera back around her neck.

"Jealous? Of my non-committal, free-spirited brother? I think not."

"You do sound a bit resentful."

"I just don't like watching him waste his life."

"Am I invisible?" Denny asked, reminding Leona and Tom he was still present.

"No offense, bro," Tom said, teasing him.

"Oh, none taken," Denny stated, not upset in the least. He and his brother had many disagreements between them regarding what each other thought were appropriate life ethics.

Leona put the camera back to her eye and Tom stuck out his tongue.

"Okay. Get someone else now."

Leona turned to Steve. It was his turn to face the camera.

"Oh no, you don't," Steve said, holding his hand in front of the camera.

"Don't be a party pooper, Steve. Charlie wants shots of everyone."

"I just don't like photos."

"This coming from someone whose hobby is photography and is teaching his own daughter about that art. Hmm."

"It's all good as long as it's not me in front of the camera."

"With your looks? Come on," Leona said.

"Are you flirting with me? I'll have to tell my wife," Steve teased. "But, I don't think I have much of a say in it now, do I?"

"Smile, then," Leona said, taking his picture. "See, that wasn't so bad."

"Maybe a little. Anyway, you know I don't like photographing people. I like animals."

"Like Denny?" Tom threw that in.

"Ouch!" Denny said, momentarily wounded. "That's twice. What is it? Attack Denny day? You're lucky it's your wedding day."

Charlie had asked Steve to take the wedding photos, but he declined. Steve enjoyed taking photographs and did it well. But, there was a difference between nature and weddings. It was exciting snapping shots of a pack of Hyenas chasing down an antelope, but he could not bring himself to photograph the monotony of a wedding. He would never tell Charlie that. He just simply declined. An environmentalist, Steve had the opportunity to capture some of nature's beauty while on trips abroad. Steve was teaching Christina about flora and fauna through photography and she was learning so much. He had found his niche - teaching. He had never imagined having the patience for teaching and was amazed at the creative methods he had come up with. Before he was a parent, he never dreamed that he would home school his children; or even if he believed in it, but through their worldly travels, he found no book could ever teach her the experience she had gained.

"It's ten past two. She's never late," Tom blurted, more frustrated than ever.

Denny looked at his watch. "Yep, she's late."

Tom hurled his brother a serious-looking scowl and Denny knew it was time to keep his mouth shut. Tom was one of those people who could be pushed a long way, but when he snapped, he snapped big. Growing up, Denny knew exactly how far he could push him, and he always stopped before the breaking point. This was that moment. It had been a long time since they had tussled, and Denny knew this was not the day to rekindle the wrestling matches from the old days.

"What's the hold up?" Tom gruffed; now agitated. He ran his hands through his hair excessively and when he was finished with his fit, Leona approached him and smoothed down the wild hairstyle he had created. Tom groaned aloud and Leona whispered reassurance that things would be all right.

"You can breathe now. I believe you were right. That was their limo," Denny said, nudging Tom in the arm and pointing down the street. "And you were worried. All that stress for nothing." He elbowed Tom then pushed him toward the church entrance. "Ready or not, here you go!"

"Wait..." Tom stalled. "I want to make sure she's alright."

"You can't see the bride until she walks down the aisle," Leona interrupted, "It'll jinx the wedding."

Reluctantly, he turned to go inside.

* * *

The limo glided to a stop in front of the church and the driver opened the door for the wedding party.

Inside the limousine, the bridal party waited on pins and needles for Charlie to make the first move. Everyone held their breath. No one wanted to say anything about the bride's strange behavior so they waited in silence for Charlie to get out. This would be their cue to follow. The door opened. She sat still, glued to her seat, as if they were still in transit, her eyes unfocused, staring forward, in her own world. The bridesmaids exchanged glances between each other; no one volunteered to speak to her.

"It's time, Charlie," Catherine finally said, poking her in the arm to snap her out of the trance she was in, but she did not budge.

"Charlie?"

"All right. Give me a minute. I feel like I'm wearing cement shoes. I can't move my feet. I think I need your help."

Catherine smiled. Charlie had never asked her for help. Hiding her delight, she answered proudly, "I can do that."

"Thank you," Charlie murmured her voice barely audible.

"Okay," Catherine clapped her hands together. She knew it would be easy from here on out, because now she was in control. "All you have to do is get out of the limo, and go over and stand at the bottom of the steps. I'll get everyone here prepped. I'll be over in a second." She looked her sister square in the eyes. "You think you can do that?"

Charlie nodded, and delicately reached her hand out to the driver to assist her out of the limousine. She relinquished control to her older sister; a first for her. With the freight train of confusion that was racing through her head, Charlie knew she could not do it alone. Without turning back, she did as she was told, and went to the bottom of the church steps.

Catherine climbed out of the limo and stood outside the open door waiting. When the driver helped Iris out, Catherine took hold of her arm firmly.

"Ouch!" Iris said, glowering at the death-grip Catherine held on her. "You're hurting me."

"Be quiet. I don't want her to hear," Catherine growled sternly. "Did you give her the gift?"

"What?" Iris was confused, utterly focused on the hold Catherine had on her. "You're bruising my arm."

Catherine shushed her and whispered roughly through gritted teeth, "You better listen to me Iris." She glanced over her shoulder at Charlie, continuing, "The present I gave you yesterday, the one you were supposed to make sure she opened this morning," she emphasized again, "her wedding morning! Did you give it to her, or not?" Iris still looked baffled, and Catherine wondered if Iris had fried her brain partying too much at college. She yelled, "You know what I'm talking about! The damned old package....,"

A light bulb finally clicked on, "Oh, that one! Yeah, I gave it to her. Just like...," she stopped for a moment, thinking.

"Like what? Like what, Iris?" Catherine's eyes were wide with impatience.

"Let go of my arm." When she released it, Iris rubbed at the red imprint.

"Like what?" Catherine badgered, unwilling to give up.

"I handed it to her. She looked at it then handed it back. She told me to set it on the counter with the rest of the wedding gifts. She said they, she and Tom, would be opening all the gifts together after their honeymoon."

"Then what?"

"I told her what you said, that it was a gift for her and that it was important she open it up by herself. She said she would open it after her bath. She was just getting into the tub when I gave it to her."

"And did she?"

"I don't know. I went out last night."

"Come on, Iris. I told you that gift was more important than life itself."

"Yeah, yeah. Sometimes you're so dramatic," Iris sneered, rolling her eyes. "I gave her the gift, what more do you want from me?"

Catherine's eyes welled up. "I wanted you to give her that gift. You promised you'd make sure she opened it."

"No, you said to make sure she got it the night before the wedding and to tell her that it was only for her. I did that."

"That is not how I said it and you know it. I never ask anything from you, ever. You couldn't do this one thing for me, could you? I knew I couldn't trust you."

"Screw you, Catherine!" Iris flung past Catherine. "If it was so damned important, why didn't you do it yourself?"

Catherine opened her mouth but the voice of her daughter inside the limousine stopped her. She had forgotten Christina was within earshot.

"Mommy, I've gotta pee," Christina announced, squirming uncomfortably. "Really bad."

"Come on, honey," Catherine sighed, reaching for her daughter's hand. She knew she had stressed the importance of the task to Iris and really thought Iris had understood. Catherine supposed it was her own fault. There was too much going on and she thought she could trust Iris to do just one thing for her. Should she have told her what was inside? Catherine and Iris rarely saw eye to eye mostly because Iris thought Catherine's good intentions were overbearing.

Christina climbed out and asked, "Were you fighting about the present from the closet?"

"We weren't fighting," Catherine fibbed, "And, yes, we were talking about the old present from the closet."

"Oh." Christina peered up at her mother, eyes squinting from the sun, her cinnamon-sprinkled nose crinkled, "I could have given it to Aunt Charlie."

"I know dear," Catherine said, patting her daughter on the head. "You're a good girl."

Catherine gave explicit instructions for Tina to go to the restroom and come directly back to the foyer of the church, telling her the wedding was about to start.

Catherine met both her sisters at the bottom of the church steps and began giving instructions on what each of them needed to do. She fluffed and lifted the train of Charlie's dress. All she had to do was get them through the wedding. The reception would be easy.   "Just breathe," Catherine whispered aloud, saying a prayer for strength. She was already exhausted, and the day had just started.

* * *

On cue, as the bridal party stepped into the foyer, the violinists began playing the first song in their repertoire, the one Charlie had chosen specifically for its calming effects, Mozart's *Eine Kleine Nachtmusik in G major*. Charlie knew how she'd feel the moment the song began and hoped it would have its usual effect - serenity. but for some reason, today, the song gave an opposite effect - fear. At the moment, she could not think of a thing that could take away her edge; a handful of valium perhaps, and she was not a hundred percent sure of that.

Charlie opened the door and stood in the doorway, allowing the cool summer breeze to cool her. She touched her face and still felt warm. Looking over her shoulder, she saw Catherine back in the foyer preoccupied with Christina and the rose petal basket. Leona walked into the foyer and they made eye contact.

Charlie waved her over. "Hi," she said nervously.

"Hi, sweetheart. You ready, because it's now or never!" Leona said, raising her eyebrows up and down.

Charlie smiled weakly. "You make it sound so...so..."

"Natural?" Leona said, winking. "I don't think I've ever seen you so nervous."

Charlie blinked rapidly. She did not want to cry. If she started, she feared she would never stop.

"You're doing the right thing, if that helps."

Charlie jolted slightly, completely miffed. Was her best friend reading her mind? Were her thoughts that transparent?

"Hold it right there." Leona put the camera to her eyes and adjusted the lens. The sun radiated off her veil making the white even brighter. "You look like an angel..." The camera snapped. "Hold still..." She lined up another shot, "It looks like you've got a halo shining above you."

Charlie smiled weakly. Click. Wind. Click.

Catherine approached; her face furrowing. Charlie was in too fragile a state to have a camera poking in her face. "Leona?"

"I just had to get that shot." She turned to Charlie. "You ready?"

Charlie nodded and they swarmed toward the entrance of the church.

* * *

At the outside entrance of the rectory, the room adjacent to where all their guests were seated, Tom and Denny stood waiting for the Pastor to come tell them it was time to stand in front of the church.

"Denny, you should probably head to the front now." Tom said, nervously.

"Ethan said he'd come get me when it was time."

"Why don't you go ahead? Just in case..."

"Are you tryin' to get rid of me?" Denny teased.

"No. I'm afraid..." Tom changed what he was going to say. "I just want to get this thing started. The waiting is killing me."

Ethan came through the rectory and joined them. His ears must have been burning.

"See, I told you he'd come get me. Contrary to what you want to believe, I was paying attention in rehearsal."

"Okay guys. See you at the altar," Tom said, pushing them along. He wanted to be alone for a moment before it all began.

"Don't be nervous." Denny smacked him on the arm.

"I'm not," Tom declared a little too quickly, "I don't get why everyone keeps saying that."

Denny reached into his jacket pocket, and his eyes widened when he found it empty. He patted his pants pocket, and quickly checked the other one.

Tom panicked. "Don't even say it!"

"The ring! I can't find the ring!"

"Shit, Denny!"

Denny pulled out his hand in a fist and opened it, the diamond sparkling brilliantly in the sun, "Ah ha!"

"That's not funny."

"You should've seen your face," Denny uttered, laughing hysterically. "That was priceless."

Ethan laughed, too. "For a brief moment," then he punched Denny in the arm, "And not cool."

"Get out of here," Tom said, shoving them both down the steps. They were laughing as they rounded the corner of the church.

Tom kept an eye on them until they disappeared around the corner and then turned to go inside. He could not shake the sensation that he was being watched. His hunch was right, but it did not stop him from jumping when he saw Charlie standing in the doorway.

"Hey, I'm not supposed to see the bride!" he exclaimed, covering his eyes. "It's bad luck."

Charlie reached for his hands and pulled them away from his face. He stared into her big brown eyes, wondering if it was sadness that he was detecting. He could feel his anticipation turn to apprehension.

From the outside door to the pastor's office, they could hear the trio of violinists inside as they began the song they had chosen to play just before, *Here Comes The Bride*." They were so far behind schedule. Tom hoped there were other songs in their repertoire for fillers.

"The bridal song's next," Tom said, bringing it to her attention. "I should be standing at the altar right now.

"I know."

Tom cleared his throat. It was suddenly dry and he was afraid to ask what was wrong. "Then turn yourself around and get to the front of the church. I will see you on the inside. Just like we practiced last night."

Charlie fidgeted with her hands, her dress swishing as she twitched.

"Charlie?" Tom asked softly, his voice as dry as toast. "Is something wrong?"

"I can't go through with this."

"What do you mean?" Tom asked, disappointment clear, although he tried to remain calm. He laughed nervously, trying to brush away what she had just declared.

"Tom, I'm not joking. I can't marry you."

He looked at her for a long moment, their eyes locking. "Charlie, this is just your nerves talking. Shit, I felt the same way this morning."

Her eyes doe-wide, "You did?"

"Well..." He reached for her hand. "No. I didn't. I can't lie. I knew from the moment I met you that I wanted you to be my wife and the mother of my children."

Charlie jerked her hand away from his, "I can't believe you just lied to me."

"Just take a deep breath, darlin'. We can do this," he smiled at her although he truly wanted to shake her and make her wake up.

"I was just thinking..."

He did not let her finish, "Thinking? What is there to think about? It's a great day. Everybody's here," he waved his hand over the parking lot, "Giving their blessing. We'll get married, have a great party...then Aruba...,"

"I can't."

"It's just nerves. Trust me."

"Tom, this is not my nerves speaking. I just woke up and had this epiphany." She looked away from him, out to the parking lot. She was too afraid to look him in the eyes.

"Get in the church," Tom blurted, pointing down the walkway that led to the front of the church. It suddenly occurred to him that there was a chance she might change her mind. He tried a new approach.

Charlie interrupted him forcefully, her voice unexpectedly powerful. "No!" she commanded. "Listen to me!" She did not want to hurt him, but there was no other way. He would not listen to her. She opened her mouth to speak, but her voice dried up, which triggered her eyes to sting. She needed a sip of water; no she needed her voice to be strong, but for some reason it vanished with her courage.

She coughed a couple times and tried to swallow to wet her throat to no avail. Her mouth was open wide yet the words were invisible. Why couldn't she say the right words to make him let her go?

Tom finally spoke when she could not. "What exactly are you trying to say to me, Charlie? That you're afraid of a little wedding? If that's so, I've got some information for you, darling." He could not mask his frustration. "We're not the first couple to get married. People do it every day," he laughed, trying to mask his sarcasm.

"What if I...What if I carry the gene?" Charlie asked hoarsely, and then coughed.

Tom's smile faded.

"I think I have it."

Tom rubbed his eyes then glanced at his watch. He took a deep breath and stepped toward Charlie. It was when she stepped away from him that the wall finally broke and his anger flooded the gates of his restraint.

"Charlie, how many times have we gone over this?" He answered for her, not giving her room to reply. "Many, many times. It'll be alright, baby." He leaned in and kissed her on the forehead. He brushed a wisp of loose hair out of her eye, "Is that what this is all about?"

Charlie tried to speak, but he put his finger to her lips, not sure he was ready to hear what she was about to say, and continued, "There's a good chance you don't carry the gene. They only suspect that it's hereditary because your mother and grandfather both died from a muscular disorder. You know that."

"But...," Charlie tried to speak again, but he stopped her another time.

"And even if you do...I still love you," he touched her shoulder, finally sure he had her convinced her, "I'll take care of you."

Charlie jolted awake, as if she had just touched an electric fence. She pulled away from him.

"You'll take care of me? You've never even known anyone with Lou Gehrig's disease, let alone watch her die. You have no idea!"

"I know your mother's death was hard on you, but you can't keep dwelling on it. It's unhealthy."

"That's easy for you to say. Both your parents are sitting inside the church. You have no idea how...," she whirled her arms in a huge exaggerated circle, "...this feels."

Tom glanced over his shoulder. "Keep it down. Everyone's gonna hear." He lowered his voice again, trying to speak calmly, hoping she would follow suit. "Charlie...let's just get through the wedding and we can deal with your...," he paused, changing his words, "...with this later. You and me together. Now, come on. Everybody's waiting on us." He looked deeply into her troubled eyes with trepidation because he could not read her expression.

It was in that fleeting moment Charlie realized he would never understand, nor would he allow her to ever leave him. She swallowed the lump that welled in her throat then looked up, hoping the angels would write in the sky what she should do.

"The truth of the matter is...," she closed her eyes and said a quick prayer for strength and forgiveness, "I don't love you anymore."

Tom was stunned, and it took a moment for him to catch his breath, "What?!"

Charlie looked up at his face and felt crushing shame for the pain she had initiated and in a fleeting moment, she almost took it all back, but she knew she could not. The voice in the back of her head, the devil one that seemed to help her find the cruelty she had summoned, would not allow her to.

Tom stared at her, unable to speak, stunned by what she had just revealed.

For effect, she repeated, this time in a voice barely above a whisper, "I don't love you anymore."

Tom, wordless, stared at her for a moment and uttered, "You don't?"

Charlie nodded, "And...I don't want to compromise my life right now..." She could not believe she just said that. "I want to focus on my singing career. I can't do that if I'm married." She couldn't believe how easily the hateful words kept coming.

"This is ridiculous!" Tom balked loudly. Now it was he who did not care who heard. "You're not making any sense! I've always supported your music! If it wasn't for your singing, we would never have met. Why are you saying this?"

"I'm sorry, Tom. I really am," she turned away from him, going down two steps and turned back to him. "I don't want to get married. Not now. Not ever."

"Ah ha!" Tom's finger pointed at her, "What is it? You can't marry me? You won't marry me? You don't love me anymore? Or...or you just don't want to get married? Because those are all different things! I don't think you even know what you're saying!"

Charlie turned and continued down the cement steps.

Tom panicked because she was leaving and there was nothing he could say to make her come back. "You're sorry? Have you completely lost your mind? We've got a church full of people in there waiting for you to walk down the aisle so we can get married. People who have come a long way to support our...," he laughed ironically, "...Our love for one another. You can't back out now! Please?"

It was the "please" that made Charlie stop walking. Her shoes, once again, felt like they were made of cement. She whirled around to face him and could not bear seeing the sadness she had created. Her shoulders sagged. The weight of her shame had become unbelievably heavy. No one would ever forgive her and she did not know if she deserved their forgiveness. But, if she went through with it, she would never forgive herself.

"It's for the best," she said firmly.

"Don't you think you could have told me this yesterday? Or last week?"

"I tried, but you wouldn't listen."

"You said you don't love me anymore, but I think it must be more along the lines of hate, because only hate could make you do this to me."

Charlie took two backward steps toward the street and turned around and began walking. She was about fifteen steps from the street and she was going to make it there if it killed her.

"You're out of your mind!" Tom yelled after her. "You know that? You're crazy and I don't care who hears!"

Charlie whirled around. He had succeeded in making her mad. She marched angrily back toward him not stopping until she reached the bottom of the steps. She tried not to cry. When alone, it would be a different story. She would allow herself tears, but not until then. It did not stop her voice from quivering and she was barely able to suppress her emotions, "If you knew me at all...Tom Mahoney...," she fisted her chest, "...Really knew me...you would understand!"

"I thought I knew you! You said *I do*! You said yes to be my wife! I'm not the crazy one here! You've become obsessed with this death wish of yours. Sometimes I think you would be happy if you found out you had A.L.S. and were dying."

Charlie covered her face with her hands, letting loose the flood gates of the dam of emotions she was holding back.

Tom ran to her and took hold of her shoulders firmly. He spoke gently now. "Charlie, let's go through with the wedding. I know you're afraid, but don't do this to me. You can leave me tomorrow; just do this for me today."

Charlie muttered more to herself than him, "If I did, I would never leave."

"Good. That's what is supposed to happen. I love you. Marry me. I'm begging you. Please."

Charlie writhed out of his grasp and turned quickly. She had to get away from him, the church and all the people inside. She sprinted across the parking lot. This time she did not turn around when he hollered. She could not look at what she had done.

Astonishingly, she made it to the grass that edged the sidewalk, which had only been ten running steps. Charlie was even more amazed when she reached the blue house that neighbored the church. With all the fortitude she could call upon, she forced herself to not look back at what was now the past, and to look forward to the future. The only goal she had was to get far away from the wedding. What fueled her strength was the power of a promise she made to herself. Make it to the end of the street and everything would be okay.

Chapter 3

∧

Later that afternoon back at Charlie's house, everyone stood around. No one knew why Charlie had left the church. She had been acting strangely, but everyone had mistaken her behavior for nerves. When Catherine, Steve, Leona, Iris, and Christina arrived at her house, they could not find her. Catherine flung open the curtains to the sliding glass doors, letting light in. That was when they saw her.

Charlie, still wearing her wedding dress, stood in the surf staring out into the vast water. Leona and Catherine moved cautiously outside except for Christina, who jumped down from the deck and ran excitedly to the beach. Iris followed with a champagne bottle in her hand and they ran around playing in the sand.

Catherine and Leona stood on the deck watching Charlie. They stared in silence, not knowing what to say or do as the incoming tide took Charlie's train in and out with each crashing wave.

"What a mess! My family's an absolute mess! What went wrong? I just don't get it. Today was perfect. Look at this day!" Catherine exclaimed, both hands in the air. "Not a cloud in the sky." She looked to Iris, who was dancing along the beach, gulping from the bottle of champagne. "And then there's Iris. She's like a shoelace coming undone a little more with every step. We are a mess, I tell you."

Leona listened. It was what she did best. "We all have our problems. I don't know what to think."

Steve walked out onto the deck with two hefty sandwiches. "Christina!" he hollered, "Want a sandwich?" He turned to his wife and Leona, "I don't know if I could have waited until the reception to eat. I was starving." He took a huge bite as he walked down the steps onto the sand. Christina, like a roller bird running away from the tide, ran to her father and plopped down in his lap.

"Christina is always so at ease with Steve," Leona said, "He's such a good father."

Catherine smiled. "She's so much like him. Steve is just so easygoing. Unlike my side of the family, where everything is a debate. If I say black, Iris says white, and Charlie says pink. That's how different we all are. I think we're just a tad on the neurotic side, if you ask me."

"Every family has their dysfunction," Leona said as she pulled her wind-blown hair from her face, wishing she had a clip to pull it up. "Christina's such a doll. She's got your beautiful hair."

"And my toes," Catherine smiled lovingly. She looked down at her feet. "Yeah, she has my long, square toes." Catherine, still smiling from her thoughts, looked at her daughter, "Yeah..."

Christina climbed onto her father's shoulders, sandwich in hand, as Steve took off, bouncing her as he ran.

"It's odd, you know. I can look at her and pick out every part on her body and name who it resembles."

"Funny about genetics," Leona said, looking to the sky. "Where did that cloud come from?" As she asked, the sun crept behind the lone cloud, casting white rays on the ocean, giving the brilliance that Heaven was up there, and the "Pearly Gates" were nearby. The light highlighted Charlie's dress catching Leona's attention. "Look at Charlie. The light! It's beautiful. She looks like a cover of a romance novel..." Leona gesticulated, trying to find the perfect name of the novel, ""Love Lost..."

"This is all too weird for me...," Catherine interrupted, not seeing the beauty the artistic Leona saw, "...And she won't talk about it. Tom is a great guy. I thought she was so in love with him."

"Well, we don't know what happened. Maybe he cheated on her."

"Right," Catherine answered sarcastically. "He isn't the type."

"I'm sure she'll talk when she's ready."

"When it's too late and she realizes the mistake she made."

"Uh huh!" Leona said shaking her finger, "Don't judge. No matter what, she's your sister and you need to be there for her."

"I've always been there for her. That's my problem. I take on their problems. I just hope she realizes what she's done before it's too late. You just can't do that to someone and expect them to forgive you," Catherine sighed, "She's messed up. And I always thought I was the most messed up in the family," Catherine looked out at Iris, who was now wading in the surf, "Then there's Iris," she shook her head and laughed aloud. "And who would Iris be in this romance novel? A lost spirit, no doubt."

Leona interrupted and pointed down the beach to a scruffy, pot-bellied man swinging a metal detector from side to side, "Look! There's Fabio, a knight in shining armor!"

Catherine laughed and Leona grabbed her camera. She set the lens to capture the odd scene. Catherine turned and stepped down off the porch onto the sand. She struggled with her dress and almost fell, regaining her balance as she walked across the sand down to the water's edge.

"Charlie, your dress! You're ruining it!"

Charlie did not appear to hear.

"Charlie? You're going to catch your death!"

Would that be so bad? Charlie thought to herself. After what she had done today, she wondered if she could ever live with herself. Her mother's sweet voice echoed in her head, "This too shall pass."

Hiking up her dress, Catherine ventured cautiously to the surf's edge. A large wave crashed onto the beach and knocked Catherine off balance. She screamed as she fell into the water. Charlie and Iris turned to see their soggy sister struggling to stand again. Iris began howling hysterically, causing Steve and Christina to turn around. Steve rushed toward the water, crashing into the surf to Catherine's rescue.

Catherine's patience was frazzled as she held back tears of frustration. Steve splashed to her rescue, trying to control his own laughter. Finally, she found the humor in the situation and she, too began to laugh. Steve swooped her up and twirled his wife around in the water. Christina took this cue as permission to enter the water, and splashed full force into the surf. Steve released his wife and plunged backward into the water, disappearing. He shot straight up out of the water, invigorated.

Leona, back on the deck, camera to her eye, snapped away, making it a "Kodak moment".

Chapter 4

∧

The bar was dark except for the neon beer sign that hung above the pool table. Still in their tuxes, Tom and Denny sat at a table in the rear of the bar. The bar was a dive, but it was perfect for their mood. Their table was covered with empty beer bottles, a couple of shot glasses, and a fifth of whiskey.

Somberly, Tom sat with two chair legs in the air, leaning back against the wall. The events of the day kept racing through his mind. He kept wondering if there was anything he could have done to have changed the outcome. Denny straddled his chair and polished off another beer.

"You think she really meant it?" Tom finally asked.

"I dunno," Denny answered, not knowing what to say. He was just as dumbfounded as Tom. "Didn't even see it coming." He could tell it was going to be a long night. Denny poured himself a large shot of whiskey.

"Do you ever get the feeling you're spinning your wheels and not going anywhere?" Denny asked. He downed the shot, winced, and exhaled. "This stuff must be watered down 'cause I'm not gettin' drunk." He turned and motioned for the bartender to bring more beers. Tom disregarded Denny.

Denny continued, "You're just gonna have to suck it up, bro. Give it some time," he yawned and stretched. "Everything's gonna work out." The bartender slammed down two more beers and grabbed a handful of empties. Denny took a fresh beer. "She just needs a little space. I know, I've been there. Sometimes you just gotta pull out for a while."

"Shut up!" Tom finally snapped. "What do you know?" He was growing tired of his brother's useless chatter.

"I'm getting love advice from my fickle brother who can't stay with someone more than a few days. I must be as pathetic as I feel."

"Hey, I just know about needing personal space."

"Personal space? You sound like a friggin' therapist. Not everyone feels the need to pack up their entire life every three weeks the way you do."

"You gotta do what you gotta do. I choose my own destiny."

Tom's chair slammed down on all four legs. Rage suddenly flushed through him. Where was Denny's support? His loyalty? He wanted comfort from his brother, not identification with the woman who stood him up. Tom got in his face. "You think so?!!   You're just a spoiled kid who can't get his act together!"

"Wait a minute! Don't take your shit out on me. I wasn't the one who dumped you."

Tom glared at his brother because his offensive words slapped redness across his face. Tom could not remember the last time he was this angry with his brother. The stare broke when Denny shoved his chair away. He stood up and moved towards the pool table.

"Come on. Let's shoot some pool," Denny said as he grabbed the triangle off the overhead beer light. He looked back at his brother. "I'm not the enemy here."

Tom sat down in his chair and assumed the same position he had earlier, leaning against the wall. Denny was right. He was not mad at him. He was just mad at the world. He did not understand why life was dumping on him. He was an honest person. He paid his taxes. He was always on time for work and he gave money to the homeless. It did not make any sense.

"Too bad the jukebox is busted. Country music would sound pretty good right about now," Denny started singing, exaggerating a thick southern twang. He was on a mission to make his brother laugh. *"...Crazy...I'm crazy for feeling so lonely...."*

Tom put his head in his hands. "First stood up at the altar, now serenaded by the shittiest singer on the planet! God, please let me be dreaming!"

Denny started racking the balls. Then he sauntered over to Tom, still in character, *"Crazy...I'm crazy for feeling so blue..."*

"Get away from me!"

"Hey, pilgrim," he said, doing his best John Wayne, "What're you reckon you gonna do about that there honeymoon of yours?!"

He grabbed a pool stick from the wall and gave it a twirl. His voice now back to normal, "Man! That's where you should be right now. No, we should be there right now! Aruba!" Denny said aloud, although he knew his brother was not listening. He did not mind speaking to himself. He knew that before the end of the night, he could convince Tom to take him to Aruba. Then he would get Tom laid and everything would be okay. Denny lined up the cue ball for the break and smacked it. Balls flew across the table. Two stripes dropped into the corner pocket.

Chapter 5

∧

Fresh out of the shower, her body wrapped in a bath towel and her sandy brown hair dripping wet, Iris walked into the living room. As she climbed onto the couch, she cringed. Her head was pounding from all the champagne.

She grabbed the remote and flipped on the television. Surfing through the channels, she found nothing but old reruns. "Summer television programming; boring!" She rolled her neck and flipped off the television and scanned the room for something to do. She spotted the pile of unopened wedding gifts overloading the kitchen table all the way to the floor. One package in particular stuck out like a sore thumb. She glanced at the place on her arm where Catherine had grabbed her earlier. To her surprise, it had not bruised.

She went to the table and picked it up. The package had called to her, the old worn wrapping and Catherine's bizarre behavior piqued her curiosity enough that she decided she was going to find out what all the fuss was about. Nobody was in the room. She would simply peel away the end, sneak a peek, and then put it back. No one would be the wiser. She looked over her shoulder, and then stripped away the old scotch tape that miraculously still held the wrapping paper together.

It was an unlabeled videotape. She walked over to the television, turned it back on, and carefully put the tape into the VCR. She scanned for the remote, found it in the coffee table, and went to the couch and plopped down. Her towel nearly fell off, so she readjusted and got comfortable. She was ready to find out what the big mystery was all about.

Snow initially filled the screen and Iris watched the static screen for more than a minute. She was beginning to think it was all a big joke and was about to hit the fast forward button when she heard a door open down the hallway. It was Catherine. She was down the hall. Quickly, Iris hit the power button on the television and the screen went black. Catherine walked through the living room and then into the kitchen. Her mind was on something else, so she had not noticed the guilty look on Iris' face. Iris faked a yawn as she watched her sister open the refrigerator and grab a can of Diet Coke then watched her walk back through the room and down the hallway to the bedroom she had come from. She had been completely oblivious.

Iris yawned, for real this time, as she fluffed a throw pillow. Getting comfortable she laid back. She flipped the television back on and yawned again. She shook her head, trying to wake up, which caused her head to pound more. It felt like a metal ball was rolling around inside her skull. Hopefully the painkiller would kick in soon.

Her yawns were coming in rapid succession and the snow-filled television was not helping. Without realizing it, Iris blinked and her eyes did not open back up. She fell instantly asleep.

The tape finally began to play to a mute audience. An unsteady camera taped an empty chair until suddenly a woman appeared on screen.

"Hello, Charlie...,"

At that moment, Christina flitted into the living room, heading directly for her sleeping aunt. She lightly touched Iris' eyelashes with her fingertip, giggling when Iris' hand flew up and slapped her own eye. Iris opened her eye and pushed Christina away.

Christina turned toward the television when she heard sound coming from it. Drawn as if she were hypnotized, she stood in front of it, watching intently.

(The woman on the television smiled nervously)

> *"I wanted you to know how much I love you and how much I wish I could be with you on your wedding day...I know I haven't been the best example of courage or happiness, but I want to encourage you...,"*

Christina sat quietly in front of the television, glued to the screen as if she were watching cartoons, not really knowing what she was watching.

* * *

Out on the back deck, Charlie drank a bottle of beer. She had two other bottles lined up on the deck all awaiting their turn.

She wore her favorite green terry cloth bathrobe wrapped around her tightly. A cool breeze brushed her neck and she flipped up the folded collar. Against her better judgment, she wore this particular robe - the one Tom had given her last Christmas. She had silky robes, the ones from Victoria's Secret, but never an oversized terry cloth. She had always wanted one but never seemed to buy one. The terry cloth robe was one of those items she figured she would add to her "wish list." This way, on birthdays or Christmases she would get something she actually wanted - gifts that she actually wanted to keep. Not that she ever returned anything; she believed a gift was a gift, so she kept them all. But her storage closet was overflowing with bath soaps and trinkets she would never use.

The wind began to pick up. The decorative flag that hung from her deck flapped wildly, snapping like a wet towel with each strong gust. Charlie watched a flock of seagulls scuttle by, their twig legs making crosses in the sand as they scoured the ground for any remaining morsels left over from tourists.

A single tear rolled down Charlie's cheek as she looked onto the horizon. All she could see was the hurt on Tom's face. She gulped down the last drop of the first beer. Two more to go. The alcohol did not erase her thoughts as she had hoped.

Poor Tom, she thought to herself as she opened the second mini bottle. She wished she could wake up and all this would be a bad dream. She knew she had handled it wrong. The timing was poor and it was simply bad manners leaving him with a church full of people. Where was the courage last night? God knew she wanted to do it then. That would have been better. But he was so happy. She was happy. Everyone was happy. She was so upset with herself. She could taste the disgust.

The last remaining curve of the sun sizzled below the waterline and the sky grew darker. When a lightning bug buzzed past, it dawned on her how long she had been standing there. It was getting colder, but she could not move her feet. She did not deserve to feel the warmth inside. She wanted to feel as cold and heartless on the outside as she felt on the inside. This was the punishment she deserved.

Charlie wiped away angry tears that streamed down her face; burning paths through the lingering remnants of her wedding make-up. If she had had the courage to stop the wedding beforehand, things would have been different. How could she live with herself? Why did she have to wake up knowing what she had to do? Last night, she was confused, but this morning she knew. It was not like she had some enlightening dream, giving her a revelation on her life. She just woke up knowing that if she loved him, she would have to leave him. There was no other alternative.

She wondered if people would think that Tom had done something to deserve being left, humiliated at the altar. She decided she would write a letter to everyone taking full blame. If anything, Tom did not deserve to be scorned. He was too good of a man.

Tears continued streaming down Charlie's face. If she was going to survive this, she would have to be strong. These would be the last tears she would shed for her loss. She would give herself tonight.

* * *

In Charlie's bathroom, Catherine stood over the tub wringing the salt water out of Christina's dress. Her own dress hung on the towel rack, dripping non-stop onto the hardwood floor. From underneath the sink she grabbed a towel and put it under to soak up the water. Steve walked into the bathroom and grabbed Catherine from behind while she was bent over.

"Oh my..." she exclaimed, standing up while she continued to wring out her dress.

"What a day!" he whispered into her ear then kissed her on the back of the neck, "How about taking a break?"

"Almost done, okay?" She put Christina's dress next to hers.

"You think Charlie's gonna be alright?" Steve asked.

Catherine, suddenly exhausted, leaned back against Steve. He wrapped his arms around her.

She sighed aloud, feeling very comfortable. "I don't know. I don't know if I should be concerned or angry. She's not saying anything. I don't even think she's talked to Leona about it."

"So what do you want to do?"

"I think Charlie, Iris and I should spend some time together...try to be a family." She turned toward her husband, to see his reaction. She had no idea how he would take her decision to be apart. She hoped he would see where she was going with the conversation. He was a fair person and most of the time saw the situation from her point of view.

"Whatever you think is best." Steve grabbed her waist and pulled her in, hugging her tightly. Catherine relaxed. She knew he would understand.

"You and I are becoming such a "one" that we're going to meld together."

"I know you care for your family. Anyone who is loved by you gets the best attention."

"I think I have the most understanding husband in the world. I was expecting an argument or something."

"The trip is only ten days...and I agree, this is messed up and somehow, I think you can fix it. How about if I take Christina with me?"

"I'm sure she'd rather see African lions up close than hang out with the anti-Brady Brunch." They both laughed at how close to reality her joke was.

"If you don't think I should go...," Steve said, but he knew that he had to go.

"Steve, you have to go. You've been searching for more Barbary lions and you can't pass up this opportunity. In fact, it may already be too late."

"I made a call this morning. They saved three lions from the bankrupt Akef Egyptian Circus. They just abandoned those animals. The Hoedspruit Research and Breeding Center for Endangered Species has the lions in safe pens. I want to get there before the Brits do," he touched her shoulder. "Don't get excited, but one of the lions has a rich black mane that runs the length of his underbody."

Catherine's eyes grew wide, "Do you think it's a Cape lion?"

"If it is, that means it could be the last of its kind."

"There hasn't been a sighting of the Cape lion since 1830. Do you know what this could mean?"

"That's why I've got to go."

Catherine smiled at him, "I never said you shouldn't. I only wish I could be there. This could be history in the making."

"I'll take good notes and call you with updates. I only hope it's not too late. Those lions were nearly starved to death." Steve shook his head with disgust. "How could someone be so inhumane?"

"You should probably get Christina to bed. Tomorrow will be a long day." He followed her out of the bathroom to the living room.

"Shshshsh!" Catherine told Steve. "Look at our little Angel." Christina was curled up like a kitten on the floor in front of the television. The videotape had ended and there was snow on the TV again. Catherine shut it off and walked to the couch to cover Iris, whose towel was barely covering her. She reached for the crocheted blanket that was folded across the back of the couch, covering her up to her neck. At the same time, Steve scooped Christina up off the floor and carried her to bed.

Chapter 6

∧

Denny sunk the eight ball, winning the third game in a row. Victory was bittersweet. He glanced at his forlorn brother deep in thought. Additional beer bottles and empty shot glasses were strewn all over their table.

"It's not really competition if you play alone," Denny said, breaking the silence as he racked the balls up for another game of solitaire pool. He was on a roll, so he kept shooting until there were only two solid balls left on the table. He banked a double shot leaving only the eight ball for the win.

"I don't mind talking to myself," he was growing tired of trying to cheer Tom up and decided to let him grieve.

"Huh?"

"You're just sitting there beating yourself up. It's not your fault."

"Maybe it is." Tom reached for another shot and knocked it back. He stood and snatched the stick out of Denny's hand. "Obviously, something went wrong."

"Forget about it."

Denny took another pool stick from the wall and sunk the eight ball. As he reset the balls for the next game he provoked Tom.

"Aruba. Aruba. Ah-rooo-ba!"

"Fuck you," Tom lined up the white ball, waiting for Denny to lift the triangle. "Move it."

"Boy, you're a pissy drunk."

Tom hit the ball. It missed the setup and bounced onto the floor. The bartender bent over to pick the ball off the floor as he walked up with four more shots. "It's a real bitch about the wedding. Marriage sucks anyway."

Denny grimaced and pointed his thumb at the bartender, "See? It's not so bad."

"I own nothin' cuz of women," the bartender said setting down full shots and walked away. Tom shot Denny a look and Denny shrugged.

"Loud mouth!" Tom glared, seriously pissed off at his brother for blabbing his problems to a total stranger. "Is anything sacred with you?"

"What?" Denny played innocent.

"Asshole."

"Candy-ass!" Denny said, "Take your shot and shut up."

Tom butted Denny with the big end of the stick then lined up his shot.

"Ah-rooo...," Denny whispered.

Tom averted his eyes, giving the look to "cool it".

Tom pulled back for the shot.

"...ba!" he said louder. "Arrrrr...," Denny rolled his "r's" "...ba!"

Tom averted his eyes from Denny again, locking his glare. But, Denny finally succeeded in breaking his. Tom laughed, shaking his head.

"Sun, surf and hot babes! That's what you need," Denny said, downing a shot, following it with a long swig of beer that dribbled down his chin. He used his sleeve to wipe his face.

Tom broke the balls again. To Denny's amusement, the white ball bounced across the table completely missing the setup again, then cracked on the floor.

"Gimme that!" Denny laughed, as he swiped the stick from his brother. "You're banned from pool forever."

* * *

The night sky was bright due to the full moon casting an orange-yellow hue across·the sky that magically illuminated the white beach house. Lightning bugs energetically searched for soul mates; their tails blinked off and signaled one another. The nighttime air smelled of thick ocean salt, clean and crisp.

As Christina slept, Steve gently carried her to the car and placed her in the back seat. Catherine followed, carrying their wet clothes.

"Are you sure you want to stay? I can reschedule the trip," Steve said, shutting the back door lightly as he turned to his wife.

"No, it'll go by quickly. Besides, I don't think Charlie alone right now is such a good idea, especially with Iris on the loose."

"You sure you want to play mom?"

"If I don't, who will?" Catherine looked at Christina sleeping soundly in the back seat. "Her writing journal is packed with her gear. Let her take some pictures by herself. She's becoming a really good little photographer. Leona taught her a few tricks today. She's anxious to try them out."

"I'll make sure she gets her Pulitzer Prize photo." Steve hugged his wife and walked around to the driver's door, opening it. Catherine stepped up beside him.

"I'm really gonna miss you guys."

"Maybe this is a good thing. Tina's never traveled without you." Catherine nodded and Steve hugged and kissed her as he whispered into her ear. "The three musketeers become the dynamic duo."

"I'll turn on the bat light if Gotham City needs you." They both laughed.

"Okay. You want me to bring you anything on our way to the airport in the morning?

"Yeah, why don't you drop off my bag since it's already packed?"

"Okay, Bat Girl. I'm just going to leave it on the deck because it'll be really early. Tina will be asleep anyway."

"You're so good." Catherine looked at her husband with a look of deep love.

"The three sisters together again, that should be a good time."

"It's what we need."

Steve gave Catherine a long kiss goodbye and got in the car. Catherine waved goodbye as he pulled away. She stood there, staring down the empty driveway, for a long while. She could not help feeling torn between doing what she wanted to do and what she needed to do.

Walking to the front door, she wondered if she was doing the right thing. It took all the willpower she could muster to not chase him down the street. Instead, she went back toward Charlie's house.

When she reached for the door handle, it opened. At first it startled her, but she quickly recovered when it registered who was stepping through the door. A frown furrowed across her brow when she saw her kid sister dressed for a night out on the town - leather miniskirt, lace choker, dark eyeliner.

"You're going out?" Catherine looked at her watch, "At this hour?"

"I need something more substantial than chips and champagne."

"Come back in and I'll make you something."

"Charlie's cupboards are bare."

"Then we'll order a pizza."

Iris continued down the walkway. It was obvious to her that Catherine was trying to stall her, and she was not going to fall for any ploy she could muster.

"Iris!"

"They don't deliver tequila with pizza," Iris said, not turning around.

There was a rustle in the bushes, and Leona appeared pulling a few leaves from her hair. The aroma of Chinese food gave away what she was carrying in the bags.

"Hey, Leona has takeout."

"I'm not hungry for Chinese."

"You're insufferable!"

"Let her go." Catherine turned, startled to see Leona.

"I always forget you live next door."

The engine started up.

"Cut the umbilical cord," Leona said, laughing at her own joke. She handed Catherine one of the bags. "She's old enough to make her own choices, Catherine."

"Yes, but for the life of me I can't recall a single good one."

Iris waved good-bye to Leona. As she drove away, she lowered the convertible top. The radio blasted loudly, locked on a rock station. The sound faded into the distance, sounding more distorted the farther away she got, until finally the neighborhood was quiet again. Catherine watched the street, and Leona watched Catherine.

"Don't worry, she'll be fine."

"It's not that...it's just...," Catherine decided to not bother explaining. It was not Leona's business anyway.

"Whatcha got in the bags?" Charlie asked when they dropped them on the coffee table in the living room. Leona pulled out egg rolls, General Taos's chicken, rice, and sweet and sour chicken. "Enough for an army."

Charlie and Leona simultaneously flopped on the sofa, and Leona grabbed the remote control and flipped the channels, settling on an old black and white movie. Charlie sighed, which Leona took as her cue to not ask about anything.

Empty Chinese food cartons were strung across the coffee table in front of them and their bellies were full. Catherine entered the living room with a tray of hot tea. Neither one of them looked up, although they both knew she had approached.

"This will help you sleep. It's been a long day."

"I'm not tired," Charlie said, not looking away from the television.

"That's what this type of tea is for. It's chamomile and it's supposed to make you drowsy."

"Oh."

"I can't believe you're not tired. You should be." Catherine shoved the garbage on the coffee table aside, making room for the tray of tea. She sat down in the chair next to the couch and looked at Charlie. Peripherally, Charlie felt her sister's gaze burning into her face, but she did not look. After a full minute, Charlie could not take it any longer and she turned and looked back, irritated.

"What?"

"What? I was hoping you would open the floodgates."

"I'm dealing with it."

"Are you? You seem unscathed."

Charlie did not answer. She had decided out on the deck that she would deal with this on her own. She had made the decision alone, and she would deal with the decision alone. Leona cleared her throat then sat forward.

"Charlie? Why don't you go to bed," Leona said, trying to save her from Catherine's wrath.

Catherine gave Leona a look. This was a family affair and she wished the neighbor would just go home. She hated to admit that Charlie would probably listen to Leona before her. Catherine had lost control over Charlie long before Mom had died.

"I'm not tired," Charlie answered, still looking at the television, though she had not registered anything she had seen for the past ten minutes.

Catherine coaxed, "Really, Charlie, you should rest. Perhaps take a bubble bath. I'll draw it for you." She stood and walked toward the bathroom.

"Catherine. Stop!" Charlie snapped. "I don't want a bath. Okay? Leave me alone."

"I just care, Charlie. You don't have to snap at me. I just think you should relax."

Leona butted in, deciding it was time for her to help out. "She should go to Aruba and get away from everything. There she could relax."

Catherine shot Leona another deadly look. "Don't you have your own family?"

"I'm just merely adding to your suggestion. You said she needs to relax. I was simply agreeing."

"Don't put words into my mouth. You know that the last thing that Charlie needs is Aruba."

"I beg to differ."

"If you really cared about Charlie, you would see that all she needs is a little time with her family." Leona rolled her eyes and Catherine continued, "Anyway, she can't go to Aruba by herself. That's the most ridiculous thing I've ever heard. Stop putting crazy ideas into her head, Leona."

Charlie ignored them both, pretending to be absorbed in the program on TV.

"Charlie? What do you think?"

She spoke barely above a whisper. "Go by myself?"

Leona put her hand on Charlie's leg. "You have two paid tickets. Your bags are packed. Why not?"

Charlie contemplated, and the room went quiet. In that brief moment, Catherine felt a flutter of panic. Why would Leona put such a ludicrous idea in her head? She should just keep her opinions to herself, Catherine thought.

Charlie looked to Leona and nodded "yes", indicating to her friend that she should go.

"You've got to be kidding," Catherine broke the silence, troubled by the fact that she was losing control of her plan. "You can't go on your honeymoon by yourself!"

She moved over to Charlie, and crouched to eye level. "Don't you see how selfish you would look going to Aruba? It's not like Tom cheated on you and you're going for revenge."

Charlie's shoulders slumped in defeat.

Catherine continued, "I didn't give up this quality time with my family to babysit Iris. I did it so we could work on our relationship. We haven't been a true family since...well, since Mom died."

"It would not be selfish for Charlie to go to Aruba and *think*," Leona said.

"Leona...please!" Catherine lost her patience. She had had it with Leona's unsolicited comments.

Leona shrugged and turned her head to the right, looking out the sliding glass door toward the beach.

The room fell silent again.

Charlie leaned back and looked at the ceiling. She wanted them to leave her alone. She knew they were both waiting for her to choose the winner of the debate. Charlie didn't not know what she wanted to do. She just needed time alone to think.

Catherine turned to Leona, who felt her gaze, and they made eye contact. Catherine knew that Leona cared for Charlie, but sometimes she did not always have Charlie's best interests in mind. How could she know? She was not family.

It was at that moment, the stare-down with Leona, that Catherine knew she would do everything in her power to stop Charlie from going to Aruba.

Charlie shot forward, "I think it's a good idea."

"Charlie?" Catherine questioned. "I can't believe..." She stopped, the right words did not come.

"You really are self-centered," Catherine declared, as she jumped to her feet, "And I think maybe you're out of your mind. Or maybe I'm out of my mind for thinking I could make us a family again." Catherine stormed down the hall. Charlie would never understand what she had given up to stay with her sisters. She would never forgive her for that.

Leona saw the hurt on Charlie's face and got up to sit by her. She sidled in closely, putting her arm comfortably around her.

"There, there," she patted Charlie's shoulder. "It's all gonna be alright. Trust me."

On the couch, they both sat, quietly, listening to drawers slamming shut down the hallway in the bathroom. After a moment, the house grew silent. Catherine reappeared at the entrance of the living room. She had obviously been crying.

"Don't you have any tissues?"

Leona came up with an idea to make them both happy. "Why don't you take your sister to Aruba? She could surely use a stress-reliever – almost as much as you."

Charlie looked from to Catherine to Leona. Her expression gave away her true feelings. Never would she take Catherine on vacation with her. Leona smiled weakly when she realized her blunder.

"I just thought we could all spend some time together. Just the three of us, you know, just like old times." The emotions were still heavy in Catherine's voice, faltering at the end.

Charlie got up abruptly and walked to the kitchen. The pressure was unbearable. Leona and Catherine both watched her every move, Catherine through the open kitchen entrance and Leona through the opening by the breakfast nook. Both had a clear shot of the distraught woman.

Leona called out to Charlie, "You could always take Iris!"

Charlie's head shot toward Leona, and she knew the answer immediately.

"She'd probably lose her before they got out of the airport," Catherine said, reaching for lame excuses, "Or have to bail her out of jail."

A loud rumbling outside interrupted them.

"It sounds like a small plane is crashing into our house!" Catherine shouted above the sound as she jumped up and flew to the window, pushing the blinds aside. "What on earth!"

Leona, curious herself, went to the window. She saw who it was and turned to go back to her seat. "It just keeps getting better and better."

Catherine spoke aloud to herself, "I want to go to bed." She then headed for the front door, and opened it.

Chapter 7

∧

Two Harleys, one solid gold and the other aqua blue with white stripes, rumbled loudly in the driveway, each carrying a couple. The two men were trying to hold a conversation, yelling over the noisy bikes.

"Think you could ride any slower?" the guy on the gold bike taunted, but before the guy on the other bike could answer, he was distracted by a woman rushing toward them, her hands flailing wildly in the air. He smacked the other biker's arm then nodded in her direction. "Hey, Pete, look. It's your new wife!" the burly biker on the gold bike said. They all burst out laughing.

"Go away!" Catherine yelled over the rumble, and then covered her ears. "You're at the wrong house."

The bikers shrugged at one another. The owner of the aqua hog shut off his engine and Pete followed suit.

Catherine adjusted her voice to fit the sudden quiet. "It's one o'clock in the morning. You obviously have the wrong address."

Pete, the shorter and stockier of the two, had a mermaid tattooed on his right arm. He weaved slightly as he climbed off the bike trying to act cool as he quickly composed himself. His passenger, Angel, who looked nothing like her name, nimbly stepped off. She seemed to be putting on a show for everyone, flipping off her helmet as if she were stripping every inch of clothing from her body, her long black hair cascading down her back as she shook it free. She turned and smiled to no one in particular, just pleased that she still had it going on.

Catherine cleared her throat, "Excuse me. You don't belong here."

All four of them stared back at her with bloodshot eyes. Their tattoos and leather suddenly seemed to be screaming at her. Her heart began to pound rapidly. She tried to change her voice. "I didn't mean to sound so rude, it's just...it's just, you're at the wrong house."

Pete's upper body swayed in a circle as he struggled to focus. "We're with her." He pointed toward the back of the house.

Catherine turned her head to see where he was pointing, but saw no one. "There's nobody there, sir."

Pete, suddenly frustrated, asked, "What's her name, Jake?"
Jake scratched his golden beard, and then squeezed his eyes shut for a moment. It was obvious he was equally as drunk and as loss for words as his friend. "I can't remember her name."

"Pete, you were just having a conversation with her. She was right there." Jake pointed to where Iris was standing. He looked to Chastity, the Chastity, the girl on the back of Pete's bike and she shrugged. She had forgotten as well. Then, as if a light bulb clicked, he snapped his head to Catherine and announced proudly, spraying an enormous amount of spittle as he spoke, "Irish."

"That's it. Yeah!" Jake agreed, nodding toward Angel then Chastity.

Catherine scratched her head, "There is no one here by that name."

"Irish!" Pete repeated suddenly frustrated, "Where'd she go?"

"She just went in back," Jake exclaimed, his voice loud as if he was in a bar with loud music. "I'll go get her."

"Shshshsh! You're gonna wake the neighborhood."

Jake climbed off his bike and headed for the side of the house.

Catherine panicked, "If you don't leave right now, I'm going to call the police."

Angel started laughing hysterically, "Irish!" She kept repeating over and over and they all began to laugh.

Catherine covered her ears. The situation had grown completely out of hand, and she did not know what to do. Her voice became unsteady, and she almost sounded like a child. "Please go. I'm begging you. There's no one...."

Catherine whirled around when she heard clanking behind her. Suddenly it dawned on her who "Irish" was. Iris appeared from the side of the house carrying a handful of shot glasses.

"Got the shot glasses, salt and lemon. We are in business!" Iris bellowed excitedly.

Jake pulled a fifth of tequila from his jacket and held it high to the sky. They all howled. "Tequila!"

"Be quiet!" Catherine screamed and they all came to a screeching halt. "What is going on here?"

"That place down the road was charging four bucks a shot. Can you believe that?" Iris answered nonchalantly.

"Do you realize what time it is? Have you no consideration?"

"We were supposed to party today! And I was psyched to do just that. Anyway, these are my friends."

"Some friends. They don't even know your name, Irish."

Iris was suddenly in no mood to deal with Catherine. "Do you live here?" Not waiting for her to reply, "No, you don't! It's not your problem, so chill!"

"I am staying here for awhile."

"But you're forgetting one important thing. You're not my boss. So, why don't you just go to bed and leave me alone."

Catherine glared at Iris but she stood firm. She had no intentions on going to bed early. Iris acted as if Catherine was not there and passed out the shot glasses. "One for you, and you, and you...and...you! I'll have one too, if I do say so myself!" Jake began pouring shots for the girls first. Chastity, Jake's girl, the golden haired biker chick with the yellow rose tattoo on her leg, dropped her shot glass and it crashed to the pavement. Catherine jolted rigidly from the sound as Pete and Jake turned to one another and began to howl with laughter again.

"Yeah, sure! Laugh all you want," Catherine announced, surrendering to the group. Without saying another word, Catherine went back up the walkway to the house, slamming the front door behind her, which only made them laugh even louder.

"Let's go out on the back deck. We don't want to party inside because that woman you just met is my sister and she could sober any buzz," Iris said, waving for her new friends to follow her through the house.

They tiptoed and shushed each other up the walkway to the house. Overreacting, cartoon-like, they tiptoed through the front door. Each shush was followed by a snicker, and then someone else shushed a little louder, which only triggered snickers from them all. They all followed their leader through the living room. Catherine stood, with folded arms, in the middle of the living room, watching the congo line of drunks pass by. Pete saluted as he passed, and Jake snorted loudly.

"Charlie?" Catherine hollered for her sister, "I think you need to have a little talk with Iris."

Charlie came down from her bedroom, wearing long flannel pajamas, her hair twisted in a clip on the top of her head. She rubbed her eyes, sleepily.

Iris answered before Charlie could ask any questions. "It's no big deal, Charlie, we're going outside."

Charlie didn't have a problem with Iris having a few friends over. "Okay. Just keep it down."

Catherine shot a look from Charlie to Iris, shocked by Charlie's nonchalant attitude. Iris, gloating, returned a sarcastic smile. Catherine looked away disgusted.

Pete, trying to be funny, lost his balance next to Charlie's china hutch, which carried her collection of hand-blown glass figurines. He tottered and then swayed backwards. He reached his arm out to grab something, anything, to catch himself. Catherine, horrified, ran to him and grabbed hold just as his hand was inches away from knocking the hutch's entire contents to the ground. Chastity giggled as Angel went to Pete's aid. Pete turned and shushed everyone and they all burst out laughing.

"We're just gonna sit here and drink for a bit. I'll keep it down."

"This isn't your house, Iris. You can't just come plowing in here with those...those..."

Iris looked past Catherine to Charlie, ignoring Catherine completely. "We'll be quiet as mice. Nobody'll even know we're out there."

Angel knocked on the window. "Come on, Irish! Don't listen to that old stick in the mud. Let's party."

"That's it! Tell your friends the party's over," Catherine yelled, furiously. "This has gone on long enough."

Iris gazed scornfully at her older sister. "Why do you think you can always tell me what to do?"

Catherine turned to Charlie for help. "Will you please say something to her?"

Charlie leaned against the hallway wall and covered her ears. Powerless against the situation, and worn-out from the entire day, she slid all the way down to the floor. After a moment, she rubbed her face agitatedly and looked to Leona for help. She could not take another moment of her sisters' bickering.

Leona smiled and mouthed, "Aruba."

She knew she had to escape the people she called family.

Charlie nodded her head.

Chapter 8

∧

The incoming tide sent crashing waves high onto the sand. A crab danced his sideways walk from the sand back into the foamy sea. Clouds blanketed the sky, giving the ocean a grayish-green color.

The remnants of Iris's beach party were evident. An empty tequila bottle, tumbleweed stuck inside, was planted in the sand. The shot glasses were on the deck.

Catherine watched Iris through the sliding glass door. It must have been cold outside, because Iris was wrapped in a blanket sitting on the deck. Thoughts of what Iris was doing with her life overwhelmed Catherine's mind, and she wished she could just pick her sister up and shake some sense into her. Catherine was exhausted. She had lain awake all night worrying about her baby sister and her partying habits. It was baffling how Iris could get into such bizarre situations. These days, a young woman should not go to a bar by herself, let alone bring home strangers.

Catherine went to the refrigerator to get a glass of cold water. She was about to open the door when she spotted the two airline tickets to Aruba on a magnetic clip stuck to the freezer door. An idea came to her. A long moment passed as Catherine wondered if her scheme would work. After all that had occurred over the past twenty-four hours, she really did not have anything to lose in trying. Catherine took the tickets off the clip and stuck them into the waistband of her pants. Feeling reckless, she checked to be sure no one was looking.

Catherine went back to the sliding glass door and began assessing the damage. Iris, still on the same cigarette, was in the same position on the steps. Angel and Chastity were passed out on two lounge chairs while Pete and Jake slept in the sand below the steps. As Catherine watched the unconscious bikers passed out, she reassured herself that something had to be done. The situation had gotten out of control. What if these people were dangerous? They could decide to move in. Who could stop them? Iris was young and naive when it came to worldly experiences. One day, it could be the death of her, but not if she could help it.

Catherine slid open the door, and whispered loudly, with conviction, "Iris, it's time for your friends to go home."

Iris tossed her cigarette into the sand with attitude, and turned her head slowly toward Catherine, glaring for a moment, her dark eyes serious for the first time. Then she slowly turned back to face the ocean.

"Don't disregard me."

Iris ignored her sister.

"I'm serious, Iris. I want them out of here...now!"

Iris shot up like a rocket, the blanket sliding off her, and she got right in Catherine's face. Venomous anger percolated, tickling nerves that had not beckoned since childhood.

"Who the hell do you think you are?" Iris scoffed bravely, as if daring Catherine to challenge her. "You're not anybody's mother here. Least of all, mine. I don't know why you think you can boss us around. Why don't you stick to henpecking your wimpy-ass husband? That's what you do best."

Catherine was stunned, momentarily wordless. "How dare you speak to me that way? I am not in the wrong here. If you could only see how selfish you are," Catherine said, resentfully, her voice quivering. "I sacrifice so much for you, Iris."

"Sacrifice! You write a fucking check for school. A check that isn't even your money! You don't even know what work is!"

The bikers and their girls were suddenly awakened from their drunken slumber. Angel sat up, rubbed her eyes, and shook Chastity awake.

"You little ingrate!" Catherine's voice suddenly matched Iris. "I've taken care of you since Mom died. You wanted to be a hair stylist, we sent you to beauty school. Then you wanted to be a chef. How long did that last? How much did that dream cost? Now, it's art school?!"

"You would not know a life's dream if it crawled up and bit you in the ass."

Catherine jolted, anger whipping through her like an electrical current. Iris' cruelty shocked her. Catherine turned away, unable to look at her sister; unable to show her how her words hurt.

"Maybe not, but at least I know how to appreciate a good thing and be grateful," Catherine said numbly, her voice monotone and quiet. By this time, Pete and Jake were up and approaching the steps to the deck. Angel put her hand in the air to stop the guys. It was just getting good.

"Grateful! You just want me to kiss your ass! And even that wouldn't be enough for you!"

"You little...," Catherine stopped herself. She could not believe Iris was getting the best of her. She inhaled deeply.

"You better not say it, sister!" Angel spoke, coming to her friend's defense. "Leave Irish alone. She's a good person."

Catherine glanced around the group that suddenly seemed to be closing in on her. It seemed as if it were five to one. If her idea was going to work, she had better try it now, before she lost her courage. She said a quick prayer, then turned to face the bikers. Although her fear was making her knees wobble, Catherine managed a smile.

"Hey, everybody! I've got two airline tickets for a one-week vacation in sunny, exotic Aruba. Any takers?"

All four bikers stopped dead in their tracks and look excitedly amongst each other, wondering if she was for real. The silence was sobering, and Catherine knew it was working.

"But there are four of us," Angel said, excitedly.

"That's your problem," she said confidently. "Maybe if you all pitched in, you could come up with enough money to buy two more tickets. The rooms and meals are paid for." She stopped for effect. "Leave right now and you could be swimming in aqua-blue waters by tomorrow."

"Catherine! Stop it!" Iris screeched at the top of her lungs. "Those aren't yours to give away."

Catherine turned to Iris as she held the tickets toward the group. Angel grabbed the tickets and took off running toward the side of the house. The others chased her, chattering excitedly to one another. A moment later, motorcycles rumbled in front of the house, slicing through the glaring silence that separated the two sisters.

"I hate you more now than I ever have," Iris said, squinting back tears that filled her eyes. She turned around before Catherine could see them. She punched herself in the leg, punishing herself for crying. She only cried when she was angry. She did not want Catherine to misconstrue the tears to be from hurt feelings. She would rather die than let her think that.

"I know you're angry...," Catherine put her hand on Iris' shoulder and Iris angrily shrugged it off.

"Leave me alone!" Iris yelled and darted down the stairs toward the ocean.

Catherine - deflated, defeated, and degraded - finally breathed. Unaware how long she had been holding her breath, she let out all the air she held tightly in her lungs. She slumped in one of the lounge chairs, disheartened. What worried her was that the worst was not over. How was she going to tell Charlie she had given away her honeymoon?

Chapter 9

∧

"Go on!" Denny said to Tom after he shut off the engine. They both sat astride the Harley across the street from Charlie's house. The sun crept from behind a cloud, suddenly blinding and bright against their alcohol sensitive eyes.

"It's too early," Tom said, squinting, his eyes watering as he spoke. "This idea sounded much better when we were shit faced."

"Look, I want to go to Aruba. You deserve to go to Aruba." Denny patted his pockets, looking for his cigarettes, but remembered he had smoked his last one at the bar. "Don't give up now. You paid for them, for crying out loud."

"Let's come back later."

"Don't be so spineless. Wake her ass up. The flight is at ten o'clock." Denny looked at his watch. "We've got a little over an hour to be at the airport, and I suggest you shower because I'm not sittin' next to your smelly ass all the way to Aruba."

Tom could not move. "Why did I let you talk me into this anyway?"

"Tom?" Denny questioned. "Don't beat yourself up. You're not thinking straight. That's why I'm here..." Denny stopped for a moment, trying not to sound desperate. "Just go get the damn tickets."

Tom nodded. "I know you're right. Why can't I make my legs get off this bike?"

"This is supposed to be the happiest day of your life," Denny said pausing for a second, "And after all she put you through, she deserves to suffer."

Tom looked to the ground, contemplating, "Your idea sounded much better back at the bar," he repeated.

"For chrissake, Tom, Mom cried! Get even!"

Even though a part of him wanted to get off the bike and march over to get those airline tickets, unnatural forces held Tom in place, like a stone statue. He felt like his toes were hanging on the edge of a cliff, and he wanted to jump but could not. The longer he sat there, the harder it was to summon the nerve to walk up the flower-lined sidewalk.

Denny felt sorry for him, "Tom, you're one of the good guys. Don't you get tired of finishing last all the time?"

"Why don't you just cut me open and pour salt on my heart?"

"What the hell's wrong with you?" Denny shouted. "Get your ass off this bike and go over."

"Why don't you go?" Tom snapped. "It's your dim-witted idea anyway... you do it."

"I'm not fuckin' going in there. They're your tickets. You go!" Denny said, and then added, "I'm losing respect for you."

"I'm leaving," Tom yelled at Denny. "I'm tired and I want to go to bed."

"Why are you petering out?"

"Me? This wasn't my idea, little brother."

"I can't believe this. She did you wrong. Go in and get what you want!"

"You don't get it do you? The only thing I want in that house is her!" Tom yelled.

For the first time since the cancelled wedding Denny saw the situation from Tom's point of view. He dismounted, and Tom slid forward, holding the heavy bike up.

"Thank you for understanding," Tom said, barely above a whisper. He was unable to look into his brother's eyes.

Denny patted his brother's shoulder. "I'm only getting involved because I want to find a Caribbean honey with long, beautiful legs."

"And I thought it was because you cared."

Tapping his finger to his temple, "There is always a reason behind this madness."

Denny started to cross the street but stopped when a shiny lime-green Volkswagen bug whipped past him, a little too close, sending Denny's hair into a wild frenzy. Denny turned and shrugged to his brother, blowing off the fact that he was almost killed. It was when he looked both ways before crossing the street that he saw something odd. Four rough-looking people dressed in leather, people he did not recognize, were coming out from around Charlie's house and getting on the two Harleys that were parked in front of her garage.

Tom's attention shifted when their engines ignited. As the small gang took off on their bikes, they let out whoops and holler. Denny turned around in the street, and looked back toward Tom, who was also staring with shocked disbelief.

Denny walked back to Tom. "Wow, that's kinda weird. Must've been some party!"

"She had a party?"

"I told you it wasn't too early to come over."

"Let's go!" Tom demanded furiously.

"What about Aruba?"

"Fuck Aruba."

Denny could not remember the last time he had seen Tom outraged about anything.

"You should be angry!" Denny said, trying to be agreeable. "I'll be right back. Let me go get those tickets."

"I'm serious, Denny. Let's go now!" Tom said sliding forward on the bike, taking the driver's helm. "If you won't take me home, I'll take myself."

"You're not driving my hog."

"Try and stop me."

Denny smirked and opened his mouth to say something smart, but Tom stopped him. "Don't even try to make a joke about this one, Denny, or I'll kick your ass."

"What?" He asked, biting his cheeks, unsuccessfully hiding his amusement.

"Fuck with me, I dare you. I'm about ready to snap." Just to show Denny he was serious, Tom turned the key and started Denny's Harley. It grumbled loudly. Tom raised one eyebrow daring Denny to test him.

Denny stepped up to take the reins of the bike. "Slide back."

Tom sat firmly. It was he who was messing with his brother now.

"I refuse to be a passenger on my own bike. Now slide back."

"I will when you wipe that smartass smile from your face."

Denny pressed his lips together, making them white, and he opened his eyes wide. "There."

Tom stood, allowing Denny to climb on, and then he slid back.

Chapter 10

∧

Leona, preoccupied with the effort of wheeling her luggage cart across the lumpy lawn, did not notice Denny and Tom as they drove away. Because of the morning's dew, Charlie's freshly mowed grass was gathering in clumps on the wheels.

Leona tried to hide the pressing guilt that was eating at her. She could not believe that she had persuaded Charlie to go to Aruba. Now she hoped it would be the right decision. One thing Leona knew for sure, Charlie needed to get away from the chaos surrounding her.

It was a struggle, but she finally made it to Charlie's front door after giving the uncooperative cart a few swift kicks. Leona delivered, her usual knock and entered on her own, blazing a green trail behind her on Charlie's hardwood floor. Charlie, who stood in the kitchen, turned around and began laughing at the sight of Leona tussling with the cart.

"Quit laughing. Whether I'm at the grocery store or I'm golfing, I always get the misbehaving carts. It must be a conspiracy."

"Ever think that it could be the operator?"

Leona swiftly kicked the cart, and it flew across the carpet. "The thing was possessed. I swear."

"I think I'm ready," Charlie sighed.

"I know you're sad, I can see it, but I want you to know that I will be there a hundred percent for you."

Charlie smiled. There was nothing she could say, or would say. She just wanted to get on with things.

"I've got tanning butter, oil, and spray...," Leona opened her bag. "And spf 4, 8, 15 and 30. "I think we're all set!"

Loud voices from outside interrupted them. Leona looked to Charlie and rolled her eyes.

"They've been at it since the...," Charlie could not say *wedding*. That word would not be in her vocabulary for a long time. The sliding door to the kitchen opened and suddenly there was no need to finish her sentence. Catherine and Iris' voices were in full volume, and Charlie covered her ears to drown out the sound.

"You can kiss my ass, Catherine!" Iris bellowed as she ran past Charlie and Leona down the hallway to the bathroom. Catherine, close on Iris' heels, followed her through the living room, but froze when she saw that Charlie and Leona were fully dressed to go.

"Ooooh...hi." She forced a smile and waved stiffly. "That Iris, she still acts like a teenager. It must be that artist's lack of sensibility."

"Must be," Leona answered agreeably, although she did not really agree.

"What was that all about?" Charlie's asked, her jaw clenching tightly. "When will this Hatfield and McCoy routine end?"

"Don't worry about it. It's between us."

"And the neighbors?" Charlie added, and then looked at her watch, "Well, we better call a cab...," Charlie smiled at Catherine. "...Unless you wanna drive us to the airport."

"Oh, you guys were serious?" Catherine asked, even though she knew the answer. Playing dumb was never her strong suit.

Charlie rubbed her face, perturbed, and then gave a look to Catherine expressly implying that she was tired of the games. Catherine began dancing nervously and was at a rare loss for words. Catherine got flustered and began to tremble.

"What's wrong with you?" Charlie asked, thinking her sister was going to faint. "Are you alright?"

Iris opened the bathroom door and yelled, "Why don't you tell her what you did?"

This time it was Charlie who was yelling, "Iris, shut up!" the bathroom door slammed shut again, "Catherine? What is it?"

Catherine took in a deep breath. "I don't think Aruba is such a good idea."

Charlie snapped angrily. "That's it? That's what you've been wasting my time with? Damn it all, Catherine! Can't you ever butt out of my life?"

Leona looked quickly to Charlie and patted her arm, but Charlie pulled away. She had some built up frustration, and it seemed that Catherine was going to be the one taking the brunt of it.

"I'm not trying to control you...," Catherine spoke quietly, trying to gain control. "I just don't think it's wise for you right now. Why don't you give it some time?"

"I don't really think that you have a say in this. It's my life. We're dressed, we're packed, and we're going. No ifs, ands, or buts about it."

Charlie turned to Leona, "Will you call the cab?"

"Sure," Leona said, as she set her purse down on top of her big flowered suitcase.

"You can't go," Catherine blurted aloud.

"I've shown amazing restraint, but believe me when I tell you my patience is wearing thin."

"Listen to me," Catherine tried to explain what she had done.

"Look here, Catherine. It's my decision. And I've made it."

"I'm not saying you can't go. I'm telling you it's impossible...."

Charlie dropped her suitcase. "That doesn't even make sense, Catherine."

"It's not that. It's just that... Really, I'm not trying to control you. I'm thinking of us." Catherine licked her parched lips and continued, "I thought since Iris is here for such a short time and we haven't been together in so long, we could spend some quality time as a family."

"Oh, so you and Iris started without me?" The sarcasm flew easily off Charlie's tongue, and she heard Leona giggle from behind her. Charlie turned to her friend, and Leona plopped down on the couch.

Charlie glanced at her watch. "Don't sit down. We've got to go."

"You go ahead and take care of things. Aruba can wait."

"She's right. Aruba can wait."

"Catherine. Stop it!"

"Look, Charlie, I did what I had to do." Catherine began to tremble again, this time more visibly than before, "I know I overstepped my boundaries, and I'll make it up to you."

"Quit speaking in riddles."

"Sit down. I can't talk to you when you're yelling."

Charlie sat down on her suitcase, and released her purse from her shoulder. It dropped to the floor with a thud. Catherine watched the purse fall and stared at it for a moment.

"I don't have all day."

"They were ganging up on me," she turned to Leona for reassurement, "You saw how big they were, right?"

"Who?" Charlie was confused. Leona suddenly got the notion that something good was about to happen. She leaned forward, anticipating the news that Catherine hesitated to broadcast.

"They would've taken over the house. Iris would have ended up in a biker commune within a week. The Hell's Angels would have made your house their summer home."

Charlie threw her hands in the air, exasperated, "I give up! What the hell are you talking about?"

"I gave them the tickets," Catherine blurted, finally freeing the truth she hesitated to admit.

"You did what?!" Charlie uttered, taken aback by Catherine's revelation. Had she heard her sister correctly?

"I had to get rid of them. The bikers...the tickets were the only thing I could think of."

Charlie glared at her sister, trying to absorb the absurdity of what Catherine had just told her. The house was silent, except for the faint ocean sound outside. Charlie slowly turned her head in Leona's direction. "Can you believe this?"

Leona, not knowing what to say, simply shrugged. She decided to let Charlie deal with this situation.

When she was finally able to speak, she replied, "Those were my tickets Catherine! They weren't yours to give away!"

"You're right. And I'll give you the money back for them as soon as Steve gets back. I swear!" Catherine stated.

"That's not the point. I was planning on leaving today. It's kind of convenient that this all works out for your little plan of family time. You never cease to amaze me."

"That's the pot calling the kettle black if I've ever seen it...and...you!" She pointed in her sister's face, "You of all people don't need to be going on a honeymoon by yourself anyway." Now it was Catherine whose voice was loud and defensive. "Yes! I admit that I was wrong to give away your property, but I will stand behind my actions. It was for the best. You will see that someday."

"Oh and perhaps I'll thank you for it, too!" Charlie snapped sarcastically.

"You should be thinking about what you just did and how it's affecting everyone."

Those words stung and Charlie suddenly stepped back. She no longer wanted to be in this conversation. She did not want to explain her life, her pain, and her decisions to Catherine. She would never understand, and Charlie didn't care if she ever did.

Without saying another word, she picked up her suitcase, turned, and headed into her bedroom. Catherine and Leona watched Charlie walk from the room. After she left, Catherine looked at Leona, who was sitting back on the couch with her feet propped up on her suitcase.

"You're pushing them away, being like that, you know," Leona said.

"Like I planned this, Leona. If you had any sense, you would know that a vacation by herself is the last thing she needs right now."

"I think Charlie knows what's best for her. She's a grown woman."

"Don't you care about her? She's a walking time bomb, ready to explode."

"Sweetheart, she's not the only one."

Catherine huffed down the hallway and went to the bathroom door. She had forgotten Iris was in there.

"Oh no you don't, Catherine!" Iris yelled from behind the locked door. "You already had your yell at me for the year."

Catherine turned, found the nearest unlocked door and went inside.

Leona sat in the living room alone. She could not help feeling sad for missing out on the trip and spending quality time talking to Charlie. Catherine would never understand that Charlie wouldn't ever open up to her.

"It's always an eventful day at the Hunter home," Leona spoke to herself, hurling her heavy bags back onto the broken luggage cart.

Chapter 11

∧

"This isn't the first time Catherine's done something like this," Charlie said, "And it won't be the last, either."

Charlie and Iris were walking along the foamy edge of the surf. They had walked so far down the beach that Charlie's house was a black dot on the horizon. It was a chilly morning, so they were both dressed in long sweaters and jeans. Partly cloudy skies gave way to the sun, which brightened up the sky for a moment and then darkened a bit as a cottony cloud passed, sending golden rays to the ground.

"I hate feeling like I'm under her thumb," Iris replied, "She's so damn arrogant." Iris tiptoed out of the way of a wave that crept farther than others had. Charlie let it run over her tennis shoes.

"Your shoes are getting wet."

"I know. I'm already numb. Really, what damage could a little cold water do?"

"Really," Iris agreed.

"You shouldn't let Catherine get to you," Charlie advised, even though she carried her own hostility.

"Yeah, easy for you to say. She doesn't try to run your life."

"Ha!" Charlie let out a sarcastic laugh, as she stepped in front of Iris. "Oh, yeah? What about this morning? I can't believe she actually gave away my honeymoon!"

"You should have punched her."

"That's real grown up," Charlie laughed and went back to walking along the beach. Iris followed, suddenly quiet. Charlie continued a moment later, "That thought did cross my mind, though."

Iris laughed, "That would have been funny."

"I don't think I've ever been so mad at anyone before."

"I can't believe you didn't hit her. I came so close last night. She shouldn't mess with me when I'm drinking tequila. It makes me crazy!"

"Iris, you've always been crazy!"

"Maybe you need to get a little crazy once in a while, too."

"I'm afraid if I let loose and start flipping out now, I might not stop."

Just then, a wave rushed up around their ankles, and Iris cursed aloud. "Shit! I was trying to stay dry."

"The tide's coming in," Charlie said as another wave enveloped her feet. She did not mind the cold water. It matched her emotions.

The surf was rising higher and higher, sending wave upon wave crashing onto their feet. The last one caught them by surprise. They both screamed and laughed as they jumped over the edge and ran further up on the sand.

"Well...now that I'm not going Aruba, and...well you know," Charlie stammered, "I can't just sit around. I've just got to focus on what little bit of my life I have left and make the best of it. I think I'm gonna call the guys and set up a little jam tonight. I'm sure Spiro won't mind."

"Who's Spiro?" Iris asked.

"The owner of the club I play at. Why don't you come down to the club with me?"

"Tonight? You're going to sing at the club tonight? You're kidding, right? Don't you think it's too soon to go back to work?"

Charlie looked at her for a moment and then brushed past her. She wished everyone would quit asking her questions. She understood that leaving Tom at the altar was a big deal, but why did everyone think they knew what was best for her?

Iris could see the turmoil on Charlie's face and felt bad for giving advice. "Look, ignore me. I just sounded a little like Catherine. Sorry."

"I can't just sit around. I've got to do something. Don't ask any more questions, please, because I can't explain it. Just come with me tonight and be there for me."

"Okay."

"Don't sound so excited."

"No, it's not that..."

"You might have fun."

"Oh, I always have fun," Iris ribbed her with her elbow. "I'm just...oh, never mind. I'll enjoy myself."

"You always do, you wild woman," Charlie teased, then they walked in silence for a long moment. Her smile faded as her thoughts caught up with her.

"Charlie?" Iris questioned. "You sure you don't wanna talk?"

Charlie looked at her and gave a smile that came too quickly.

"Oh, I was just thinking that I need to put new strings on my guitar – don't let me forget."

"Wait." Iris stopped Charlie, jumping in front of her and grabbing hold of both shoulders, "You've got to tell me one thing. Is Catherine's going? Because, if she is I'm not. Nothing against you."

"You'd better get used to seeing her. She's probably going to be hanging out at my house a lot while Steve and Christina are away. She doesn't like being alone. In fact, I can't remember her ever being without them." Charlie stepped out of her path and continued walking. "But I'm sure she won't go tonight. I'm not even going to tell her where I'm going. So don't you mention it either. That's the last thing I need, more Catherine crap."

"You don't have to ask me twice. In fact, I've got an idea. It's a sure fire way to make sure she doesn't go. We can put her to work. You know how Catherine likes tasks?"

"Like what?"

Iris began listing aloud, using her fingers to count. "First, she could buy groceries for the week, and I've got some dirty laundry. Maybe she could clean your floors..."

"You're mean!" Charlie hit her arm. "Besides, what's wrong with my floors?"

Chapter 12

∧

That night, Charlie stood on a modest stage, singing to a small but enthusiastic audience. The stage lights brightened the club, but they also made it hot. Tall fans waved back and forth, cooling the musicians insufficiently. But without them, the stage would be unbearable.

Denny was tending bar. He began pouring a beer when he saw Iris coming toward him. He tipped the glass, spilling out the excess foam that frothed over the rim, and slid it to her as she walked up.

"Tell me something," Denny said as he pushed an empty ashtray forward, inviting her to stay and talk to him for a minute.

"What?"

"What's going on with her?" Denny pointed at Charlie onstage.

"Don't even ask, Denny. I'm just here for the ride."

Two handsome college boys walked into the bar and Iris watched them sit down at the table nearest the dance floor. Excusing herself from Denny, she sauntered through the tables, toward her table, bypassing theirs. She fancied the big armed, dark haired guy wearing the backward Brown University baseball cap. She took her time passing in front of their table, just so he would notice her, and then sat down next to Leona at the table at the corner of the stage.

Charlie finished her song to scattered applause and whistles from the audience. She smiled and thanked the audience graciously. She did not feel like singing anymore. From her first step on stage, it occurred to Charlie that singing may not have been a smart decision. Her stomach was in knots. Fighting the feelings seemed impossible. Erasing Tom from her mind was going to be harder than anything she had ever done in her life. Singing used to be the easiest release, but it did not seem to be working now. Never before had she felt like all eyes were on her, judging her. She knew it was impossible for the audience to know about her troubles, but it felt like they all did.

It suddenly occurred to her why everyone was staring. She was standing on stage in dead silence. The music had ended and she was standing in front of the microphone, deep in her own thoughts.

Ethan nudged Charlie, "One more?" Ethan turned to the band mates and they all shrugged. Some of the members made their living off gigging, so it was a rare occasion for them to say no.

Charlie shook her head no, replacing the microphone in its stand.

Ethan was surprised. Usually they had to pry Charlie from the stage. "You alright?"

"Yeah...I...,"Charlie looked back out at the thinning crowd. "We can talk later."

"Uh...okay." He did not know what to say. Nobody did. When she showed up to set up the equipment, there was an uncomfortable silence. Ethan associated that sensation with the feeling of dread that comes when somebody dies and you don't know what to say to the bereaved.

Charlie turned back to the audience and spoke. She flipped the microphone back on. "Thank you all for coming. We'll be back Saturday night."

Charlie stepped off the stage and walked past the table where Leona was sitting. Leona had her camera to her eye and began snapping off shots of her. Charlie put her hand up to block the flash.

"Leona!"

Leona kept firing as Charlie escaped to the bar. Denny had a bottle of beer waiting for her as she approached. Charlie gulped half of it down then placed the icy bottle against her sweating face.

At first, Denny did not know what to say to her. He thought for a moment then said, "You forgot to tell them to tip the bartender on the way out."

"The only reason people are in the bar is because we were here, so give me a break." Charlie took another big swig. "Besides, I thought you only tended bar for the endless supply of women...or is it for pinball machine storage?"

"Hey, leave my beloved pinball machine out of it." He dumped out an overflowing ashtray and wiped it out with a bar towel. "Speaking of storage, you know where I can park it for a few days?"

"Not again! Have you ever stayed with anyone longer than three weeks?"

"It's not my fault. She did not believe that the reason I stayed out all night was because Tom got dumped...," Denny stopped mid sentence. "Open mouth, insert foot."

Charlie looked away.

"Uh, shit. Sorry about that."

Charlie did not answer. Not that she would know what to say if she could. She did not want to talk. Period. Not now, not ever, and especially not with Denny. Granted, she had been Denny's friend long before she met Tom. In fact, Denny was the reason she had met Tom. Denny was never the friend she confided all her secrets to. He was more like the friend you went out with when you wanted to escape reality and have a few laughs. Besides, she knew blood was thicker than water, and when push came to shove, Charlie knew where Denny's loyalty would be.

"Look, Charlie...I didn't mean it to sound like that," Denny said apologetically.

Charlie turned completely around and faced her bandmates on stage. They were swiftly clearing up.

"I'm surprised they haven't come up for beer yet."

"This whole night has been bass-ackward."

Charlie turned her head to the side and shot him a look; "Whatever are you implying?" then took another drink of her beer.

Denny pushed the issue, although he did not really know why. He had never been one to pry into the "whys" of things. This way, he would never be expected to explain his own actions, which were unexplainable most of the time. But Tom was his brother, and something inside pressed him to ask. "So, have you guys even talked?"

Charlie scrunched her face. He just had to push. "You're the last person I expected to bother me." Charlie downed the remainder of her beer. Then she turned back around to face him. "I should go help them."

Charlie slid the empty bottle to him. He caught it as it glided smoothly off the edge of the bar. They made eye contact for a fleeting second, but she looked away.

Denny grabbed her hand. "You should." She pulled away quickly, as if she had just pricked a cactus. He began wiping the bar. "Go talk to him."

She could not look at him, so she concentrated on the hard-wood floors. "Doesn't anybody have anything else to talk about? I came here to get away," she whispered quietly. She really thought that tonight would be easy. She'd go sing away her cares. Escape reality. "Why can't everyone just let it go?"

For once, it was Denny who was at a loss for words, but Charlie broke the unexpected silence. "I gotta go, Denny. Thanks for the beer," Charlie said without looking up. It was difficult to look at him. Guilt was a funny thing. It was an emotion she did not want to get used to.

"He's free-falling," Denny hollered when she was half way between him and the stage.

Charlie covered her ears when she heard his last words and continued walking, blocking out what he had just said.

Denny watched Charlie for a moment, half-hoping she would come back, but knowing she would not. He would not know what else to say to her if she did. Talking to her was like trying to rationalize with a drunk.

Charlie did not go on stage. She was unable to confront the guys about her disaster on the stage. Instead, she went over to Leona, who was packing up her camera gear. Charlie pulled a chair from the table and turned it around, sitting with the back forward. She looked up to Leona with wide eyes as helpless as she felt.

"This too shall pass," Leona said as she pushed bangs out of Charlie's face. "I got a couple of really nice shots of you on stage." Leona told her as she stuffed the rolls of used film into the side pocket of her leather camera bag.

"You got here late. I looked a lot better earlier."

Leona zipped the bag shut. "I would've gotten here earlier, but I was on the phone talking to someone about you."

"Oh, yeah?" Charlie smirked. "Your psychic or your shrink?"

"I haven't seen the shrink in years and you know I've been wanting you to go see Gerardo for a long time. He could have spared you all that...that stuff from Saturday. You know, the wedding and all."

"Of course, I know. I was there. I'm sick to death of everyone bringing it up!" Charlie snapped. Immediately she was sorry for the tone she used with her best friend. "I didn't mean to be short with you. I'm sorry." Charlie smiled, "It's just that you're Leona the patient. Leona the just. You're the one person I know who never judges. I wasn't expecting to hear about my mess ups from you."

"I'll try to be careful not to mention it in the future."

"I'm sorry. Please go on, please." Charlie forced a smile, to show that she was sorry.

Leona pulled up a chair and sat next to Charlie. "This music producer from L.A., well, we were lovers twenty years ago, when I was Iris' age. Anyway, he's just moved back here and started his own label. I told him about you. He wants to meet you."

"Are you serious? You better not be teasing me."

"I'm serious. He's produced some big names. He wants me to bring you by the studio tomorrow. That's why I was taking some extra shots. I'll develop them tonight when I get home, and we'll take them with us."

"Why didn't you mention him before?"

"I wasn't ready." Leona shrugged, "But I do know he's going to love you."

"I don't know what to say. I needed some good news, Leona, and you just made my day," Charlie said, excitedly. She grabbed Leona's hand and squeezed. Charlie thought about her demo and stopped smiling.

"What is it?" Leona saw the change of her expression.

"I was thinking about how rough my demo is."

"Charlie, I think he should see you sing live. You and Ethan, acoustic. I'm sure you'll be recording a new CD...on his label!" Leona beamed brightly. She loved being the hero.

"Oh, my God!" Charlie put her hand to her mouth. "I need to go treat my voice to some herbal tea."

"Get a good night's rest," Leona added. "You need to be alert and mentally prepared for this meeting." Leona grabbed her stuff, and Charlie danced around her as they exited the bar. On the way out, they grabbed Iris away from the two guys she had been flirting with, and Iris followed their lead. Charlie gave Iris a whirl and the two sisters hugged, laughing hysterically.

Denny watched the three exit the bar. He wondered how Charlie could appear so happy and unaffected when Tom was a total wreck. If what Charlie and Tom had was not been real love, then he did not know what was. Their failure took away any hope he had for true happiness.

Chapter 13

Λ

"It's three-thirty in the morning," Catherine mumbled under her breath as she sat alone at the kitchen table watching the second hand slowly tick. She wondered where her sisters were.

Catherine could not get the big mistake she had made that morning out of her head. They both were mad at her. How long would her punishment last? Leaving without telling her where they were going was only the beginning of her sentence. Iris would hold a grudge for a long time, but she was used to that. She and Charlie rarely fought, so she had no idea what wrath would come from her. Maybe if she replaced the tickets, Charlie would forgive her.

Catherine reached for a fashion magazine on the telephone stand by the table and began leafing through the pages, just looking at the pictures. Unable to focus even on the pictures, she pushed it toward the center of the table and glanced back at the wall clock. Only ten minutes had passed.

When she heard keys rattling in the front door, she quickly reached for the magazine again, pretending to be reading it. She did not want her sisters knowing she was waiting up for them.

Charlie walked through the door first with Iris close at her heels. They were laughing loudly. Both went into the kitchen, intentionally ignoring Catherine and continued their conversation as if Catherine was not in the room.

Iris was speaking, "...and I can sing back up on that one song. You know the one...," she began singing.

"Whoa! Stop please. My ears are bleeding."

"I sing great! You're just jealous," Iris said, laughing. Singing was not one of her talents, and she knew it But, she liked singing and that would not stop her, even if it was audio abuse to anyone within ear shot.

"You couldn't carry a tune if it had handles," Charlie teased, and Iris laughed a little too loud at the joke. Charlie tossed her keys on the counter and Iris watched the toss, getting dizzy and swaying, slightly.

Using the counter to keep her balance, Iris started singing again, her voice painfully off key. Catherine closed the magazine, listening, amused by her sisters' chatter.

"I can't believe we are even related," Charlie said.

"What? I sound good," Iris said, stopping only to answer her sister before crooning out of tune again, only this time exaggeratedly worse.

"You're right. Forget about my singing career, sister. You shouldn't settle on being a back-up singer. Front row, center. That's you! Maybe this guy'll sign you, too!" Charlie said mockingly.

Testing the waters, Catherine decided to join their conversation, forcing laughter in her voice, "What's going on?"

Iris' laughter faded. Her smile vanished as quickly as an eraser wipes chalk from a blackboard. "Uh, I'm going to bed."

The tension in the room became dense, and for an instant the three stood perfectly silent. Charlie hoped Iris was not going to unleash her ugliness again and was relieved when Iris walked out of the kitchen and headed down the hallway.

"Good night, Charlie," Iris hollered from down the hall. Suddenly, she began to sing again.

Charlie hollered to Iris as she headed down the hallway, "Don't quit your day job. Oh wait...what day job?"

"Funny girl!" Iris teased as she shut the door. She had chosen Charlie's rehearsal room to sleep in rather than the couch, not minding the futon. The room was overfilled with boxes, amplifiers, guitars, and anything else Charlie could not seem to find a place for in her house but could not live without.

It suddenly occurred to Charlie that she was alone with Catherine, and she did not like that. She was not ready to speak to her yet, even though the anger was no longer there. Charlie had to stick to her guns. It was the principle. What Catherine had done was wrong. Iris, on the other hand, would be mad for a long time. Charlie supposed her easygoing disposition had something to do with being the middle child. She seemed to be the pacifist, the tolerant sibling. Her temperament was just the right combination to offset sibling arguments. When they were kids, she would always end up being the mediator between the two.

Charlie, suddenly hungry, opened the refrigerator for a snack. She could hear Iris singing through the closed door and giggled aloud. It was funny how different all three of them were, especially with their artistic ability. She could not draw a 3-D box, and Iris could not sing the birthday song with one right note.

"I guess she's still upset with me," Catherine said as she came to the counter and sat at the barstool facing the inside of the kitchen. When Charlie did not answer right away, Catherine picked up a folded newspaper on the counter and began combing out a rumpled corner, "And I suppose you still are, too."

"I am still pissed, Catherine," Charlie admitted, shutting the refrigerator door and turning to face her sister. She was not really angry with Catherine any longer, but she knew she should be, so she forced the resentment. Catherine needed to be taught a lesson. She knew silence would be the worst punishment.

"You weren't there, Charlie."

"I'm going to bed," Charlie disregarded her statement, not wanting to rehash the situation again. "I'm tired."

"You're not even going to give me a chance to explain, are you?"

Charlie took a long, hard look at her sister. An overwhelming feeling of pity swept over her. She noticed the dark circles under her eyes, the torment etched deeply. A flash of her mother's face came to her. Catherine looked the most like their mother, from the facial features to her expressions. Just like her mother, Catherine was a worrier.

At that moment, Charlie decided to forgive and forget. She no longer wanted to carry on the facade that she was still holding a grudge. Even though giving away her airline tickets was wrong, she knew that deep down, Catherine knew what was best. She knew that she would have been miserable in Aruba without Tom, although Charlie would never admit the truth to her sister. That information would go to the grave with her. Catherine would use information like that as fuel to meddle more.

"You going to stay here? Or go home?" Charlie opened the dishwasher and began loading the dirty glasses from the sink. She had hoped Catherine would say she was going home. It would be much easier tomorrow when Iris got up. Charlie did not want to deal with any more chaos, but it was probably inevitable if Catherine chose to stay.

"I don't mind sleeping on the sofa. Saves me having to drive home every night."

Charlie squeezed her eyes shut, even though she had known the answer. "You're gonna stay here every night?" Charlie asked, shutting the dishwasher.

"Don't sound so disappointed."

"I'm not. I didn't mean to sound that way," Charlie lied. She was and she could not hide it. All she wanted was for Iris to go back to Florida, to college, or wherever, and for Catherine to go home and leave her alone. A-l-o-n-e.

"I didn't think you'd mind. The three of us hardly ever have a chance to be together," Catherine explained.

Charlie saw through Catherine. She knew her sister was on a mission to rectify what had gone wrong between the three of them after their mother died. Catherine was trying too hard to make amends and her guilt was apparent with the monthly paychecks she dished out to whatever school program Iris wanted. Charlie donated to "Project Iris" as well, but for completely different reasons. Even though she knew Iris would never complete any project she started and was incapable of making responsible decisions on her own, she didn't care about that. Charlie gave because it kept Iris out of her hair and far away from her life. She wished Catherine would have gone to Africa with Steve and Christina. Now she was stuck with her. Catherine had never really been by herself. She had gone from living with her mother and sisters right to living with Steve. Soon after they got married, their mother had gotten sick and then they all went their own ways. Charlie loved her sisters but she wanted things the way they were, with everyone living their own lives.

"It will only be for a few days?" Charlie asked as she flipped off the kitchen light.

"A week at the most," Catherine answered, following Charlie out of the kitchen into the living room.

"Well...okay," Charlie conceded. "I guess I'll have to ignore you both."

"It'll be okay. She can't stay mad forever."

"Leona set up a meeting with a producer tomorrow. His name is Reno McChesney. Have you ever heard of him?"

"The name kinda sounds familiar."

"Anyway, my point is that the last thing I need is stress. So, please, don't try too hard. Just let her cool off...then she'll come to you." Charlie turned off the living room lamp, leaving the room pitch black. Then she walked down the hallway leaving Catherine alone in the blackness.

"Do you still have that futon in the guest room?" Catherine asked, speaking to Charlie's shadow.

"That's not a guest room. It's my rehearsal room, and Iris is using it. I don't think you want to share with her. Just come sleep in my bed." Charlie turned on her bedroom light, illuminating the path for Catherine to follow. When she got to Charlie's room, she saw her sister rummaging through her top drawer. She pulled out a nightshirt and handed it to Catherine, who accepted it.

"I did bring my own clothes, you know," Catherine said, as she unbuttoned her pants.

Charlie snatched it back, "You don't have to wear it."

Catherine took it back from Charlie, "No, I want to."

Charlie climbed under the sheet as Catherine sat at the end of the bed, looking into the mirror on the dresser as she brushed out her braids, her long hair waving perfectly. As Catherine combed her own hair, she watched Charlie's in the mirror. Charlie's eyes were closed. As Catherine watched her sister, she wondered what terrible thing had happened to make her sister do something as drastic as leaving Tom at the altar.

Charlie sat forward, grabbed her pillow and fluffed it. She caught Catherine's gaze through the mirror, and Catherine moved her eyes back to her own reflection.

"Do you wanna talk?" Catherine decided to ask. It was the first real opportunity she had had to speak with her sister.

Charlie yawned and leaned back onto her pillow. She closed her eyes, "Wow, I can't believe how tired I am."

Catherine turned on the bed to look directly at her sister. "Have you talked to anyone? You can't just hold all this in," she waited a moment for Charlie to respond. "I'm not suggesting that you have to talk to me. God forbid. I'm saying you should talk to somebody. Maybe Leona, or a shrink, a bum on the street. I don't care. Anything is better than holding it all inside."

Charlie, her eyes still closed, rolled onto her side, turning her back on both Catherine and her reflection. She did not want to get into this. Catherine was the one person she would never talk to about what she had done. Catherine had the perfect marriage, the perfect life and the perfect solution to any crisis.

"I would rather you tell me to shut up than blatantly ignore me."

Charlie began to cough, pretending to have a tickle in her throat. "I think I'm getting sick." Charlie felt her own head for effect.

Catherine got up and went to Charlie's side. She felt her head but it did not feel hot to her. "Want me to get you some aspirin? How 'bout some tea?"

"No, I think I just need to sleep." Charlie coughed again. "Are you gonna stay up?"

"No. Sorry," Catherine said, climbing under the sheet, "I really don't mind getting you something if you need it."

"You're trying too hard."

"You shouldn't disregard a kind gesture. You're misinterpreting my intentions."

"I'm sorry," Charlie replied as she reached for the book she had been reading from her nightstand. She tried to read.

"So that's it?" Catherine asked.

Charlie did not answer. It was hard to concentrate, and she kept reading the same paragraph over and over. Giving up, she closed the book and replaced it on the nightstand.

Charlie flipped off the light. Her nightgown was twisted underneath her, and she could not get comfortable. After flipping and flopping incessantly, Charlie said aloud, "I usually sleep in the nude."

"And I usually sleep with my husband."

"I know."

The bedroom fell silent for a long moment.

"You asleep?" Catherine whispered.

"Trying."

"Sorry. I was just thinking about Tina," Catherine said. "I can't sleep with her either. She's wiggly like you."

"Oh," Charlie paused, "Do you remember that time Mom took us camping and didn't bring enough sleeping bags? I had to share mine with Iris. God, I'll never forget that night. I couldn't sleep at all. I felt every little movement she made. I could feel her breathing."

Catherine rolled over, facing Charlie. "Funny how we get so used to sleeping with someone..."

"I'm still not used to it," Charlie confessed.

"I miss Steve."

The room fell silent again.

Charlie started to say something, but decided against it. She could not find the right words to make her sister feel better. She did not want to tell Catherine that she too was missing her bed fellow. She was afraid to delve into that subject even if it was only Catherine speaking about Steve. Her own memories flooded her mind. About two months before the wedding, Tom and Charlie had rented a guesthouse on Block Island. They rode mopeds and stopped at all the pubs, visiting with the other tourists. She squeezed her eyes trying to shut out the memory.

"I'm so lonely without my family," Catherine continued, not taking the hint that Charlie did not want to talk. "You know, this is the first time since we've been together that we've been without one another.

"Oh?"

"Yeah. When Christina was six months old, we traveled to Tanzania together."

"They'll be back before you know it." Charlie patted her arm. "You're a good mother and wife."

"I didn't think you ever noticed."

"I did," Charlie confessed.

The street lamp shone through the window, casting illuminated shadows from the blinds across the room. Between those shadows, Charlie could see one of Catherine's tear-filled eyes. She leaned over and kissed Catherine on the cheek. She felt Catherine smile.

"Goodnight, Kit," Charlie said, rolling over, her back to Catherine.

"Goodnight, Chuck."

Charlie snickered.

Chapter 14

∧

Iris sat on the back steps of Charlie's deck, smoking a breakfast cigarette, and thinking of nothing in particular, just relaxing. She watched an army of red ants march through a knot in the wood. When she looked up, she saw Fabio wagging his metal detector along the beach, scanning for treasures.

She realized, as the figure got closer, that the woman on the beach was Catherine. Iris groaned aloud. She contemplated snubbing the cigarette out and going inside and avoid to her, but when she looked at her cigarette, there was too much left to enjoy, so she thought otherwise.

"How can you smoke first thing in the morning?" Catherine gasped, out of breath. Her face grimacing at the mere thought of smoking a cigarette.

Out of spite, Iris took a long drag then blew smoke rings into the air. Catherine shook her head, laughed, and then invited herself to sit next to her sister.

Catherine saw that Iris did not move over for her, but she also did not complain. It was a start. Iris took another long drag off the cigarette and the two sat in silence.

Catherine broke the ice. "I've got homemade Belgian waffles on the menu for breakfast, with strawberries and whipped cream." Catherine smacked her lips "We could have breakfast out here on the deck." She waited for Iris' response, and she ebbed again when Iris did not answer. "Well, what do you think?"

"I just want coffee," Iris said when she finally spoke. If she did not say something to her now, Catherine would be pestering her all day long.

Catherine tried to hide her pleasure, "I bought hazelnut coffee beans." Catherine added, "I know how you love flavored coffees."

Catherine got up, went up the stairs, and crossed the deck to the door. Iris, after a fleeting hesitation, stood and grudgingly joined her sister.

"I'll make the coffee," Iris grumbled in a monotoned voice, "Yours always sucks."

Still smiling, Catherine purred, "Whatever."

"And wipe that shitty grin off your face. You didn't win. I just can't stay mad at you forever."

Catherine mockingly wiped the smile from her face. Iris rolled her eyes and turned away quickly before Catherine caught her smiling.

Chapter 15

∧

Tom, Denny and Ethan played basketball with a group of neighborhood regulars at the Providence YMCA. The gym squeaked as skidding sneakers amplified off the walls. Tonight, their competitors were Union Local 252. The team usually was no competition for them, but tonight proved to be contrary.

Tom was distracted. Usually he carried the rest of the team, but today he was off. Ethan passed the ball to Tom, and it bounced off his head.

"Hey!" Tom shot Ethan a dirty look. "Watch it!"

Denny stole the ball and scored a three-pointer from half-court, and he hollered as he and Ethan high-fived. "The Denman saves the day!" He bragged as he strutted around the court.

"You gonna play or dance?" Tom snapped.

"What's eating you?" Denny retorted, "Get your head out of your ass and back in the game."

Tom glared, and Denny stepped back.

"You wanna play some poker tonight?" Ethan asked, swiping the ball from his opponent. They tussled back and forth. Ethan won.

"I'm in," Denny hollered as he stole the ball from Ethan and went for a lay-up.

"Hey, we're on the same team."

The game got serious for a while and they played hard.

Tom was lost in the middle of all the action, one step behind everyone. He could not shake what Charlie had done to him. A part of him did not want to believe her, but she sure had a way of showing him how she really felt. How could he love someone who could fall out of love with him? Maybe she never loved him in the first place. He could not imagine loving anyone but her.

"Tom! Snap out of it. We're losing here." Denny elbowed his brother.

"Denny, you think I'm too nice?"

"What?" Denny swiped the ball from the Italian bodybuilder on the other team and shot. Missed. Ethan rebounded and shot. It bounced off the rim and circled around and around. They all waited to see if it would drop. It did, and Denny's team cheered. It was the other team's ball.

"You think I'm too nice a guy? Maybe I should..."

Denny interrupted, "Slap 'em around?" They all laughed.

"Right, Denman, and I suppose you pick your dirty underwear up off the curb 'cause you're a tough guy," Ethan said as he stole the basketball from the one they called Stretch, who happened to be six foot four. He took it down the court and sunk it. Stretch was uncoordinated, so his height worked against him. The Local 252 did not get far before Ethan struck again, stealing the ball for another two points. As Ethan gyrated around the court, dancing in jubilation, Tom and Denny caught their breath.

"Will you snap out of it?! We're losin' here! You're buying, 'cause I'm not the one who's fucking up."

"Ethan's the one saving us," Tom chided.

"What is it, Tom?"

"I mean, maybe if I woulda..."

"What?! Forced her to walk down the aisle?" Tom got clobbered in the melee for the ball, knocked to the ground by the more aggressive players.

"Yep. You're just one of those chumps who gets taken every time," Ethan said as he gave Tom his hand to help him up and the rest of them played on. They both ran to catch up with the group at the other end of the court. Denny was still trying to stay in the game. He jumped in the middle of the group, and Tom followed.

"Did you see that movie...," Denny paused when the ball was thrown to him and then passed it before catching his breath. "...Where the guy gets dumped...and he pledges to treat his next...girlfriend...really shitty..." He stopped to breathe again, and continued, "Because he decides...that women stay with guys who treat them bad?"

Tom stopped and bent over, resting his hands on his knees, "And I suppose you agree with that?"

"Sometimes it seems that way," Denny shrugged, then patted him on the back, "But, if it's not in your nature...it's not in your nature."

Chapter 16

∧

Reno McChesney, was a long-haired Sixties child. He sat behind the control panel in the studio control room that he created in his basement. The equipment was state of the art - too elaborate for the average, run-of-the-mill basement-recording studio. Charlie was impressed by his equipment and the potential his facilities might offer.

Reno nodded his head to the beat of the music as he bit his bottom lip. Charlie thought he looked like Bill Clinton when he did that. She and Leona sat beside him in black leather chairs, watching him curiously, as they listened to the songs Charlie had recorded acoustically for him.

Inside, Charlie could barely contain herself. A couple of times she thought she would toss up her lunch. She opened her purse and snuck two Tums. What if he did not like it? What if he told her to give up her life-long dream? Music was the only thing she had left. If only the song would hurry up and end, he could put her out of her misery.

Finally, it ended and Charlie and Leona watched Reno anxiously, awaiting his stamp of approval.

The silence was intense.

Uncomfortable in her seat, Charlie kept repositioning herself. It was not until she began seeing stars that she realized she had been holding her breath. She gasped aloud, feeling embarrassed when Reno and Leona both looked at her.

"I'm nervous," she laughed. It perturbed her that he was not saying anything. She was not getting any vibes from him, either good or bad. All he was doing was fiddling with the controls in front of him, oblivious to the tension filling the room.

"Well?" Charlie blurted out impatiently.

"Well what?" Reno answered casually, not looking away from the dials and buttons.

Charlie laughed nervously, not knowing what to say.

Reno whirled around in his black leather chair and looked directly at her. Charlie's stomach dropped and she suddenly did want to hear his solicited criticism.

"Leona told me you were talented, Charlie."

Charlie glanced at Leona, who winked. Charlie smiled quickly, turned back to him.

"You've got a unique sound," Reno turned to Leona, "You were right. I really think we've got something here." He spun back around to the control panel and cued the music back to the beginning. The song began again. After a minute of playing, he said aloud, "Yeah, I really do."

Leona nudged Charlie and she looked at her with wide-eyed elation.

"And I've got more. Stuff that Ethan and I have been working on for such a long time."

"Great. Are you ready to work your ass off for the next few weeks?"

"The sooner, the better."

"Let's schedule some recording time and get started."

Charlie grabbed Leona's arm and squeezed excitedly. "I can't wait to tell Tom..." Charlie blinked, and shook her head. Leona started to say something but Charlie stopped her. "Don't."

Leona raised her eyebrows.

"It was a slip, that's all. Please don't dwell on it." She could not believe she had just said that. With all the effort she'd done to try to forget about him, it disturbed her that he just popped into her head the first moment she'd let her guard down. When her mother had died, it took years for her to get out of the habit of picking up the phone to call her. She associated the two the same way. She would have to learn to disassociate her thoughts of Tom.

Leona watched Charlie intently. When Charlie realized Leona was staring at her, she mouthed, "What?" and turned in her chair away from her.

* * *

Iris, wearing ratty cut-off jeans and black high top boots, bopped along an empty side street on the outskirts of Providence. Strapped to her back was her exhausted and faded backpack. The city's streets were clean. Iris thought that unusual for a big city. Providence, at one time, had been dirty and dangerous, but now the city was attractive and safe. She walked over the bridge that overlooked Waterplace Park, down at the outdoor ice skating rink and then to the new mall. She smiled at what Providence had become.

Iris walked five blocks, scanning the old buildings, looking at the architecture of bricks and mortar, fully wrapped-up in the nostalgia of this New England city. An old Cadillac rumbled up beside her with two guys in the front. The window was down, and Iris recognized the song playing within.

"Excuse me," the music reduced and the guy in the passenger seat asked, "Do you know where Route 1 is?"

Iris stopped. Squinting from the midday sun, she checked out the handsome duo. She smiled, walked over to their car and leaned into the passenger window.

"Where you going?" she asked.

The guys looked at each other.

"We're heading west." It was the driver who answered.

"All the way out to the West Coast?" Iris asked excitedly.

"Nah, just over to Westerly," the driver continued, "Misquamicut Beach."

"Oh." Iris looked sad for a moment, "I can't help you. I'm not from around here."

"Where are you going?" the passenger asked.

"I'm just looking for stuff to sketch. How 'bout I draw either one of you?"

The guys looked at each other, puzzled, "Are you for real?"

"You could just say no."

"Uh, I've just never been sketched before," the driver confessed, "What do you need to do?"

"It's no big deal. See that bar right there?"

They both followed her finger.

"I'll trade you...a sketch for a beer."

The two looked at each other and shrugged.

* * *

Catherine sat on Charlie's floral couch, folding laundry. The sun filtered through the window, leaving a warm square on the carpet beneath her feet. She used to have a cat that would nap in the sun patches on the floor. She felt like that cat.

Catherine was worn out from the simple tasks of household chores. Fatigue was something new to her and she did not like it. Hoping it would alleviate some of the exhaustion, she had begun a regimen of vitamins but either they were not working or they had not kicked in yet. She hoped it was the latter.

Catherine ran through the list of chores she had done. There was nothing out of the ordinary. She had just cleaned the kitchen, dusted, and folded a few baskets of laundry. Why was she so tired?

Catherine went to the fridge for a soda, hoping the caffeine would rejuvenate her energy. While she was in the refrigerator, she spotted the chuck roast she needed to put in the oven. She had prepared it all the night before, marinating it in her own secret recipe. She could not wait for the aroma she knew would fill the air. It occurred to her, while she was salivating over the roast for dinner, that she had not eaten lunch and supposed that that was the reason she felt so weak. She went to the bread box and pulled out an open bag of chips. It was the perfect snack to tide her over until dinner time.

She sat on the couch, folding laundry and eating her chips, as she watched her favorite daytime soap. It was her only vice, and she was proud of it. She had started watching the show back in the early days, and it just seemed to be getting better and better every year. When she and her family went overseas, she set the tape recorders to record on all three televisions, each one to tape for a different week. They had never been gone longer than three weeks at a time, and she loved nothing more than sitting in bed at night, after Tina was asleep, playing "catch up."

Catherine waited for commercials to load her arms with folded towels and clothing to put them away. Her arms were fully loaded when the telephone rang and for a moment Catherine was confused as to what to do first, answer the phone or put the towels away. She dropped the load onto the kitchen table and answered the phone.

"Hello? Mommy?"

"Hi, baby! I miss you!"

"I miss you, too." Her angelic voice echoed over a bad connection.

"Daddy's taking me on a safari tomorrow."

"That's wonderful, sweetie."

"And remember Nate? From last year?"

"From last year's expedition? Yes I do."

"He's coming with us."

"He is? Well, tell him hi for me, okay?"

"Okay."

"What else have you been doing?"

"Taking pictures. Daddy's showing me how to be a good photographer," Tina declared proudly, sounding more innocent and adorable over the phone than in person, "And I took some pictures 'specially for you."

"Really? What did you take?"

"I can't tell you!" Tina sang. "And I'm big now, so you can't trick me into telling you."

"I love you, baby," Catherine's eyes welled. "I can't tell you how much I miss you," She was almost sick with the overwhelming yearning for her daughter,

"I miss you, too. Bye, Mommy. Daddy wants to talk to you."

By the time Catherine could choke out a goodbye to Christina, she had already passed the phone to her father.

"Hello, darlin'," Steve announced in his deep, passionate voice, and Catherine inhaled deeply. It was not until the phone call from them that she realized how much that she missed them. It was almost unbearable.

"Has Christina forgotten me?"

"Don't be ridiculous. She speaks of you constantly." This made Catherine smile and she wiped away hot tears.

Steve spoke about the job and how good Christina was being. He admitted that he did not think they would be gone longer than a week, which gave her relief.

Catherine told him how all she had been doing was fighting with her sisters. He laughed when she told him about the bikers and agreed that she had done the right thing. If she had to choose one quality that she liked best in Steve, it was that he stood behind her, even if he thought she was wrong. He would always see situations from her point of view.

"So, why did you hire Nate? I didn't think another salary was in the budget?"

"I want to come home. I don't like being without you. Nate will help me get the job done quicker."

"You're going to make me cry."

"Why, darlin'?" Steve asked with genuine concern.

"Because you're too good to be true. I can't believe that I'm so lucky to have you."

"No, I'm the lucky one," Steve said. Catherine heard Tina's voice in the background. "Christina's wants me to tell you that she's been a good girl. Just like she promised. I'm even surprised."

"I'm not. She's a good girl."

"You did a great job with her," Steve complimented. "You're a good mother."

"*We* did a good job with her," Catherine corrected him.

* * *

Iris sat opposite the two guys she had propositioned to sketch. The three of them sat at a table in the brightest part of the bar, which happened to be near the front window. She was sketching the passenger first. He introduced himself as Richie, while the driver, Gary, watched in utter amazement as the likeness of his friend appeared on what was once plain white paper.

A curious redhead wearing Levi cut-offs and a black tank top stopped to watch on her way to the restroom. She too was drawn, mesmerized by Iris' obvious talent. She pulled up a chair.

"I'm Natalie. You don't mind if I watch, do you?"

"No worries," Iris said cheerfully as her hands whipped quickly across the paper. Each stroke evolved into Richie's face.

"Wow! That really looks like you!" Natalie declared in awe. "I'm serious, you're really good."

"Thanks!" Iris beamed proudly, "I need practice, though."

"You're kidding, right? You're awesome."

Iris returned to the drawing, pausing for a moment, inspecting her work, "You really think so?" Iris found it hard to believe she was so good. Would anyone buy her work? Not that she really tried to sell her art. There were times she was broke and needed rent money, but it never occurred to her to sell her art.

"It's like a photograph."

"It does look like you, Gary," Richie agreed. "Too bad the subject is so ugly."

"Let me see," Gary got up to look, but Iris held the drawing against her and gently pushed him back down.

"Not yet."

He sat back down, disappointed. But as quickly as he sat down, he stood back up and tried to peek over the top.

"Uh uh," Iris shook her head back and forth as she pulled the sketch away again, "Not until I'm done, I said. Trust me."

Iris felt the pressure to produce quality work, so she worked diligently to create the best likeness of Gary that she could. Iris asked Natalie to hold the picture so she could step back and assess. Everyone watched as she turned her head sideways and then back straight again, looking critically. After that, she put her hand to her chin and squinted her eyes. When they saw Iris' face widen with a big smile, their enthusiasm was satisfied. When she approved of her own work, they all exhaled.

Iris went to the picture and turned it around for Gary to see.

"Wow, you're really good. Richie, you're right. It *is* like a picture." He shook his head, smiling. "That's amazing, Iris."

"And all for the small price of a beer," Richie pushed his friend out of the seat. "It's my turn. Get up, Gary." Gary stood, and Iris handed him his picture.

Richie, took off his hat, fixed his hair and then turned to the bartender, "Get the little lady whatever she wants."

Chapter 17

∧

"No way," Tom said as he backed down a tightly winding staircase, hefting one end of a very large pinball machine. At the top of the stairs, Denny carried the other end. The object they lugged looked more like a casket than a pinball game.

"Why do you do that?"

"What?"

"Begin in the middle of a conversation you've been carrying on in your head." Denny did not give him time to answer because he smashed his pinky and nearly lost his grip. "Shit! Watch out for my fingers! That hurt! Swing your end."

"Damnit, Denny. This is ridiculous," Tom grumbled as he did as he was told. He nearly lost his footing when all the weight of the pinball machine was put onto him. After a moment of silence, "There's no way I'm apologizing. I'm not the one who walked out."

"Start from the beginning. I have no clue what you're talking about."

"I'm not wrong for being upset," Tom stated, as the metal balls inside rolled from side to side, interrupting his train of thought. "Here's my dilemma. If I hold a grudge and refuse to talk to her, then I'm only hurting myself. She's gone completely crazy."

"I agree with you there."

"Agree with what? That I'm right and I shouldn't talk to her?"

"No. That she's crazy."

"Denny, you're not helping here."

"I never said I wanted to help."

Tom set the pinball machine down. "I'm helping *you*, aren't I? For the fiftieth time, I've helped you haul this stupid pinball machine from girlfriend's to girlfriend's. The least you could do is help me work my way through this."

Still holding his end, Denny tried holding up the machine so it would not topple down onto his brother, "Come on, this is too awkward and heavy to hold."

Tom did not budge.

"All right! I'll listen! Just pick it up." Denny's hands were getting wet with sweat. "Hurry, it's slipping."

Tom did so, and Denny sighed with relief.

"Now, as you were saying..." Tom said, not giving up.

"I don't know what you want me to say. I saw her the other night, and she seemed...well...kinda..."

"Over me?" Tom finished Denny's sentence, as he smashed his hand between the wall and the pinball machine. "Son of a bitch!" Tom balanced the pinball machine with his knee and right hand as he shook his injured left hand.

"Now we're even." Denny mocked Tom's pain. The machine began to wobble. "Be careful! Don't drop it!" Denny bellowed at him, "You know this is my baby!"

Still shaking his hand, Tom frowned at his heartless brother, "You know you, really are a dick."

"Come on, wuss!" Denny retorted, "Your hand's not hurt."

"This girl better be the one, because this is the last time I'm doing this!"

"Let's just get it into the truck in one piece," Denny said curtly as they struggled with the heavy machine the rest of the way down the staircase.

Tom gave Denny an exasperated look.

"Quit trying to make me feel guilty. I already said I'd listen to you."

"Never mind."

When they finally reached the bottom of the winding staircase, Denny set down his end. He did not know where to start. "You know...you could've made her check it out way before the wedding. You should have gone with her."

Tom blinked at Denny, shocked that he had said something serious. Now it was he who was at a loss for words.

"Don't you wanna know?" Denny prodded, "I would."

Tom picked up his end of the object and nodded for Denny to do the same. "Your new girlfriend...what floor is she on?"

Denny was shocked Tom was ignoring him. Tom turned his head to the side, making sure the path behind him was clear since he was walking backward. Denny picked up his end of the pinball machine and helped carry it through the doorway outside.

Huffing, Denny answered Tom's question. "Second."

Tom rolled his eyes and muttered an obscenity under his breath as they lugged the object toward Tom's truck. "Why don't you ever pick a girl that lives on the first floor?"

Tom's face was flushed, and Denny wondered if it was from carrying the pinball machine or his frustration with life in general.

"What? I should change my pick up line to, 'What floor do you live on' rather than 'What's your sign?' Denny said rolling his eyes. "Stupid!"

"No, what's stupid is a man who doesn't have his own place. What's wrong with you?" Tom asked. His anger was now uncharacteristically provoked.

They hefted the pinball machine onto the bed of Tom's white Chevy truck. The metal balls were still rolling around, banking quietly over deadened bumpers. They both watched it, waiting to see where the ball would end up. When it stopped, they both, in step, turned and walked back up the pathway. Tom looked at the front lawn. Denny's clothing and personal effects were strewn across the lawn. More of his things were broken.

Denny looked up, embarrassed to find his underwear and socks hanging from the oak tree in the front. "I give new meaning to airing my dirty laundry."

"That's for sure."

"I can get the rest of this stuff." Denny scuttled quickly, picking up loose articles of clothing. He spotted his empty laundry basket and began filling it with the laundry. Once the basket was filled, Denny found an empty duffel bag and began stuffing more of his belongings into it. Tom joined his brother in picking up his life. They both were in the same boat, rejected and alone. He felt sorry for Denny, but he knew he would recover. Denny went through a break-up so often, he was used to it.

They crossed the lawn together, collecting things from the bushes, the tree, the grass and the things that made it as far as the street. An elderly woman, walking a tiny Belgian boat dog along the sidewalk, stopped and watched for a moment, then snubbed her nose in the air as she ambled away.

"You never answered my question," Denny finally said, wondering if he really wanted to bring up the touchy subject again.

Tom ignored him, bending over to pick up a broken Pez dispenser. "You still have this?" The dispenser was one of the ones Denny had collected - Scooby Doo. "It's gotta be worth a lot of money."

Denny grabbed Tom's arm and said, "I thought you wanted to talk." He snatched the Pez dispenser out of his hand.

Looking Denny square in the eye, Tom asked, "Of all the questions, that's the one you ask?"

"Don't you wanna know, Tom? If it were me, I'd have to know."

"Drop it," Tom blurted out angrily as he turned toward the house. Crouching by the front porch, he began scooping what used to be the belongings of Denny's junk drawer.

Denny followed Tom. He paused before speaking, choosing his words carefully, "I mean that's pretty heavy. If my wife-to-be was going to..." He could not say the word, "But on the other hand..."

Tom stood and darted toward Denny, stopping directly in front of his face. "What if she does carry the gene?" Tom yelled, red-faced and angry.

"What if she does? Are you saying that if she found out...?"

"Would I marry her anyway?" Tom suddenly grew over-anxious, "Would I marry someone I knew was going to get sick and die?"

Denny stepped back, allowing his brother some space.

Tom kicked a broken piece of plastic with his shoe. "It's scary, man. And I'm no fucking hero..." Tom ran his hands roughly through his hair, aggressively. "...but I love her."

"Why don't you tell her that?" Denny looked down and realized that he was standing in the guts of a busted lava lamp. Colored goo stained the lawn purple. He bent down to pick up a piece of the broken glass.

"Don't you think I've tried?"

Denny grabbed a pair of old shorts and began wrapping the busted lava lamp in it. "Maybe she needs to hear it again. Obviously, it's something that's on her mind twenty-four seven."

"I'm not fuckin' begging." Tom snapped.

"Then there's your answer," Denny said as he crossed the lawn, tossing the lava lamp mess into the back of Tom's truck. He slammed the tailgate shut and wiped his hands on his jeans. Tom followed him like a lost puppy.

"Oh, did I tell you that she's singing at the club tomorrow night?"

Tom's face turned white. "She's singing again?" He shook his head, "I don't care. She doesn't really love me, remember? Besides, I would not want to come between her and her new biker friends."

Denny shrugged. He had said all he could say. Tom needed to figure out his own life before he could advise another on theirs. Scanning the front yard, the mess looked like the aftermath of a tornado. He knew it would take the rest of the day making the yard look like it had before. The sound of a drip distracted him. He looked at the ground then followed the trickle upward. It was the lava lamp slime dripping onto the bed of Tom's truck, staining what was once white paint.

Normally, he would have gotten upset, but his senses were dulled. He just did not seem to care about anything anymore.

Chapter 18

∧

On her daily ritual of inspecting the city of Providence, escaping the confines of Charlie's house and Catherine's shadow, Iris walked along the city streets, looking into boutique windows. Her leather skirt was short. Her black boots were long, accentuating her long, tanned legs. The suede jacket she wore was Charlie's, but she figured her sister would not mind. It was a brisk Spring afternoon.

On his way through town, heading towards the coastal drive, Denny passed on his Harley. She was dancing and walking. Nobody could miss her in her mini-skirt, doing the sidewalk rumba, and he chuckled at the sight. He turned around in the street and pulled up beside her. Unsuspecting, Iris was startled, but she recovered with a bright smile. She yanked the earphones off.

"Hey Denman!"

"Hey there, little girl. Wanna ride?"

"Do you even have to ask?" She laughed and climbed onto the back of his Harley. Her best friend at college had a Yamaha 500, and it was great tooling around town on that, but it was nothing compared to Denny's Harley.

The streets were lined with oak trees, with leaves that were beginning to bud. The smell of gardenias filled the air. Iris inhaled the beauty. After riding around for a half an hour or so, Denny pulled over, on the edge of a hill overlooking the city's capital building. He stopped the engine.

"Let's look at the view."

Denny parked his Hog, and they both climbed off. Without words, they walked to a waist-high wooden fence. He sat down, patting the grass indicating Iris should do the same.

"I'll have to have you bring me back up here to do some sketching. This place is beautiful. I'd like to draw the city in the background, but put this hanging branch in the forefront.

"I can see it," Denny said as he closed his eyes to envision Iris' picture. "If you draw it, I'd like to get a copy of it."

"I'll draw it for you."

Denny turned around to check on his Harley.

"It's okay," Iris said, watching him, "Nobody's gonna steal your bike. They'd have to contend to me first," Iris made a fist and swished it in the air.

"Be careful, slugger," Denny said, clasping her fist and then kissing it, "You could hurt somebody with those weapons. You've registered them, right?"

Iris laughed and pulled her fists back, "What's that building?"

"That's the Turk's Head building. I think it's almost a hundred years old. I'm not sure. Providence has some cool buildings, huh?"

"Yeah. I was drawing some of the architecture yesterday."

"Providence used to be a bad place."

Iris gave him a look of doubt.

"Crime." Denny said.

"Really? It's so clean." She did not understand why Denny had brought her up here to talk about Providence. What were they going to talk about next? The weather?

After a long moment, Denny said, "Tom's pretty messed up. She really did a number on him."

Now she understood Denny's behavior and why he had been so awkward at first. "The whole thing's a trip."

"Do you even know what happened?"

"I tried to ask her about it, but she wouldn't talk. Any time it comes up, she just skirts the issue. I figured she'd tell me when she was ready."

"I've been around them the entire year they were dating, and let me tell you this, if anybody was in love, it was them."

"At first, I thought it was Tom's idea, or that he had gotten cold feet. But, when I saw the way she adjusted, I knew she was responsible for everything. Plus, any woman would be devastated if he had called the wedding off."

"Yep. Charlie laid it on him just like that. Blindsided the poor bastard. He didn't even know what hit him. I guess she told him she didn't love him anymore."

"How do you know all this? Did Tom tell you?"

"He told me that she said she didn't want to marry him and she didn't love him anymore."

"That's bullshit."

"You think I'm lying to ya?" Denny asked as he turned his head to face her.

"No. Not you. Her. I don't believe she doesn't love him. Do you? She's mad about the guy. Or at least I thought she was."

"That's what I thought, but that morning after the non-wedding..."

Iris snorted aloud, "Non-wedding. That's good."

"Can I finish?" He asked, her laughing made him chuckle.

"Sorry." Iris bit her cheeks, "Go on."

"Tom and I came by the house to pick up the tickets to Aruba, and these bikers were pulling out..."

"Oh shit," Iris scrunched her face.

"What?"

"He thought she was having a party?   Those people were my...guests."

"You really do like Hogs, don't cha?"

Iris raised her eyebrows up and down. "Someday, I'll own one of my own."   She rolled her neck, stretching her sore muscles, "Poor Charlie. She really must've been really freaking out to do something so drastic. I mean... this whole business...and no explanation. And the worst thing is, she won't talk about what she's afraid of," Iris stood and dusted her rear end.

"What's that?" Denny asked, although he knew the answer. He wanted to see if Iris knew.

"It," Iris kicked rocks under her feet. She did not look at Denny, but continued before he could ask what "*it*" was, "I think she thinks she has what Mom had."

"Do you think that's it?"

Iris nodded and then sat back down on the fence.

"It is scary. Do you ever think about it?"

Iris looked at him. He could read the answer by the look of fear in her eyes.

Iris looked away from Denny. "I try not to. I've got this way of getting rid of negativity when it gets into my head. I don't dwell on it like Charlie does. It's on her mind all the time. I'm not saying I'm not afraid to die, but I just don't think about it."

"So, you escape your fears."

"No, I just don't think about them."

"That's escaping, darling."

"No, if I get *it*...," she said, "Then, God forbid, I get it. I will deal with it."

"And?   That's it. If it happens, it happens?"   Denny persisted, curious to see if she believed what she said.

Iris kicked the toe of her boot against the fence pole, almost losing her balance as she tried to dislodge a pebble that was embedded under the metal tip, "I don't know. I mean, what do you do? It's hard to test for something like A.L.S. It's more like a process of elimination. But she doesn't have any symptoms...none of us do."

"What are the odds?"

"About the same as finding a straight man who isn't afraid of commitment."

Denny laughed and Iris joined, although hers was more of a nervous laugh.

"Be serious."

"I'm trying. I think it's something like fifty-fifty odds."

"Iris, maybe she is showing symptoms. I mean, if she's so freaked out, do you think maybe she does have it?"

"Now you're scaring me. My heart just dropped to my stomach."

Denny put his hand on top of hers. "I'm just asking. I swear, I know as much as you do. It's just that Charlie seems kinda crazy leaving Tom the way she did."

Iris breathed out, relieved. For a second, she actually thought Denny had brought her here to tell her that he knew Charlie was dying or something. She could taste the bile at the back of her mouth and wished she had some water. "Denny, they don't know much about the disease, but there are two types, and we have the genetic kind in our family. Which means it's fifty-fifty that any one of us could get it. Fifty-fifty that our kids will get it. I was curious about why Mom died. I was only fifteen, and I wasn't really around when she was sick. Since then, I've done a little research on the internet, but it's scary researching something you could have, especially when there is no cure."

"What do you mean, you weren't around?"

"I was being a selfish brat," Iris frowned at the memory of herself. She jumped off the fence and scuffled her feet in the rocks, then looked at Denny. She suddenly felt like she understood where Charlie's fear had stemmed from and empathized with her. "Maybe if I was about to get married and thinking about the future along those lines...you know, children...till death do us part, maybe I'd react the way Charlie did. I may not agree with how she handled the situation, but it's not my place to judge her."

Denny stepped down from the fence, following Iris' lead that it was time to go. "Yeah...I kinda agree with you there. I was just trying to be there for Tom and listen to him. It's hard, because Tom's a good guy, too. I love Charlie and now talking with you, it all makes a little more sense."

Iris turned to go back to the Harley, but Denny grabbed her arm and turned her to him. He held her for a long moment and her heart pounded nervously. Denny, following his natural instinct, stepped closer, and Iris bit her bottom lip. She did not know if she wanted what was about to happen.

Denny read into her expression and he snapped out of his habit. It still did not stop the urge he had to kiss her. He found her irresistible, but he knew she was too young for him. Plus, Charlie would kill him. Denny pulled her in closely and kissed her on the forehead then stepped away.

"You're a good kid, Iris."

Iris smiled. "Denny?" Iris cocked her head sideways, looking at Denny with her artistic eye. "Can I sketch you?"

Chapter 19

∧

Catherine sat on the back deck drinking her morning ritual of Hazelnut coffee, with extra cream – no sugar. Her blond hair was pulled up in a claw clip, and she was still wearing her robe and slippers. She closed her eyes and breathed deeply. The clean salty air filled her lungs. Seagulls squawked as they fluttered all around, diving toward the remnants left in the sand by a couple Catherine had watched sharing breakfast on the beach.

As Catherine drank her coffee, she thought about Steve and Tina. She wondered what they were doing at that very moment. She hoped they were safe. Safaris could be dangerous, especially searching for lions. But she trusted Steve. He knew what he was doing. She wished she was there with them.

It had been a year since they first started going to Africa, but it seemed like yesterday. She could picture herself there with Steve and Tina. She knew where they were eating breakfast; she could envision the basket weaver sitting under that big, shady tree at the corner by the market. She loved to watch the old woman's dry hands intertwine leaves and branches, twisting nothing into the most elaborate, store-quality baskets. Even though at that very moment in Africa her husband and daughter were sleeping, she found she related what they were doing to her time zone. She supposed it was less confusing that way.

They had called and left a message for her. She really wished she had not missed their phone call. She needed to hear his comforting voice. She smiled, thinking about the message he had left. He was excited, rambling about his findings. He had said the lions they were tracking could be a mixed breed from the Cape lion, and they were running DNA analysis to determine whether the lions originated from the South African Cape lion or the Barbary lion. She was missing all the excitement.

The wind began to pick up a little, and a cloud rolled in front of the sun. Catherine pulled her robe shut tightly, a shiver cut through to her bones.

A loud thud on glass gave Catherine a start and she looked at the sliding glass door from which the sound came. When she saw what it was, she began to laugh hysterically. Iris, still in her pajamas, and apparently still groggy, had walked right into the glass door.

She slid the door open, "Thought it was open," then rubbed her head, "Glad you got a good laugh."

Catherine would not stop laughing.

"I'm sorry," Catherine said, trying to regain her self-control.

Iris pulled a pack of cigarettes out of the elastic waistband of her purple-and-white-striped pajamas and put one in her mouth. She pulled a matchbook from behind the cellophane and struck a light, then climbed up and straddled the ledge of the deck, fully aware that Catherine was watching her and was expecting her objection for smoking momentarily.

"How can you do something so disgusting so early in the morning?"

Iris ignored her.

"And where were you so late last night?"

Iris took another long drag, looking at the ocean's surf. Finally she answered, "Catherine...don't start."

"I only say these things because I care."

Iris hopped off the railing and headed for the stairs leading to the beach. She walked straight for the water.

"Iris?" Catherine called out after her.

Iris did not answer.

"You wanna go to a matinee? Charlie's holed up in her music room again."

Iris flicked her foot in the water and the thrill of the cold New England ocean rushed all the way to her spine. Her body shuddered from the chill. Iris whirled around and hollered over the roar of the surf to her sister, "Maybe."

Catherine smiled, then 'Okayed' with her hand to let Iris know she understood. Catherine began to laugh again. Only this time, it was out of mischievousness. A big wave was heading straight for Iris and she was about to get soaked. The natural urge was for her to warn, but as she watched it swell fully into a big curl, she decided it was payback time. Catherine waved at Iris, distracting her from seeing the wave. She could not help fighting that twinge of guilt surging through her, but it did not stop her.

As Iris signaled back to Catherine, the wave enveloped her knocking her down, arms and legs rolling with the wave, completely soaking her to the bone.

Catherine's laughter overpowered the ocean's roar as the wave brought Iris safely to the water's edge.

Iris stood, looking like a drowned rat, half in shock, as she watched her sister doubled over with laughter on the deck. Iris signaled Catherine again, only this time with her middle finger.

* * *

In her rehearsal room (the same room Iris had taken over as her semi-permanent residence), Charlie sat at her keyboard working on a new song. She had not been inspired to write a single lyric since before the wedding, and now it seemed as if the words and music were just pouring out of her like truth serum's effect on a liar. She sang quietly to herself as she went over and over the lyrics;

> *"Whisper words of frustration,*
> *deep breath, exhale and sigh.*
> *Making sense of confusion,*
> *But we don't see eye to eye.*
> *Flailing arms in a pool of sweat,*
> *I think I'm gonna drown.*
> *I thought I found my soul for life,*
> *But of course, life let me down..."*

Tears welled up in her eyes, and her emotions seemed to open the floodgates. She did not want to cry. She did not have time to deal with those issues now. Focusing on her music career and forgetting the past was all she had time for. Dwelling on the unchangeable would never give her peace of mind. It was now, more than ever, that she needed to focus.

Charlie grabbed a tissue and blotted her eyes, angrily wiping away the tears. How long would it take for that painful churning to get out of the pit in her stomach? Would she ever be able to breath without thinking about him?

Charlie stopped writing and looked upward; she closed her eyes and said a prayer for strength. She knew that God understood why she did what she did. He would forgive her. If only she could forgive herself.

* * *

Tom stood, staring out the window of his office, deep in thought. Although he appeared to be kept - black suit, stylish tie, hair combed perfectly - he was the complete opposite.

Tom had walked to the window to get away from the telephone, because he could not seem to control his fingers. They were betraying him. He did not want to talk to her, but his reflexes seemed to think otherwise. After he dialed her house four times and hung up before she could answer, going away from the telephone seemed the only alternative.

Though he would not admit it to Denny, he believed he should have gotten the Aruba tickets from her and gone away. He needed to do something different, or else he was simply going to go insane. He might even get himself fired. The real issue was that he could not focus on anything other than Charlie. The day before, or maybe it was the day before that, (they all seemed to blur together), George Martin, his boss, sent him home because he had forgotten to shave. George seemed to be patient and understanding, but Tom knew that business would always come first, and he had to get his shit together.

He knew he would have to get on with his life. She did not love him anymore, and a person could not be any clearer with their feelings than the way Charlie had been. He wondered if he could ever love anybody else. It just hurt too damned much.

Tom rubbed the back of his neck. He glanced at the clock. He had an hour before the San Francisco clients would be in their conference room. He was ready for them, thanks to George and his assistant, Clara. They both deserved the commission on this client, because he did not do a thing.

Tom returned to his desk and glanced at the telephone again. He picked up the phone, opened one of his desk drawers and put it inside, slamming the drawer shut.

He felt smug for beating the urge, but as soon as he felt superior, he felt humbled when he remembered that Charlie was probably in Aruba at that very moment, basking in the sun, drinking mai tais and margaritas, watching the sun move slowly across the sky, holding back time.

Tom kicked his foot into the carpet. Was he a glutton for punishment? "Quit thinking about her," he mumbled aloud. Why could he not be more like his brother, insensitive and uncommitted? He never thought the day would come when he would believe he should follow in his younger brother's footsteps. Maybe Denny could teach him the art of not loving. It couldn't be that hard. If Denny could be that way, then could he? They were genetically connected and resembled each other physically, but that was where their similarities ended. The genes split somewhere, and Denny got all the insensitivity chromosomes while he had ended up with the sappy leftovers.

Tom stood, rolling out a crook in his neck, and went back to the window. He tapped his fingers, then stopped when he began to drive himself nuts. He wrapped the cord to the Venetian blinds around his wrist, wishing it was a noose and his fist was his neck.

A knock at his office door brought him out of his reverie. Tom turned around to see his boss, standing in the doorway.

"Tom, you got the report for the China project?"

"Oh, um, it's right here." Tom went to his desk, which was disheveled with loose papers and manila files. "It was right...."He shuffled through papers and found it buried beneath a stack of files. "Here it is."

George took the file from him and shot a disapproving glance at Tom's desk. "You alright?"

"Fine. I'm fine." Tom lied, raising his eyebrows to exaggerate good health and mind.

"I've never seen your desk look so...."

"I know," Tom interrupted defensively, shaking his head, embarrassed. "I really am organized; it just looks like I'm not."

George looked at him, indulgently tolerant to Tom's circumstance. "You really should have taken this time off. I'm worried about you."

"Really, George, don't worry about me."

"Well..." George chose his words wisely, expressing that he was also concerned about the company. "You're the Man down here. We can't afford to have you A.W.O.L."

"I'm fine." Tom could not even look George in the eyes. He knew he was outright lying to him. "Trust me."

On the other hand, George saw right through Tom's pretense. He smacked the file against his other hand, "Could have fooled me," he placed the file under his arm, "Let's go get some coffee."

Chapter 20

∧

The nightclub was hopping; people were packed shoulder to shoulder. Word around town got out that Charlie's band, New Horizon, was playing, which always drew a big crowd of locals. Denny was behind the bar, drawing up mostly pitchers of draft beer for the college-aged crowd.

Denny's newest girl of the week, Gina, a short, bubbly brunette with bobbed hair that curled under her chin, stood at the waitress station at the end of the bar. She was talking to another young woman. Denny made his way back to the waitress station to fill Gina's order, two pitchers of Budweiser and a bottle of Heineken. She introduced him to the woman next to her as her kid sister, Heather. Heather resembled Gina in facial features of big, round eyes and full pouty lips, but she had waist-length blond hair that she wore both teased and big. Her slender frame stood two inches taller than Gina's did, and unlike Gina's black shorts and white tee shirt uniform, Heather sported a spandex miniskirt.

Charlie and her bandmates were playing on stage for the cheerful crowd. They were in their fourth and final set for the night, about five songs into it with six to go. The fast song the band played was one that Ethan had written long before he was with his prior band. The dance floor was hopping.

Iris was resting at a corner table near the dance floor with a bottle of beer in hand, her hair wet from perspiration. She put the icy cold bottle to her forehead and neck to cool herself down. She moved her body as she watched Ethan jam on his guitar. After his solo, he looked at her first for approval, then gave her a quick wink as she smiled back approvingly.

Wearing a cowboy hat and Wranglers, looking sexy and many years younger than she was, Leona sat at the table where Iris stood, snapping photos of Charlie on stage.

Gina stopped by their table to deliver fresh bottles of beer, compliments of Denny. They both raised their beers high to Denny, then toasted each other. Like a lost puppy, Heather followed Gina from table to table. The two returned to the bar, and Denny leaned over the bar and stole a kiss from his new girlfriend. When he finished the kiss, he saw Tom standing before him.

"Hey, bro! Glad to see you decided to get out of the house." Denny climbed back underneath the lift and went for a Bud Light, sliding it to his brother.

"I can't believe I'm down here."

"Be cool. Did you meet my girl, Gina?"

Tom looked at Gina and tipped his bottle to her before taking a big swig.

"And this little beauty is her sister, Heather." Heather smiled at him, gushing immensely.

Tom looked from Heather then back to Denny and then shook his head. Denny knew his brother had come down here to talk to Charlie. How could he think that he would even be interested in meeting another woman? Tom tossed the bottle back and drank furiously.

Heather patted Denny's arm. "This is your brother? Wow! Your father must be really handsome."

Tom, bottle to mouth, averted his eyes at Denny and Denny shrugged coolly.

"You gotta be kidding," Tom said under his breath only for Denny's ears. Tom guzzled the remaining beer in his bottle then set it on the bar.

"You want another one?" Denny asked, not waiting for him to respond. He slid his brother another. He was afraid Tom would say no and leave. Denny knew that Tom needed to get out of the house and be around people. He had asked Gina to bring Heather out as a distraction. It would be a bonus if a love connection happened.

Tom took the second beer from Denny and turned away from the bar, stepping toward the table area. He leaned against a pillar and took a mouthful of beer, swallowing it slowly as he watched Charlie sing. It took all his courage just to turn and look at her and even more just to watch her. Anxiety danced in his stomach at the mere sight of her on stage. He wanted her back so badly. In the year they had dated, he had made it a point to go to at least one gig a week. She always told him he didn't have to, but what she did not realize was that he took pride in her talent, even though he had nothing to do with it. He loved watching her sing.

Gina prodded Heather to go talk to Tom, and after a few nudges she picked up her Cosmopolitan and sidled up next to Tom by the pillar. Unconsciously, Tom moved away from her, oblivious to Heather, who was watching him watch Charlie. The song ended and the room applauded loudly. The next song began and Tom instantly recognized it. She had written it for him. How could he forget that day? They had just finished making love and he was still in bed. Charlie was nude, standing in front of the mirror. He could see the front of her body in the reflection and her backside was facing him. She caught him admiring her. As she began to turn to him, she sang, making up the words as she went along. She was always good like that, spoofing with songs from the radio. She was quick with lyrics.

Charlie on stage sang:

I'm in your eyes...I'm in your hair.
I'm in the mirror when you stand there and stare...
I'm in the teeth of your triumph and smile...
I'm gonna put you in my pocket for awhile...

Tom was brought back from his thoughts when he realized Heather had been chattering to him. All he caught was that she was doing something about just getting some art done, or something.

"What?" He was annoyed. He really wanted to hear the song. "I can't hear you over the music."

Heather, not taking the hint, yelled louder over the music. "Wanna see my tattoo?"

Tom looked at her confused, touched his ear with his left hand, playing off that he could not hear her. He wanted her to leave him alone. He turned his attention back to Charlie.

Heather tugged on his sleeve, "I said, do you want to see my tattoo?"

She enunciated every word clearly, making sure he would definitely understand her. Why would she not go away? Damn Denny for putting him in this position! All he wanted to do was be with Charlie. Before he could answer her question, Heather jutted her hip up and with one hand pulled her little spandex skirt half way down her ass. Tom's automatic reaction was to look. He saw a brightly colored butterfly tattoo on the soft whiteness of her skin.

It was at that very moment Charlie spotted Tom across the crowd and through the dancers. When she saw Tom, he was looking at a woman's exposed butt. Charlie's heart fell. Her stomach churned, suddenly overwhelmed with anxiety. Charlie flubbed the next line of the song. Then she stumbled on the one that followed. Ethan looked at Charlie then followed her gaze to Tom. He pushed her away from the microphone and went into the guitar solo early. The band members all shot each other confused looks, but they recovered smoothly.

Charlie flicked off her microphone, thankful that Ethan had saved her. She watched Ethan, afraid to look back into the crowd. She had hoped that Tom had been an apparition, a mind trick. She squeezed her eyes shut then opened them. The lights were bright. When she looked back out into the crowd, she saw that her eyes had not deceived her, that he really was standing there – with a woman. Without thinking, Charlie ran off the stage.

Not knowing what she had missed, Leona watched helplessly as Charlie darted off the stage. She knew she had to go to her friend. Grabbing her hat, she pushed through the crowd and made her way to the back room.

Ethan turned to the band and gave them the cue for the end of the song. They dragged the song out, knowing it was the last one for the night. Ethan stepped to the microphone and addressed the crowd.

"Alright. Thank you," the crowd cheered and clapped. "That's it for tonight, folks. See you next week. Don't forget to tip your bartender and waitresses." He looked at Denny who gave him a "thumbs up."

Tom looked around at Denny. Had he missed something? He had only looked away from the stage for less than a minute and the band was done. Where had Charlie gone?

Denny shrugged and continued serving beer.

Before Tom could look back at the stage, Heather took his head in her hands and turned his face to her breasts.

"I'm gonna get another one..." Heather took his hand and put it right on her right breast.

Tom pulled his head away. "That's great."

"I think so," she beamed.

Tom wanted to get away. The girl was not taking a hint. Walking away from her, he strode to the bar and set down his empty beer bottle. Hot on his shadow, Heather followed, and Tom ran smack into her. He held his breath while his anger was building.

Tom turned back toward the bar, "Excuse me, Denny!"

Denny finished ringing in a sale at the register before her turned his head.

Tom pointed toward the stage with his thumb, "Are they playing another set?"

"Nope. Shoulda got here earlier," Denny shrugged, shutting the till. "Want another beer?" He reached in the cooler as he asked.

"See you later," Tom reached into his pocket for his keys.

"Hey! Don't go. It's early. Why don't you hang out a while? At least have another beer, since I opened it for you."

Heather walked up and put her arms around Tom's neck. "Yeah. Let's party. Denny told me that you're getting over a broken heart. I'd love to help you mend it. I don't mind being a rebound."

He peeled Heather's arms from around him, "No, thanks. Maybe in another lifetime."

"Uh, Okay?" She stood confused.

Without saying another word Tom walked out of the bar with both Denny and Heather watching him. Heather turned to Denny, "Hey, Denny. You said we were going to party."

"Don't take it personal."

"Is he mad at me?"

"Not at all. That's just how he is. He plays hard to get. In fact, I think he likes you."

"Oh. I think he's kinda sweet."

Gina slapped Denny in the arm for lying.

* * *

Charlie paced among stacks of boxes in the back room, which also fronted as her dressing room. Beer posters of scantily clad women were plastered all over the wall. Leona sat on a stack of beer cases, watching her friend pivot back and forth.

"Talk to me. What happened?"

"What the hell is he doing...?" Charlie rambled, "Who does he think he is flaunting himself...and with a bimbo too...I thought he had better taste...?"

Leona interrupted, "Whoa! What are you talking about? Who?"

"Him!" Charlie bellowed.

"Calm down, dear, you're all over the place. What are you talking about?"

"Tom! Didn't you see him?"

"Tom? No, I didn't see him. Are you sure it was him?"

"Yes! It was Tom. I know my fiancé." Charlie shook her head. "Ex...ex-fiancé." She hoped Leona hadn't caught her flub, but by Leona's expression, she could tell that she had. Charlie continued defensively. "Anyway, that's not the point. He had this bimbo on his arm! What a jerk!"

"Where was he?"

"He was standing by the pillar, pulling some Barbie's skirt down." Charlie picked up a Styrofoam cooler and threw it across the room. "I can't believe you missed it. He was there...in front of everyone...making a fool of me."

"Take a deep breath, Charlie, and try to calm down." Leona went to Charlie and began rubbing her back. "Are you very sure? Because this doesn't sound like something Tom would do."

"Whose side are you on?" Charlie snapped, pulling away from Leona. "You're supposed to be my best friend. You're acting like I'm crazy. Everyone else thinks I'm crazy. I don't care what others think of me, but I do care what you think. I know what I saw."

"Nobody thinks you're crazy. We're all just concerned for you. As for me, I'm simply trying to find out what happened."

Charlie blinked and stared at Leona's slim, pleasing face. She moved her eyes to the ground, hiding the shame she felt for not trusting her friend.

"Come here and sit down." Leona patted the beer cases, and then sat down herself. She patted again, and Charlie finally gave in.

"Ever think that maybe he's trying to make you jealous," Leona hinted.

"Jealous?! With a cheap hussy like that?!" Charlie tried to stand but Leona put her hand on her leg to hold her in place. Charlie glared at her friend, but Leona kept her gaze locked, determined to be strong and to make Charlie see from her point of view. After Charlie stopped squirming, Leona continued.

"Think about it for a second. He probably got shitty advice from Denny. Doesn't bringing a floozy down here sound more like something the Denman would do?"

Charlie shrugged. "Do I look that cheap? I mean, am I like that girl and I never noticed?"

Leona laughed aloud, shaking her head back and forth. "Boy, you're on a roll now."

"I'm not imagining this, so quit!"

Leona threw her arms in the air, surrendering. "Look, you need to take a chill pill." She leaned over Charlie like a buddy on a barstool, moving way into the boundaries of Charlie's comfort zone. "And I've got a medicine cabinet full of what the doctor ordered." She raised her eyebrows up and down. "Hmmmm?"

"Maybe." Charlie slid off the boxes and stood with her back facing Leona. "Whether he knows it or not, I was doing him a favor by not marrying him, and regardless of that fact, it doesn't mean I wanna watch him pick up sleazy bitches right in front of me."

It took her a moment for Leona to take in what Charlie had said. Never before had she mentioned any reasons as to why she had left Tom at the altar. The air was suddenly heavy.

Leona proceeded cautiously. "A favor?" Leona asked, arching her eyebrow.

Charlie whirled around, her brown hair following a second later. "Yes! I'm sparing him a whole lot of heartache in the long run."

"A favor...that's what you're calling it?"

Charlie covered her face, hiding her humiliation. Leona would never understand. At that moment Charlie knew she could never try to explain herself to anybody again. Charlie felt alone. More alone than she had ever felt.

"You want to go home?" Leona asked after a long period of waiting.

Charlie pulled her hands from her face. Tears darkened the circles around her eyes. She shook her head.

"You can't sit here all night."

Charlie wiped her eyes with her hand.

Leona snatched Charlie's purse and took Charlie's arm in her hands, tugging gently until Charlie took her cue to stand. Leona towed her friend all the way to the door, flipped out the lights, and closed the door behind them.

"All you need is a little fresh air."

Charlie nodded numbly.

* * *

Ethan rolled his microphone cable around his wrist and arm while the rest of the band packed away their instruments and equipment. Breaking down the stage was the only part of playing in a band that he disliked. Iris stepped up onto the stage without being asked to help. She began dismantling the microphone stand. She tilted her head sideways and threw a smile to Ethan. Her hair fell onto her face, covering one eye, and she flipped it back.

"Hi! I'm Iris, Charlie's sister. I don't think we've been officially introduced." Iris threw out her hand like a determined politician.

Ethan smiled, looked at her hand and said, "So formal." He set down the cord that was wrapped into a neat circle and shook her hand anyway. "I'm Ethan and I remember you from the...uh...wedding."

"Yeah."

"You looked pretty. I remember that."

"Thanks," Iris said pressing her lips together until they were white, a nervous habit. Iris licked them, and the color came back to their full pouty pink.

"You don't need to do that," he pointed, referring to Iris dismantling the microphone stand.

"I don't mind."

"Well, we kinda do. This stuff is fragile." He patted the stool that Charlie sometimes sat on during ballads. "You can sit right here and keep me company, if you want."

Iris beamed, as she slid onto the stool, imitating a sultry singer, looking innocently sexy as she got comfortable.

"Are you a singer, too?" Ethan asked as he picked up an amplifier and placed it next to the microphone stand.

"Only in the shower."

Ethan laughed. Something about her made him not want to take his eyes off of her. He did not know if it was her big round eyes that looked innocent or her heart-shaped face that accentuated each feature. Her face lit up when she smiled. He realized that he was staring, so he looked away feeling foolish.

"And the car."

Ethan picked up two amplifiers and carried the equipment off the stage, heading toward the van outside the side door. Still wanting to help, Iris picked up the microphone stand and followed him toward the exit.

Ethan turned to see his new shadow. "Uh, that stays here."

"Oh." Iris blushed. "I just feel stupid sitting there watching you work."

Ethan winked at her. "I'll be right back."

* * *

Outside, in the parking lot, Charlie dug a path in the gravel as she walked back and forth. Leona thought she had finally gotten Charlie under control back in the liquor closet, but once they were outside, the fresh air rejuvenated the panic. Leona knew she would never get Charlie to calm down, so she gave up. She leaned against Charlie's car, hoping that her friend would run out of fuel soon.

Charlie stopped pacing when she saw Ethan walking from the nightclub, heading toward his van with an armful of equipment.

"Shit. I need to talk to him."

Leona turned, "Ethan will understand. Really, it can wait until tomorrow."

Charlie stepped in front of Leona, the gravel-crunching stopping for a moment, "No, it can't wait. I got so angry, I didn't even apologize to him for walking off the stage the way I did. That's so unprofessional. He must think I'm a real nutcase."

"Go talk to him if you must, but I need to get going."

Charlie walked toward Ethan and Leona hollered after her, "Don't be too harsh on yourself. He'll understand. I'm gonna go get my stuff inside. Want me to get your stuff?"

"Okay," Charlie said, not even looking back, marching full speed ahead toward Ethan. When she reached him, she suddenly pulled back. Maybe Leona was right. This could wait until tomorrow. Charlie crept up on her toes, trying to quiet the crunchy gravel, and turned back to her car which was at the other side of the parking lot.

She took a few steps, then stopped and watched Leona sweep up Iris – who had just bounced out the club door–in her arm like a square dancer, and danced around with her in a circle, doe-see-doeing her back into the club.

Charlie tiptoed away from Ethan's van. She heard a footstep and whirled around with a fright. When she turned, she was standing face to face with Ethan. He had a big grin on his face.

"You scared the shit out of me!" Charlie blurted, slapping him in the arm.

He laughed aloud, but stopped when he saw that Charlie was not laughing. After a moment, Charlie opened her mouth to speak, but Ethan stopped her.

"Don't," he smiled. "I'm cool. We all are. As long as you don't make a habit of it," he chuckled.

"Thanks," Charlie looked down at her feet. She felt foolish, even though they all forgave her. She kicked some gravel with her shoe.

"It wasn't very professional. I know that. It got weird. I felt myself leave my body and watch as this other person took over and freaked out."

Ethan reached behind his ear and pulled out a cigarette and lit it, "Been hanging out with Shirley McLaine lately?" He blew the smoke through his nostrils, "Like I said, don't worry. I don't think anyone even noticed," Ethan scanned the parking lot. "Did Tom leave?"

"I knew it!" Charlie exclaimed, punching her fist into her leg, "I knew I wasn't crazy. He *was* there!"

"Yeah, I saw him," Ethan said as he took a long drag then crushed the cigarette beneath his feet; the gravel crunching softly under his Birkenstocks. Charlie followed him back to the van.

"I hope he left. I don't think I could handle another confrontation."

Ethan grabbed a cord that had fallen from the van. He picked it up and wound it around his arm and wrist then tossed it into an open box. "I know it's none of my business, but have you guys even talked?"

Charlie shook her head.

"I don't want to tell you what to do, Charlie, but I think you should clear the air. It might have a negative impact on your singing...especially in the studio."

"What do you mean?"

"Recording a new CD with Reno is the break you've been looking for, Charlie. Reno knows his stuff, that's for sure. If you've got all this pent up emotion, it's going to affect your voice, your vocal cords, and your spirit."

"Don't they always say a broken heart makes for the best songs? Maybe I could pull something good out of this nightmare I call my life." Charlie faked a yawn, "Ooh. I'm tired. Time's ticking and I've got a long day tomorrow." She forced a phony smile.

Ethan shook his head, "You're not going to take one word of my advice are you?"

It seemed that everyone had advice for her, but she did not see these people doing anything to improve their own lives. She wished everyone would just quit asking her questions. It was not anybody else's business.

"You need anymore help?" she asked, changing the subject.

"Nope. Iris is helping."

"Uh, huh. I'll believe that when I see it," she teased Ethan, pointing her finger in his face, "You better watch out for her. She's a handful!"

Chapter 21

∧

Charlie entered the kitchen wearing a business suit and carrying her briefcase. Her healthy brown hair was swept up into a bun and little wisps accentuated her face. She set the briefcase down by the fridge and opened it for the orange juice. She poured a glass and stood in the middle of the square kitchen, watching Iris outside on the deck through the kitchen's sliding glass door.

She wished she did not have to work. Her boss was not expecting her in until the following week, but she could not sit around and wait, especially with her sisters watching her every move. It was time for her to get back into her real life. Perhaps her singing career would take off and she could quit selling real estate. But until that time, she had to get used to the fact that nobody else was going to take care of her. She had made sure of that when she removed Tom from her life.

Catherine walked into the kitchen, still wearing her cotton pajamas. "Oh, no, no, no. What do you think you're doing?"

"Uh...drinking orange juice."

"I can see that," Catherine picked up the daily newspaper that was still rolled up and unread from the counter and swatted Charlie in the arm. "You're not going to work."

"Look, Catherine. Don't start with the mother hen routine, please. I've been sitting here...and...and I can't just sit around here for the rest of the week."

"Charlie? This can't be healthy," Catherine needled. "You need to spend some quality time fixing...whatever's wrong with you."

Charlie pulled her trump card, "Hey, I could be relaxing in Aruba, but...," she slugged down the rest of the juice.

Catherine blinked at her then looked away, "That's a funny one. You weren't out there, Charlie."

Charlie put her glass in the sink and picked up her briefcase. "You have to understand that I can't sit here with my thoughts. I've made my bed, and I'm trying to lie in it. Don't beat me up about it anymore."

"Beat you up? I'm just concerned."

"I know you are, but give it a rest. This motherly routine is growing tiresome."

"Fine."

"Good.

"Whatever."

"Oh, and do you think you and Iris can get through the day without killing each other?"

"What do you mean? We're getting along fine," Catherine turned around to look at Iris, who was now walking along the edge of the deck, cigarette in mouth, baby doll pajamas flowing in the wind. "Alright, she does get on my nerves a little."

"You got my number at the office if you need anything. But if you guys start fighting, call 911 'cause I don't want to hear it," Charlie laughed aloud at her own joke. As she grabbed her purse, she caught Catherine frowning disapprovingly.

"You need to stop trying so hard," Charlie said, exasperated. Charlie had been on her own for such a long time, she could not remember Catherine ever taking care of her. She rarely asked Catherine for her opinion, even though Catherine usually put in her own two cents whether it was solicited or not, and she hated it. This was where she and Iris agreed implicitly, only Iris probably hated it more that she did. Financially dependent on Catherine, Iris put herself in a position to be obligated to listen to Catherine.

Charlie tossed her briefcase and purse onto the front passenger seat of her car and slid behind the wheel. It was a sunny day, so she pushed the convertible button and the top opened, letting the morning sunshine warm her.

Charlie looked out at the lawn, realizing she needed to have the neighbor's boy mow it. Suddenly, a thought occurred to her. She threw the car into park, got out, and walked to the center of her lawn. Using both of her hands, she tugged and pulled the *For Sale* sign out of the ground and angrily flung it across the yard. Charlie clapped her hands together, walked back to her car, and drove away.

Chapter 22

Λ

The office was abuzz with the weekend gossip about the Charlie Hunter wedding scandal. Groups of sales agents gathered around the water cooler as others grouped together at one another's desks.

Bill, round and thick, in a white collar shirt and tie, looked jovial despite his tie being three notches too tight. He was the lead real estate agent in the office three years running, with Charlie a close second. He was talking to glossy Red Lips Liza (what everyone in the office called her behind her back) and Annette, whose bright red hair was short and shear, in a pixie cut. Annette was the newest agent at the office and a longtime friend of Liza. She had gotten tired of watching Liza make the "big bucks" while she slaved away at the beauty salon.

Bill pulled his Roosevelt glasses up to his eyes and elbowed Liza, interrupting their Monday morning gossip. Liza whirled around and saw it was Charlie. The entire office hushed, quiet as they watched Charlie go into the manager's office and shut the door. Then the room filled heavily with chatter.

"I wonder if she's going to quit," Liza asked, "If so, I'm taking her sales leads."

"You're a sensitive one, aren't you?" Bill commented.

Almost everyone from the office had gone to Charlie's wedding. Over the weekend, everyone in the office speculated about what had happened, each day's gossip exceeding the previous one.

"Uh, oh." Liza said as she sipped a drink of her coffee, "this is going to get interesting."

"Didn't she have this week off?" Annette asked, "I would have at least taken the week off. That's for sure."

"Oh my God, I don't know what to say to her," Liza looked at Bill, concern furrowed her penciled eyebrows.

Bill shook his head, "Nothing. That's what you say. Nothing. But you women, you can't do that, can you? You gotta make an issue out of everything."

Liza wadded the napkin from her muffin and threw it at his face. Annette laughed aloud as she watched uptight Bill's face get hot with anger, and she coughed when he scowled at her for laughing. Bill was the wrong person to have on her bad side.

* * *

Charlie left her boss's office unscathed. She had not planned to reveal anything to her boss other than she was coming back to work. Luckily, her boss was on a conference call with their Dallas headquarters, so she entered and exited without having to answer any questions. As she left, she could not help but notice the entire office staff watching her. Charlie quickly looked away, not wanting to see the pity in their eyes. Pity was the last thing she wanted from anybody.

She picked up a file from her "in" basket and rummaged through it, not absorbing anything she read. Everyone was looking at her, so she tried to appear busy. She wondered what everyone was saying. It was the laughter that made her stand strong. She threw her shoulders back and inhaled deeply. It didn't matter what they all thought, she told herself. Charlie lifted her eyes and scanned the room. She caught the brief glances of apprehensive eyes before they looked away. Charlie sighed aloud, realizing the day would be a long one.

Charlie went to the front counter to get her messages. She sat in the secretary's chair and flipped through the message book, but she stopped when she heard more giggling. Charlie squeezed her eyes shut tightly as anger rose inside of her. How could these people laugh at her? She thought they were her friends. How could they all be so insensitive?

Charlie bolted up from her office chair, and it rolled to the wall and it slammed against, "Look! I'm tired of...," Charlie stopped dead in her tracks.

Staring back at her from the reception area was a man and woman, snuggling closely, both wrapped up in their own little world. They both looked at Charlie like deer caught in headlights.

"Oh, I'm sorry," Charlie felt two inches tall. "I thought you were somebody playing a trick...," she stopped, and scrunched her face. "I feel stupid. I thought someone was messing with me...," she shook her head, trying to start all over, "Is someone helping you?" She forced a plastic smile.

"We're looking for a house. My...," she looked at the man, "Husband called a couple weeks ago and spoke to Charlie Hunter," they pressed their foreheads together and giggled.

"I'm Charlie Hunter," Charlie walked around the partition to officially greet them, "Yes, I remember you. You're the newlyweds I spoke with last week," she took a deep breath and gulped.

They both looked at each other and back to her, nodding enthusiastically.

"We thought you were going to be gone. You mentioned that if you were out, we were to speak to Bill."

Charlie steeled, trying to speak calmly. Her body shook and she could feel her knees knocking together. She told herself that she could do this. "Plans changed," Charlie announced briskly, slapping her arms to her thighs, "Now, I printed an MLS listing with the condos that were in your price range. I have that back at my desk."

The couple looked to each other with excitement.

Charlie smiled back at them. "Let me get the file and keys and we'll be on our way."

Charlie's heart pounded as she left the waiting room. The newlyweds were inseparable, just like she and Tom used to be. Her stomach burned, and she bit back the orange juice that wanted to come back up.

At the cabinet, she rummaged for the keys to the three houses. Even though her hands were shaking, she finally found them. On her way back to the couple, Liza motioned for her to come over to her.

Charlie shook her head and turned away from her. Liza was the biggest gossip in the office. Anything she said to her would be exaggerated by the end of the day. She refused to be the source of her own office gossip. Charlie could hear nosey Liza approaching because of the sound of her heels on the terrazzo floor. Would everyone just leave her alone?

Charlie herded the couple out the door before Liza could get to her. As she drove away with the happy couple in the back seat, she saw Liza and a few other office people staring out the window at her.

The five-minute drive to the first condo seemed like an eternity. When they finally arrived, Charlie decided to let the couple roam the house on their own. She did not feel the need to pressure sell, that was not her style. She knew they were serious buyers, because she had them pre-qualified with the bank first. This way, her time was not wasted. The girl's parents had given them twenty-five thousand dollars for their wedding gift, which they were ready to put down for their starter home.

Standing alone in an empty living room, jingling the keys in her hands, Charlie listened to the romantic murmurs of the newlyweds as they roamed from room to room. It saddened her to hear them kissing; the empty rooms amplified the echo of their playfulness like a slap in the face.

Charlie dug a tissue from somewhere between the layers of her purse and dabbed it at the corners of her burning eyes. She did not want them to see her cry. She knew she had to stop crying because her nose would turn red, which would be a dead giveaway.

She opened her mouth wide to inhale air deeply. Maybe Catherine was right. Going to work was not a great idea. She wished she were in Aruba, baking in the sun. How was she ever going to get used to life like this? Life without Tom? Life without love? She needed to get away from everyone, these newlyweds, her sisters, work, even away from Rhode Island. Charlie cursed aloud, damning Catherine for giving away her tickets to Aruba.

* * *

Tom sat at his desk twirling a pencil between his fingers. The afternoon sun crept behind the clouds, casting a dreary shadow inside his skyrise office. He dropped the pencil, and it fell on the floor. After staring at it for a long moment, he finally bent over to pick it up.

George Martin walked in unannounced. Tom, startled by the sudden sound of footsteps, slammed his head on his desk when he sat up.

"Ouch. That sounded like it hurt."

Tom rubbed his head, grimacing, "It did."

George took a seat opposite Tom. "How's it going, Tom?"

"My head will be fine."

"You know what I'm talking about."

"I'm okay I mean, everything's on target."

"Good, in both regards. I just got off the phone with Mitzutech and they want to push the meeting up a week. How do you feel about that?"

Tom considered the proposition. "We're ready. Everything's in order."

"Good. It's probably going to take some schmoozing. You up for that?"

"As long as it involves alcohol," Tom said, half serious. He knew what the job entailed – many cocktails, late hours, open tab, and of course, women.

George smiled, "It's nice to see you getting your sense of humor back," George's expression got serious, "You should have Donna make arrangements for you to fly out tomorrow morning."

"Tomorrow morning?" Tom asked, sliding forward in his chair. He realized that his entire demeanor had changed and he sat back slowly. He did not want George to think that he could not handle the deal. The team had worked six months on their advertisement, and now they liked their initial idea. Soon it would be time for them to sign contracts. "Tomorrow would be fine."

"You wouldn't be actually doing the presentation until Thursday, but I think you may want to be there a couple of days to get yourself together and on their time zone, before any serious negotiating begins."

Tom's tension subsided. "You're right. I can check out the facilities after the last renovation."

"And...it'll give you something to focus on."

Tom nodded in agreement. "You're right. This is what I need. Go overseas, get away from everything."

"I'm sending one of the designers and our corporate attorney, just in case there are any contract changes. I want this contract signed, sealed and delivered to my desk the minute you're back in town."

"I've got it."

George stood, looking at Tom, not fully convinced that Tom was ready. Tom's team had been working on this campaign for many months. Landing it would have the business sitting pretty for a long time. Even though he personally did not think Tom was ready to go overseas and pull this campaign together, Mitzutech felt comfortable with him. Pulling Tom from the deal could blow it all to bits.

"Why don't you go home now? I'll have Sally run the documents to your house. Go pack, rest, and get ready to make us all a lot of money."

Chapter 23

∧

Iris left the house for what was becoming her daily ritual of going into the city to sketch pictures. She tossed her backpack on her back and pulled her braids out from underneath the shoulder straps. As she walked, she wondered how she was going to tell Catherine that she was not going back to Florida State. At twenty-one, she finally knew what she wanted to do with her life. Art was her life. It was all she thought about. She saw the beauty in all of God's creation, and sometimes the feeling to capture all its beauty was overwhelming.

Iris cut through a field of tall grass. The wind blew the yellow straw back and forth, making it dance in a mystical pattern. Iris stopped to watch the different swirls sway, as she tried to figure out how she could capture that on paper.

When she reached one of Providence's busy city streets, she crossed it. She scanned for something to sketch: the bus station, the grassy courtyard where the business people spent their lunch, the tall buildings. But nothing appealed to her. She had already sketched the courthouse and some of the old buildings and there weren't any unusual-looking people roaming the streets. How was she going to use her talent to make extra money on the weekends if she could not find anything to draw?

A three-legged dog staggered across the road nearly getting hit. It was a scroungy runaway mutt. Although its hair was dirty and matted, the dog was still adorable. Iris followed it to the alleyway where it stopped to eat the remains of a melted and oozing ice cream sandwich that someone had dropped. She had found her subject, if only she could get him to stay still. Iris opened up her backpack and pulled out her peanut butter and jelly sandwich. She broke off a piece of it and held it in her hand as she edged in closer to the dog. The dog sat, showing the manners of a long lost house pet. She tossed him the bite and he scarffed it down quickly. When he finished, he sat back down and gazed at her with deep, dark eyes. Iris broke off another piece, quickly opened her sketchpad and pulled her charcoals out of the zipper pocket of her pack. When the dog was done with the bite, he sat at attention. Iris' hand darted quickly across the paper, as she magically transferred the image to her pad.

After twenty minutes or so, the dog grew tired of waiting for another bite. An ice cream truck jingled by and the dog took off, chasing it. Iris called after him, but he kept running. Iris slid down the brick wall she was leaning against and finished her picture from memory. When she was done, she set it against the wall and stepped back to assess.

Afterward, Iris walked downtown looking for the sandwich shop she had eaten at the other day. They had the best turkey roll-ups, and her stomach was growling just thinking about it.

As she rounded the corner, she stopped suddenly, unsure which way to turn on the street. The streets were confusing to her. She could not ask for directions because she had forgotten the name of the shop. The sound of someone playing guitar and singing made Iris stop dead in her tracks. Recognizing the voice, she hastened her step. Iris followed the voice around another corner. Her instinct was right. It was Ethan. Iris' stomach swirled with excitement. She had been looking forward to seeing him again at Charlie's next gig the following Saturday. And, here he was. She watched him admiringly. Ethan sang to the few individuals who were either standing or passing by. At the end of the song, he opened his eyes and saw Iris standing before him. He stepped toward her.

"Hey sunshine!"

Iris smiled then asked, "Is this your day job?"

"Nah, I practice outdoors. If people want to throw money, that's okay."

"That's so cool," she nodded.

He motioned for her to sit by him on the curb. Iris followed like a loyal puppy. Ethan saw the sketchpad under her arm. "Can I see?"

Iris shook her head no. She did not want him seeing her work. It was too rough to share, "I have better stuff back at Charlie's. This is just practice."

"Let me be the judge of that."

"I'd rather not show you."

Ethan put his hand on it, and cautiously pulled it from under her arm, and Iris did not fight him.

She made excuses as he opened it, "It's nothing, really."

He leafed through a few pages critiquing her work with an occasional "Hmmm," and "Uh, huh."

Iris' stomach cramped. She did not know if it was pangs of hunger or nerves. She wished she had not let him look, "I'm better than this."

Ethan did not answer her, he just continued flipping from page to page. Each leaf exposed an elaborately detailed depiction of the subject she had illustrated. He could no longer contain his true feelings. His "Hmmm's" turned to "cool" and "awesome" as he flipped through the entire book.

"Practice makes perfect," Iris made one last excuse as he shut the notebook.

"No, you're good. Better than good. Charlie said you were going to school, but she didn't say what you were going for."

"I'm not an art major. I was trying to finish my mandatory classes as I decided what I wanted to major in. It wasn't until recently that I knew what I wanted to do."

"Are you on a break?" Ethan asked as he handed her the sketchpad. "It's the middle of semester."

"Yeah, well...sort of. I came up for Charlie's wedding, and now it looks like I'm kinda stuck here for awhile." Iris looked to the ground, trying to hide her shame. She did not want to tell him she had failed and would not be returning to Florida State.

Ethan cued to her sudden change and asked, "What is it?"

Iris thought about not telling him, but decided against it. "I kinda failed some courses. My friends and I liked the nightlife a little too much." Iris covered her face, "I'm so embarrassed."

Ethan took her hands and removed them from her face. "Don't worry about telling me. I never thought I was smart enough to go to college."

Iris snorted as she burst out laughing, "You're just trying to make me feel better," she looked upward, as if her eyes were searching for words in the sky, "I haven't told my sisters yet, but... I'm not going back to Florida. I'm going to San Francisco."

"That's cool."

Iris felt invigorated just saying aloud, "I've been thinking it over and came to the conclusion that I need to get away from all my friends and take my schooling seriously. I want to go to art school at San Francisco University. They have a good program."

"Oh, yeah? When you goin'?"

"Pretty soon," she rolled her eyes, "When I get the courage to tell Catherine. She's been paying for my education. Charlie helps too, but it's Catherine I'm afraid to tell. She thinks she's my mother sometimes."

"Why San Francisco? Rhode Island School of Design is one of the best in the country," Ethan pressed curiously.

Iris shrugged. She was embarrassed to give him the real answer.

"You can tell me."

"I've never shared my dream with anyone."

"I'm really curious."

An impish grin curled across her lips. "The sky...Mount Shasta...the fog. It's far, far away from my sisters and, San Francisco State really has a good art program."

"I was there once a couple of years ago. I was playing with a Pearl Jam cover band. They were pretty good."

"Really?" Iris asked, genuinely eager to hear about his West-Coast adventure. "That's so cool. I want to try something new. I'm tired of recognizing the same old stuff, day in, day out."

"I know what you mean. I could go for a change like that." Now it was Ethan who was being reeled in to Iris' fantasy. "I really liked it out there. Life is so kicked-back."

"Imagine...the Golden Gate Bridge, Half Moon Bay, Sausalito." Iris used her hands to explain. "I love the way the bay windows are painted different colors. And the air is really clean. And they have great bookstores. And healthy foods. And it's not too hot in the summer or too cold in the winter..."

Ethan watched her, completely mesmerized by her vitality. When he first met her, he thought she was adorable, but he would never have pursued it. But something in him changed, and he wanted to take her in his arms and hold her tightly. As Iris rambled on, he watched her intently, slightly aroused by the way her mouth curved to the side when she spoke and how her eyes sparkled with excitement. He had never seen eyes that dark. It was as if the pupils had overtaken the iris of her eyes.

"...and Chinatown has the best Chinese food!" Iris stopped, realizing that Ethan was staring at her. She could feel herself blush.

"Wanna grab a coffee?" Ethan asked, not wanting the moment to end.   .

Chapter 24

∧

Charlie was curled up under an afghan on her bed, hoping for sleep to erase the memories of the day. Spending the day with the newlyweds had really put a toll on her. She wondered if she could get out of bed and do it all again tomorrow.

Charlie reached for the glass of water on the bed stand and took a drink. When she went to replace it, she opened the drawer of her nightstand and took out the picture that used to rest on the stand. It was a photo of her and Tom on a mini-vacation on Block Island. They had rented mopeds and tooled around the small island, pretending they were tourists, going from beach to beach, during the day and bar to bar at night. They rented a room at a little bed and breakfast that overlooked the ocean; the room was no bigger than her bathroom, fitting only a double bed and a nightstand. It was one of the best vacations she had ever had.

Inspecting the picture, she saw the obvious happiness, and the memory of that weekend flooded her mind, almost taking her breath away. Charlie had almost forgotten what it felt like to be happy. She tossed the picture back into the drawer and slammed it shut. Why was she doing this to herself?

Charlie flipped off the light and tried to sleep. Just as she was starting to doze, a knock at her bedroom window awoke her. She jumped out of bed and flew to the window. When she looked out, she could not see anything but the moonlight over the ocean. It must have been a seagull hitting the window. Charlie went back to bed. When the knock happened again, she bolted out of bed and dashed to the window. She pulled the sheer curtains to the side and was shocked to see Tom staring back at her. He motioned for her to come outside and Charlie quickly let loose of the curtain, and it swayed back and forth. Numbly, Charlie went to her bed and sat down. She did not want to see him. She knew she was not strong enough to fight her emotions. Not after the day she had.

The bedroom door creaked opened and Catherine poked her head in, "Just thought you should know that Tom's outside."

"I see that," Charlie said. "Send him away please."

"Charlie…"

"I can't see him," Charlie said, looking away from her sister to the mountainous painting that hung on the wall between the door and the bed. Charlie could feel Catherine staring at her, but she did not budge. She did not want to see Tom. She could feel Catherine's gaze, "And quit judging me."

"Well, Charlie, you're putting me in an awkward situation...and I don't feel comfortable."

"I already told you to send him away."

"And I said that I'm not going to be rude. If you don't want to talk to him, you're going to have to tell him yourself."

Charlie growled under her breath as she got up. Her demeanor hardened.

Outside, the setting sun was already sizzling on the water. The sound of the wind sent big, crashing waves onto the surf. Tom straddled the ledge of Charlie's deck, looking out at the ocean. Charlie observed him through the sliding glass door before she summoned the courage to step outside and confront him. Why was he making her life so impossible? She had made a blunt statement by leaving him on their wedding day. Why was he making it so difficult for the both of them?

She slid the door open, and Tom turned when he heard the door glide on its track. Charlie warily stepped out onto the deck. "What is it, Tom?"

Tom regarded Charlie for a long moment, as gusts of air wafted Charlie's long hair into her face, then off her face, over and over again. He suddenly lost his nerve wishing he had not come to her house.

Charlie grabbed her hair and held it by her fist. "I have a doorbell."

"I didn't want to see anybody else. Just you."

"What do you want, Tom?"

"I think we've got some things to talk about."

"I don't," she said then stood immovable. She was afraid that if she said much more, she would do what her heart kept telling her to do, which was to throw her arms around him and tell him that she still loved him; still wanted him. But she knew that was impossible.

Charlie slid the door shut behind her, doing anything to distract herself. She was fighting overpowering urges that she had not felt since the wedding day. She pursed her lips together tightly. She suddenly did not trust herself.

After a long moment, Tom spoke as he climbed off the ledge and came toward her, "Charlie, I can't believe after one year of telling me that you love me, that now, all of a sudden, you don't love me anymore."

Charlie stepped back against the sliding glass door, trying to put distance between them. Her lips were white from the pressure of locking them shut.

"Stop standing there looking at me as if you don't give a shit," Tom said and then shook his head, biting back his frustration. He lowered the volume in his voice, regaining control and then continued, "Do you realize what you've done to me?" He waited for her to answer, but when she did not, he said, "You've ruined my life!"

"It didn't look that way last night," Charlie finally spoke, but as soon as she did, she regretted it. Her jealousy flared, and she spoke without thinking.

Tom was confused. "What? What are you talking about?"

Charlie turned her head away from him.

"I really don't know what you're talking about." He was panicking and it showed in his voice. Hope suddenly felt apparent to him. "Come on, talk to me."

"Don't play stupid, Tom. You were just trying to get me jealous bringing your cheap date to my club!" Charlie was fearful she would say more. She had already said too much. There was a metallic taste in her mouth, and she realized that she had bitten her lip too hard and drawn blood.

"What're you talking about?" Tom walked to her and grabbed her by the arm, his large hands circling her fragile limb. "You think I'm dating? You think I could go out only a few days after..." He stopped.

Charlie turned to face him, looking him squarely in the eyes. It was then that she decided to tell him what she had seen. "You sure looked like you were freewheeling last night."

Tom took a step back. "You do. What the hell's wrong with you?" He turned, took three steps toward the deck stairs, and then whirled back to her. "You ripped my heart out, Charlie. I can't eat. I can't sleep. I can't concentrate. All I keep thinking about is...you. I don't understand what happened. If you don't tell me what I did...I can't fix..."

Charlie interrupted him again, "Stop it," she covered her ears. "I won't do it. I can't do this...to you...to us," she reached for the sliding glass door handle, but Tom grabbed her hand.

"Don't I have a say in this? It's my life, too."

"No, Tom, you don't," Charlie exclaimed, peeling his grip from her hand, "Someday you'll understand, but for now, it's not up for discussion. It's over, Tom."

Charlie opened the sliding glass door and went inside, shutting it and looking at Tom the entire time.

He walked to it and placed his hands on the cold glass, touching her hand through the pane. She quickly removed her hand. Tom spoke through the glass to her, "How can you be so cold?"

"If you knew me at all, you'd understand what I'm doing. Go home, Tom."

She could barely look at him. His face was sad, confused, and miserable, but for some reason, she could not tear her eyes away from him. The voice in the back of her head kept giving her the dialogue to be strong. Where had this voice been when she said the stupid, jealous comments outside? But she appreciated that the voice was there now, helping her. She turned to leave, but Tom flung the sliding glass door open, the wind whipping the curtain against the wall and snapping it like a wet towel.

"I feel like I don't even know you anymore, Charlie Hunter. You are a cruel person, and you couldn't possibly be the same person I wanted to spend the rest of my life with."

His hurtful words were a slap in the face, and they stung, wounding deep within. It took a moment for her to recover, but she did. She told herself that he was hurting and saying whatever he could to make her feel the same pain he was. Could he not see that she was hurting too? She was thankful for his cruel and inconsiderate words. She wanted him to say them. She needed for him to get mad, angry enough to forget her.

"Aren't you going to say something?" Tom asked, rubbing agitated hands through his black, messy curls.

"I thought I made it perfectly clear at the church."

"So that's it? You said yes to marry me, then you tell me at the church that you don't love me anymore. Do you expect me to sit around waiting for you to change your mind?"

"Don't you get it?" Charlie shouted at the top of her lungs. "I'm not getting married, Tom. Not to you. Not to anyone. Not ever!"

Tom was momentarily paralyzed, "You can't do that! You can't stop living!" Tom said. He turned to leave, deciding at that moment to take with him what little bit of self-esteem he had left before he made a complete ass out of himself.

Charlie watched him leave, ran to the door and flung it shut. She stared outside to where he had stood only moments before. Her hand drew magnetically to the print his hand left on the pane of glass.

She fought the urge to run after him, drop to her knees, and beg forgiveness. Hot tears filled her eyes. She did not want to blink and begin their flow, showing her vulnerability. Instead, coolly, she wiped her face with her sleeve then whispered aloud, "Good-bye Tom."

Chapter 25

∧

It was sunrise. Pinkish clouds filtered golden rays in the sky, mirroring on the water. Catherine was up earlier than usual. She had watched the sunrise, which sparked an urge to walk on the beach barefoot. The vibrant water was inviting, so she rolled up her cotton pajama bottoms and walked into the chilly surf.

As the waves crashed up past her knees, the iciness shot through her body, exciting her, making her feel like she was living life on the edge. She felt like she was Iris, young and vibrant, without a worry in the world. She had not felt this carefree in a long while. A wave knocked her over, and she struggled through the strong surf to stand. She laughed aloud but quickly looked up and down the beach to see if anybody had been watching. When she glanced at the back deck of Charlie's house, she saw Iris outside smoking. Catherine motioned for Iris to join.

Iris had been watching Catherine for a while and wondered what had gotten into her sister. Catherine's attitude had changed and Iris did not know if it was permanent or if she was just trying to get along. But this, playing in the freezing cold, Iris could not help wondering what was really going on. If she did not know her sister better, she would say that she'd been on something. She was getting conflicting signals, suddenly seeing Catherine in a different light; odd and amusing.

Catherine fell again and Iris burst out laughing. But when she did not come right up Iris panicked. She shot up from the deck ledge, jumped down to the sand, and ran halfway down the beach. Before she could reach the spot where Catherine had gone down, her sister surfaced, choking and gagging on water. Iris, her heart pounding wickedly, watched as her drenched sister stood saturated from head to toe, smiling ear to ear.

Iris flicked her cigarette into the air, kicked off her sandals, and striped to her undergarments. She ran into the water just in time to catch a big wave, riding it all the way to surf's edge. The sand burned her sensitive skin, and she scrambled quickly to her feet. Looking at her body she saw that it was red in places. The sand had brazed her skin like sandpaper and it stung. Peripherally, she saw Catherine struggling to her feet. Her sister could not get up as quickly as she could. Iris reached for Catherine's arm and tugged her to her feet.

They both stood at the end of the surf, bent over, hands on their knees, completely wiped out. Catherine lifted her head and smiled at Iris. She had sand in her teeth. Iris doubled over; hilariously consumed with laughter, she fell down in the wet sand.

"You've...," Iris laughed uncontrollably, "...got sand..." she continued laughing and snorting even harder than before. She pointed at her own teeth when she realized she would not be able to finish her sentence.

Catherine knew she had sand in her teeth and knew that she looked funny. She wished they had a camera; it would be a good memory to capture. She began spitting out the sand which only made Iris laugh even more.

All the sand would not get out, so she gave in to the futility and began flicking water with her foot on Iris. Iris stood up and began flicking it right back at her. They playfully splashed each other, back and forth, until they both fell over in hysterics.

This made Catherine happy. Maybe she was finally getting somewhere with Iris? And perhaps she had made a good decision not going to Mpumalanga with Steve and Christina. This was all that she prayed for, for her and Iris to connect and become the family they should be; the family they were before mom died.

As she and Iris played, she fought back a twinge of doubt that kept gnawing at her. She was trying not to get her hopes up. Any little thing could set them back. It would be inevitable – something would happen – and she would get her heart stomped again. Of the three, she was always the sister who was getting hurt. Naturally, she would be, and had always been, the one who would pick up the broken pieces. And at any cost – humiliation, determination - she'd have the family glue to patch it up. If she waited for them to make the effort, it would never happen. They would all just simply grow apart. Iris, with her temperamental spoiled spirit, and Charlie, with her detached persona. Neither one of them would even know how to make a move toward salvation for the family. That's why they needed her.

As she watched Iris's face bright with laughter, she could not help but hope that things were getting better between them. Maybe she was loosening up and Iris was growing up; hopefully, a little of both.

Next step was Charlie. Charlie would be harder to get to because to Charlie, she didn't have any problems to fix.

* * *

Charlie kept glancing at her watch. The day was going by slowly. All Charlie wanted to do was to go home and take a nap, but that was out of the question. All the other agents were out on calls, so she had to stay in case there was a walk in. The last thing she wanted was to show homes to another happy couple. Going back to work was not a good idea, and it did not really help. It just made her more stressed.

An hour later, the door opened, and in walked a couple who appeared to be in their late thirties. Charlie showed them some fliers for houses within their price range. When they found some properties that they wanted to look at, Charlie grabbed the keys to the houses they represented. As she walked out the door, Charlie wondered what had happened to singles buying a home these days. That's what she needed right now - single people. Only until she was able to interact in the real world again. She could not take watching another young couple ogling over each other in front of her any more.

Charlie, in the bare, high-vaulted living room, sat on the ledge of the bay window, as the couple glided from room to room. As she sat alone, her mind went to the day before. It loomed over her like a shadowy dark cloud, lurking and gloomy. She had hurt him. It was wrong how she did it. She was not too selfish to realize that, nor to take full blame for it. It was the *why* that she couldn't live with. The *why* she knew he'd never understand. The *why* she knew that she would never love again.

The couple asked a question about the age of the house and she answered. They disappeared into another part of the eighteen-hundred-square-foot Victorian home. Charlie opened her purse for a piece of gum or candy. Something, anything, to get her mind away from her own thoughts. She found some Lifesavers and put a lime green one in her mouth.

The man walked into the kitchen and went to the cupboards. From the back, he looked like Tom, tall with dark curly hair. Charlie looked away quickly. Now her eyes were playing tricks on her.

"How set on the price are the sellers?"

Charlie looked up. Relief swept over her when she saw that he did not look a thing like Tom from the front. "One hundred and eight thousand was their initial asking price, and they said they would not go any lower than where it is now."

"Oh. My wife, Elaine, really likes it, but we only have ten thousand in the savings. We will need more than that with closing costs."

Charlie walked to the center partition, standing on the dining room side of the divider. "How's your credit?"

"Well, I've got some things in the past. I was married before." He shrugged as if that explained it all.

"The best advice I can say is to make an offer. It's been on the market for six months. The sellers moved to Florida and this is the last of their loose ends, so to speak."

He nodded, then excused himself to go back and meet with his wife in the back bedroom. Charlie realized he must have asked her to stay in there so he could negotiate.

When they returned, the man announced, "We'll take it." The woman jumped into his arms and squealed with excitement. They kissed, a little too long, and Charlie turned away, uncomfortably. She turned back when he asked, "What's the next step?"

Charlie's voice was quivery and she cleared her throat. She did not realize until the moment she tried to speak how much the couple had shaken her up. She needed to get over Tom soon. She just could not avoid couples.

"Like I mentioned before, that depends on what kind of financing plan you fall into, which is based on credit, money down, seller contribution. I've got banks that I work with. If this is your first home, we could try to put you in an FHA loan. You will need three percent plus closing costs. That's all."

The couple looked at her with confusion and excitement at the same time. Charlie smiled, "Come on." She scooped up the woman's arm with hers and led her toward the front entrance. The husband followed like a puppy.

"Let's set an appointment to go through all your options. There are so many different programs. I am confident I can get you qualified somehow." The woman expressed a look of fear and Charlie smiled, "It's really not as confusing as it seems." Charlie let go of her arm to lock the door behind them. "Trust me."

At the street, they shook hands and exchanged business cards, and Charlie watched them drive off in their black Durango. She did not know why she was compelled to watch them leave, but doing so made her feel even emptier than before. They were off to their perfect, loving world, while she went back to her "hell" house with the Bicker Sisters.

Charlie started her engine and looked upward to the graying sky when she felt one solitary rain drop land on her nose. Another droplet was followed by a few more. The perfect weather for any miserable mood. She raised the top of her convertible and headed home.

It seemed everywhere she looked, something reminded her of Tom. Restaurants they had frequented, streets they had roamed, the car dealership where she bought her car. She could not escape him.

The drive seemed as if it would never end. A light on her dash caught her attention, reminding her to fill her empty gas tank. Up ahead was a Shell gas station. Even the gas station reminded her of him. She sighed and turned on her blinker.

As she filled her tank, she thought about how Tom's words had hurt her, and she tried to brush away that thought. She didn't deserve the luxury of feeling pain. So what if he said that she was a cruel person and that she was not the person he wanted to marry? She made him say that. She had to see from his point of view. If she didn't, she would stop understanding his pain and cruelty and start to believe it. He had called her a coward, but if anything, she was brave. She was fighting against every grain of what she wanted to do and was doing the right thing. Still, it made her feel like shit.

The gas pump clicked off, and she replaced the nozzle and got back into her car. When she started the engine, she turned the radio up full blast, hoping the sound would drown out her thoughts, and drove toward the home she now dreaded.

* * *

At the airport, Tom stood next to his carry-on luggage, looking out the window, watching, absently, as airport personnel hustled about underneath the giant metal bird he was about to board. Occasionally, he glanced over his shoulder, toward the boarding area, half-hoping he would see Charlie coming to see him. He knew it was impossible, but he could not hide his hope.

The gate doors opened, and the prior flight exited. The people ambled off the plane, filling the boarding area until the final passenger exited. The room overflowing with the noise and excitement of lovers and family members being reunited. A young Army soldier, in full uniform, who had been waiting with flowers, was reunited in a long, passionate kiss with his sweetheart. A fresh-faced twenty-something with golden hair walked up late to the boarding area. Tom watched her as she scanned the room, making eye contact with a sad-faced man who thought he had been forgotten. Both faces brightened with excitement and they rushed, like an old silent movie, into each other's arms, kissing wildly.

He could no longer bear watching the people around him. His stomach tightened into a knot, and his heart dropped as pangs of sadness rushed through him. There was nothing he could do to get rid of the swirling feeling inside. He felt nauseated like he had just gotten off a long carnival ride. In reality, his life for the past week had been a roller coaster. He had never been able to handle that ride.

Tom gulped in fresh air, the stress making it hard to breathe. That should have been Charlie running through the gate into his arms. He wondered; *what if it was her*? Would he tell her that he loved her? Tell her that he forgave her? She was killing him. Tom unexpectedly got angry, angry with himself for being such a sap. If she walked through that door, he would make himself say that she had blown her chance with him. The tables would be turned, and he relished in the thought of her sharing his pain. Then he would tell her it was over and gloat as he dished to her the same cruelty she had inflicted on him; slap her with a reality stick and see how she liked it.

A blue-haired woman wearing bright orange lipstick was looking at him. It was then that he realized that he had been holding his breath. He imagined that his face was beat red, just like when he got embarrassed or laughed too hard. He pasted on a cordial smile and turned away. Then, he breathed. Who was he kidding? He knew if Charlie were to walk through that door, he would melt into her arms and never let her go.

The announcement for first class and people needing extra assistance was broadcasted, and Tom picked up his carry-on bag and headed for the line. He patted his breast pocket for his ticket, but it was not there. He patted his back pockets, but to no avail. He turned back around to where he had been standing and saw his ticket was on the floor. He retrieved it and got back in line to board. He hated how his mind would not focus. It was a full-time job staying angry with her. Why could he not *unlove* her like she so coldheartedly did to him? Or simply cast her aside like an unwanted shoe?

Tom found his seat, got situated and opened his briefcase. Pulling out the Mitzutech file, he decided to direct his attention to the ad campaign. He scanned the paperwork over and over, but after reading the same paragraph three times, he knew that it was useless. Closing the file, he told himself that he would use this time away to get over Charlie. He was glad he did not tell her that he was leaving the country. Let her think he had given up and gotten on with his life. Apparently, it was what she wanted and that was what he would do. He had to take care of himself and free his mind.

* * *

In a far corner of the neighborhood coffee shop, Iris and Ethan sat opposite each other, talking intimately.

Leaning forward and speaking quietly, Ethan began, "Charlie used to talk about her mother...," Ethan corrected himself, "*Your* mother all the time, but she never mentioned your father?" Ethan sat back, picked up his coffee cup, and listened.

"I have pictures of him, but I really don't know anything about him."

"Does it bother you talking about him?" He set the cup down.

"No, not really. I feel indifferent about him," Iris said, squirming uncomfortably. She had never really spoken of her father to anybody and was unsure about how she felt talking about him.

"Do you ever wonder who he is? If he's still alive?"

"Yeah...well, sometimes I wonder," Iris paused; deciding whether she wanted to continue in the direction the conversation was headed. She took a sip of coffee and made the choice to reveal what she had never told. "My father was a truck driver. He was gone a lot. My mother was always alone. I don't remember a whole lot except that she wasn't very happy. And then when he left, she was alone...more alone."

The waitress came to refill and they both sat in silence until she left.

"How long were they married?" Ethan asked.

"Something like fifteen years."

"And you haven't seen him since."

Iris nodded and then shrugged.

"Why'd he leave?"

She picked up the napkin and began twisting it nervously. This was exactly why she did not like speaking of her father. How could she tell him the truth?

Ethan saw he had made her uncomfortable. "I'm sorry for prying. You don't have to tell me."

Iris opened her mouth to speak, and then stopped. Instead, she picked up her coffee cup, sipped slowly, and set it back down. Ethan watched her, suspecting he had evoked painful memories. He whispered again, "Sorry."

"I'm just not proud to admit my father left because of me."

Ethan gave her a questioning look.

"They had to get married when she got pregnant with Catherine. Then it was a long while before they had Charlie, but I don't think she was planned, either. I don't think he was into having kids. I didn't know him, but I heard he was a free spirit."

"Hmmm," Ethan shut one eye, analyzing Iris through the other, "I can see the resemblance."

"My mom was trying to save the marriage or so the story goes. She got pregnant with me and it backfired." All of a sudden, Iris wanted to tell him everything. She considered telling him all her deep dark secrets and without hesitation. She knew that she could tell him everything and that he would never judge her.

"Wow, so she raised the three of you alone?"

"Yeah. Pretty much. Catherine was older and helped, when Mom got...um, got depressed. But, I guess I'd be pretty miserable too, if I had to take care of three kids all by myself."

"You don't like kids either?"

"I liked being one. I was kind of adventurous," she smiled and paused, remembering some of the crazy, sneaky things she had done and raised her eyebrows, "Had a lot of fun, if you know what I mean."

"I believe it," he wanted her to continue.

"You don't even know the half of it."

"So..."

"As for kids, I don't know if I like them or not. Haven't been around many," Iris took another sip of her coffee, realizing it was getting cool. She liked her coffee piping hot or not at all. She pushed the cup away from her. "What about you?"

"I think kids are the best."

"I meant," Iris laughed, "Let's talk about you. How long have you been with Charlie's band?"

"I hooked up with them about two years ago."

"Have you always lived here?"

"No, I'm from Texas...Austin, Texas. I was just passing through on my way to Toronto. I stopped into the club for a drink and met Denny. He told me Charlie was looking for a guitarist."

"And the rest is history," Iris beamed. "Isn't Denny the best? I really like him."

"Yeah, he's a good guy." The waitress stopped by to pour more coffee, but they both declined. "How serious are you about San Francisco?"

Iris looked deep into his vibrant green eyes, wondering why he would ask a question like that. She shrugged, raising her eyebrows, "Why do you ask?

* * *

At Charlie's house, Catherine opened the spare room that was doubling at Charlie's rehearsal room and Iris' temporary bedroom. She shook her head as she scanned the mess Iris had created in the already cramped quarters. Iris had dirty clothes spread across what used to be green carpeting. Clean clothes were hung on Charlie's keyboards and amplifiers. She knew Charlie would disapprove of that. Catherine held the small pile of folded laundry in one hand as she went to open a dresser drawer with the other hand. The pile fell out of her hand onto the floor. Exasperated, she bent down to pick up the laundry.

After placing the folded laundry in the drawer and making a dirty clothes pile outside the doorway, Catherine noticed Iris' sketchpad hanging out of her opened backpack. She picked it up. A rush of guilt surged through her, but she disregarded the emotion. Her curiosity triumphed and she started leafing through the sketchpad. Proudly, she admired her sister's talent. She could not help but wonder why she did not possess any of the talent either one of her sisters had. Perhaps Iris was finally honing in on her true calling. Iris had changed her major so many times that Catherine had lost count.

Catherine went to put the sketch pad back exactly how she had found it, so Iris would not know she had poked around, although technically, she did not consider it snooping if something was left out in the open for all to see. When she put it back in the backpack, Catherine noticed an envelope inside with a return address from the Dean of Academic Affairs at Iris' art school. Thinking it was a letter of commendation - because of the apparent talent her sister possessed - she rationalized reading it, since she could tell it had already been opened.

The smile disappeared from her face, as she read the unforgettable words that filled the paper. To her surprise, it detailed in specifics that her grade point average was below the minimum required. Iris had been expelled. Catherine stomped her foot on the ground furiously. She had paid good money for Iris to go to Florida State. How could she let this happen?

Catherine did not hear the front door shut, but she did hear footsteps coming down the hallway. Quickly, she tried to put the letter back in Iris' pack, exactly where she had found it, but it was too late.

Iris was standing in the doorway. Catherine froze like a child caught with her hand deep in the cookie jar.

Iris, stopped dead in her tracks, immobilized with disbelief. "What the hell is this?"

Catherine shot up, no longer feeling remorse for snooping and thankful she had found out the truth. "You've been expelled? When the hell were you going to tell us?" Catherine flashed the letter in front of Iris' face.

Iris' eyes widened, fearful at first and then fired-up with anger. She wanted to tell Catherine at the right time, "What are you doing looking through my stuff?!"

Catherine ignored the question and probed her, "When were you going to tell us?"

"I was going to tell you!"

"Oh yeah? When? After you were through sucking money from me and Charlie?"

"I don't need your fucking money! I'm not going back anyway!"

Catherine waved the letter in front of her face. "Apparently not!"

"I'm moving to San Francisco."

Catherine was taken aback, snorting aloud with sarcasm when she realized there was no way financially that Iris could go three thousand miles across America.

"How the hell are you going to get to San Francisco? Don't think I'm bankrolling another one of your pipe dreams!"

Iris angrily tossed her purse onto the bed and ripped off her jacket, looking as if she were preparing to raise her fists, "I don't want anything from you! I can manage on my own."

"Is that right? You've never even held a job."

"Oh now isn't that ironic!" Iris' voice grew louder than before. "Neither have you and you're doing just fine."

This time they both heard the front door shut. Startled by the sound, they both realized it was Charlie home from work.

"I could hear you guys from down the street," Charlie said, dropping her keys on the kitchen table and heading toward the fight in her rehearsal room. "You can't be together for five minutes without fighting, can you?"

Catherine was so red-faced and overwhelmed with anger that her hands were shaking, and she looked as if her eyes were going to bulge out.

"I caught Catherine snooping through my stuff!"

Charlie looked from Iris to Catherine.

Catherine nodded. "I'm glad I did. We would've never found out."

Charlie looked from Catherine now to Iris, suddenly feeling as if watching a tennis match. "Found out what?" she asked firmly.

"It's none of her business, Catherine...or yours for that matter."

Catherine turned to Charlie, "She got expelled," she turned to Iris, "And you better believe it's our business!"

Charlie was stunned. She had hoped her sisters would be leaving soon so she would have her home back. If Iris failed out of school, clearly that meant that she would not have any other place to go, since staying with Catherine was out of the question.

"Wait a minute. Expelled? Is that right? Iris, I thought you were doing so well."

"Leave me alone," Iris folded her arms and looked out the window. She did not feel that she had to explain her failures to either one of them. They both were doing what they wanted with their lives, and she felt like a big failure. They were the last people she wanted to expose her inadequacies to. They were also the very same people she could not live up to.

Charlie motioned for Catherine to shut up when she saw her opening her mouth to speak, and then moved in closer to her younger sister, "Tell me what happened."

"I'm going to San Francisco, so you and Catherine can rest assured I won't be taking any more of your money."

"You can't walk away from something like this, Iris," Charlie stated.

Iris turned to look at Charlie. She could always talk to her, but never the Condescending Catherine. Catherine always made her feel worse about her shortfalls.

Catherine belted out, "Give it up, Charlie, she's just gonna lie her way out of this one."

Iris turned on her heels and flew right into Catherine's face, furious at her accusation, "I've never lied to you!" Iris screamed at the top of her lungs, "Never!"

"Oh, sure," Catherine folded her arms and scrutinized her baby sister with both cynicism and distrust.

Iris threw her hands in the air, "I don't give a shit!"

"Stop it!" Charlie moved between the two. "Catherine! Leave her alone. It's hard being away from home..."

"Why do you always defend her? She's an irresponsible, self-centered, little brat."

"Why don't you just mind your own business, Catherine?" Iris asked defensively. "Don't you get it?"

"Get what, little sister?"

"No one asked you to be here. You invited yourself here. Take a hint. No one wants you here!"

"This is Charlie's house. She said she didn't mind me staying here," Catherine looked at Charlie, who wasn't responding.

"See?" Iris chastised, smiling as she gloated, "You're not wanted here. Why don't you go home?"

Iris' words wounded Catherine, her face paled.

"Iris!" Charlie screamed at the top of her lungs, her hands flew to cover her ears. "Shut up! I can't take this anymore!"

Iris was on a roll, and the cruel words flew effortlessly, "You should have gone away with Steve! Nobody needs you to play mother. We already had one! She's dead, just like you are to me. D-E-A-D!"

"Stop it, Iris!" Charlie grabbed her shoulders and shook her, "What is wrong with you? How could you be so evil?"

Catherine numbly dropped her arms to her side. The letter fluttered downward in slow motion, cutting through the air as it floated to the floor.

Catherine looked from Iris to Charlie and then back to Iris. Had Iris spoken the truth about how they both felt? Why had they not said something about it before? All along she knew that she was the outcast of the family, and it was time for her to face the cold hard facts that they would never be the family their mother would have wanted them to be. It was time for her to give up the cause. She stumbled to the doorway, her feet suddenly heavy and inoperable.

She turned in the archway, "I don't know why I even bother with you," Catherine paused for effect; her eyes spilled instant tears, "You're hopeless, Iris." Catherine turned around and left the room.

"Catherine?" Charlie called to her sister, her glare not leaving Iris.

Catherine mumbled as she walked down the hallway, talking to herself, "I should have gone with Steve."

Charlie pointed her finger in Iris' face, "This is my house! You have no right throwing anyone out of my house!"

Iris pushed Charlie's finger away, and Charlie shook her head, "She doesn't have any respect for me, Charlie! She never asks, she demands! She never considers my feelings!"

"And you were being considerate of hers just now?"

"Charlie, she treats me like I'm a kid!"

"Acting like one doesn't prove her wrong."

"I know! I can't control myself around her. She makes me crazy!"

"Iris, she's just trying to...," Charlie stopped because she wanted to find the right words to make Iris see from Catherine's point of view. "She just cares about you...us."

"That's not caring! She's a control freak! I won't let her monitor my every..."

"Iris, you're overreacting. She..." Charlie corrected herself, "We are paying your tuition, and we do have the right to know that you're failing. Why do you have to go about feeling like the world is against you?"

"There you go!" Iris kicked a shoe on the floor underneath her bed. "You know, sometimes you're just like her!" Iris picked up her backpack, shut the flap and put it on her back. "I don't need you! I don't need either of you!"

"Iris!" Charlie hollered out for her sister, but realized she was not coming back when the front door slammed shut. Charlie stood in the middle of the messy room, hands on her hips, bewildered and suddenly exhausted.

She closed her eyes and clicked her heels together, "There's no place like home." She kept her eyes shut for a long moment, relishing the silent house. For a moment she thought her "Dorothy" trick had worked. Maybe it had all been a dream and she was home alone, just like she used to be.

Cautiously, she opened her eyes. Her elation was gone. Looking at her messy rehearsal room, she knew the nightmare had been real.

Chapter 26

∧

It seemed as if everyone was buying a house, although this time, Charlie was being spared "Romance Theater." She did not really care for the woman with whom she had an appointment. Her name was Roberta. She was almost fifty, never married, and bitter because of it.

Charlie forced herself to go through the motions. She was numb, and nothing seemed to matter. But selling houses was her only form of income. She could hardly make a living off the band after splitting the money among her bandmates. The passion inside her was dying, and she found it hard to motivate herself.

"And in here, we have...," Charlie checked the floor plans because the listing agent was unable to attend, and this was the first time she had shown this house, "...the dining room."

"It's not big enough to be called a dining room," the woman disputed and brusquely ripped the paper from Charlie's grasp. Roberta scrutinized the paper, holding it steady as she squinted her beady eyes at the small type. When she saw that in fact it was the dining room, her expression changed and she shrugged, "Sorry." She handed the paper back to Charlie. "It is small, though."

There was a quick knock at the door and they both whipped their heads toward the front door. It opened and a familiar face popped through the door - Iris. Charlie widened her eyes and with them asked Iris to leave. How did she know how to find her? This was the last thing she needed, another confrontation with her sister.

The woman looked from Iris to Charlie, waiting for someone to speak.

"Excuse me please," Charlie said to Roberta, then headed to the door, "Why don't you check out the cupboard space in the kitchen and I'll catch up with you in a second."

"Hi, Charlie," Iris announced uncertainly.

"What are you doing here?" Charlie whispered gruffly, "I'm working."

"Your office told me I could find you here," Iris scrunched her face suddenly aware that she should not have come to her during work, "Sorry."

"Can't this wait?" the woman barked from the kitchen, "I don't have all day." She slammed a cupboard door loudly. "But I'm sure I can find another competent real estate agent in the city."

"Excuse me, ma'am, but it's kind of a family crisis...," Iris blurted and Charlie clapped her hand over Iris' mouth.

Charlie whirled around, "Roberta...I mean, Mrs. Santaro. I apologize for this inconvenience. I'll be with you in a moment."

"All right. But just a minute. I'll be looking around." The woman went around the corner and headed toward the back of the house, too stubborn to look in the kitchen merely because Charlie had suggested it.

Charlie turned back to Iris, took her hand off her sister's mouth, and shoved her out the door. When Iris resisted, Charlie gave her a hard shove. "I'm not joking, Iris. I've had it with you."

Iris whispered, "Stop it, Charlie. It's important. I have talk to you."

"Fine!" Charlie whispered. Charlie fixed her rumpled blouse and put the few flyaway wisps of hair that had fallen back behind her ears. "Meet me at my car in twenty minutes."

The woman cleared her throat in the other room. Charlie pushed Iris' face through the door and shut it. "Mrs. Santaro?"

"It's *Ms.*," she announced loudly from the other room, "Ms. Santaro. Do you see a ring on my finger? No." She appeared around the corner holding out her left hand. "And this place is just not right."

"Well, I have a few other listings to show you."

Roberta walked to the door, "Have a nice day, Ms. Hunter, and call me when you take your job seriously."

Charlie turned away when the door slammed. She breathed in and shook her head as she slowly walked to the window ledge for a moment and sat down. That woman was a hard sell. She probably would not have been happy under any circumstances. Charlie wondered what else could go wrong. When would she regain some sense of control?

Charlie threw her head back and growled under her breath. For a moment, she had forgotten Iris was outside waiting for her. The last thing she wanted was to deal with Iris, especially if all she wanted was to complain about Catherine.

Outside, Iris was sitting in the back seat of Charlie's blue Mustang, the top down, her feet atop the driver's seat. Her bare feet were exposed and she had her eyes shut, taking in the sun's rays. Iris did not hear Charlie walk up, and she squealed when Charlie shook her foot.

"What's up your ass?" Iris asked, taking her feet down, "There's no reason to be rude."

Charlie did not answer, she just folded her arms and waited.

"What? No sale for frosty-freeze?" Iris climbed out over the door and continued, "Someone needs to tell her that beehives went out in the sixties. How can you take shit from people like that?"

"That's part of being a sales...," Charlie stopped in mid sentence. She wasn't going to justify her job to Iris. "What was so damn important that you had to sabotage a sale for me?"

"She wasn't buyin' and you know it?"

"That's beside the point." Charlie pulled her keys out of her purse, "Anyway, where were you last night?"

Iris leaned against the car. She looked down and kicked a pebble that was at the end of her sandal. "I wanted to tell you that I'm leaving. I'm moving to San Francisco." She paused for a second, hesitating on her next sentence. "That is, Ethan and I are moving to San Francisco."

Charlie stepped back, assessing Iris, seeing if she was bluffing.

"You're not going to say anything? I said Ethan and I are going to California."

"I heard you – I just can't believe it! You get expelled from school and the answer is to move across the country. I can see why Catherine loses patience with you," Charlie tried to open her car door, but Iris slid in between Charlie and the door handle.

"I'm being serious here. We're just gonna wait for Ethan to tie up a few loose ends and then we're leaving. He's got a van and he said he'd take care of us."

Charlie closed her eyes and counted to ten inside her head. She was trying to remain calm. The counting did not work, and her eyes flew open along with her mouth, "A van, huh? You're gonna live in a van?"

"It will be exciting!" Iris' face brightened, "I can't wait."

Charlie pushed Iris aside, "This is ridiculous." She no longer wanted to listen to Iris' banter. She could not believe that her own sister was doing this to her. Iris knew how important Ethan was to her.

"I can't deal with this right now. I've got to be in the recording studio in an hour and I haven't even rehearsed," Charlie opened her car door and whirled around. "The only reason I'm not going into this right now is because I need to save my voice for recording."

"You're straining it now," Iris said, provoking her to a fight.

Charlie got in her car and shut the door behind her. She started the engine and drove away without looking back.

Iris watched Charlie speed off down the street before she realized that she did not have a ride home. Why didn't she tell the cab driver to wait? She knew Charlie had a temper. Iris began chasing her but could not catch up. Charlie's Mustang had squealed around the corner and disappeared out of sight.

Iris started walking down the street. The sky was getting dark, and it looked as if it was going to rain. Inspecting her thumb, she supposed that she would have to turn to "old reliable."

* * *

In the darkened bedroom of her own house, Catherine was curled into a ball in her bed, cold and shivering. Her hair was drenched; her light skin was pale and clammy. She had just awoken and at first could not remember where she was. It took a moment for her to figure it out. She glanced at the clock and was alarmed when she realized she had slept through the afternoon. She had missed Steve and Christina's telephone call, the one thing that she looked forward to every day.

Catherine tried to get out of bed, but even the minute effort of lifting the covers took too much energy, more than she could summon, so she stayed put. Earlier, she had felt a little tickle in the back of her throat but did not think anything of it. Now the scratchy throat had turned into a full-fledged flu.

She groaned aloud and did not feel foolish because nobody was home to hear. Overreacting was out of character for her. She was usually the strong one who never got ill.

Nightmares about her sisters haunted her sleep. What made her think she could save the family? She knew she was wasting her time. All she wanted was a normal family. A family that wanted to share holidays and have Sunday dinners together. She only wanted to do what their mother would have wanted.

Catherine was so cold, she could not stop shivering. She needed to get up and take some Tylenol, but she could not make her body move. Instead, she curled her body, pulling her knees close to her chest.

She flitted in and out of sleep, but the nightmares kept waking her. The dream repeated, and each time Iris' behavior worsened. In her dreams, Charlie joined Iris, and together they ganged up on her.

Catherine tried to stay awake. She did not want to dream anymore. They were too vivid, and because of her fever, they seemed to intensify. She questioned what was real and what was delusional, and she literally had to focus to remember the facts. She wondered if Charlie felt the same way. Charlie never chose sides; she just lived with whatever outcome that happened. Charlie never wanted to hurt anyone's feelings. Catherine sometimes wondered if Charlie even had a backbone. Would it have been so hard for her to stand behind her just once? Find one important cause and stand firm? Iris was their sister, and she was wasting her life. How could she not care that Iris was flushing their hard-earned money down the drain? With Iris thinking the world was against her, and Charlie being spineless, it amazed her that they had all come from the same mother.

Catherine couldn't seem to get warm, so she doubled the feather comforter over and piled the blankets higher. Doing so sent an unusual chill through her body, and she relished the moment of warmth to come. Curling into fetal position again, she tried lying perfectly still, not wanting to feel the coldness of any part of the untouched sheets. She feared she would never get warm.

If Steve were home, he would take care of her. She wished he was with her. He was always sympathetic when she was sick, and he babied her to extremes. What she really wanted was a cup of hot tea, but wild horses could not drag her from the bed. The thought of warm tea trickling down her throat almost brought her to the point of getting out of bed, but every time she would talk herself into doing it, she could not make her body respond.

Catherine finally fell into a deep sleep. Only this time she dreamed of her daughter and of being in Africa with them. Her daughter's long red braids were flapping up and down in slow motion as she ran through the tall grass. They were laughing hysterically, and Catherine swooped up her daughter in her arms. They twirled around and around in the air.

* * *

Charlie sat in Reno's recording booth singing, earphones on and the microphone pulled in closely. Her face expressed sadness and confusion. Dark circles revealed all the gloomy secrets she held inside. She wondered if the day would come when she wouldn't feel the emptiness any longer. Something had to change. It couldn't get any worse.

Singing was her only escape from reality, but she couldn't even summon the desire to enjoy it. This was her diversion from reality and she so wanted it back. She needed it back. Charlie couldn't get over the fact that Iris was going to California and taking Ethan with her. Why was she doing this to her? Was it her sick way of getting even with Catherine? Or had she and Ethan fallen in love? Iris knew the ultimate revenge on Catherine would be to leave without saying good-bye. She knew it would break her. Iris could be so spiteful and selfish. Iris did what Iris wanted. Charlie knew she needed to talk to Ethan.

Reno McChesney stopped the music for the third time. He stressed that Charlie needed to stay focused. Leona put her hand gently on his arm and affectionately patted him. She could see his frustration and feared that he would snap soon. She leaned into him and whispered something in his ear. He nodded and he stood up, stretched, rolled his neck and sat back down.

Leona shook her head. "That's not a break, dear."

At Leona's insistence, she got him to allow Charlie a fifteen-minute, much-needed break.

Charlie mouthed a thank-you and left the recording area. She went to the bathroom, locked the door, and put down the toilet lid. When she sat, her head dropped, shamefully. She knew she was not being professional. It was her lucky break getting a producer to back her. Why could she not focus? It had never been a problem in the past. She needed to flush the past ten days from her mind.

"Focus," Charlie whispered aloud to herself. "Don't think about anything else." She told herself that she would do with Catherine and Iris what she did with Tom. She would take her problems and throw them to the back of her mind, store them right next to the wedding mishap, with Tom, and with her mother.

Back in the recording studio, Charlie rolled her neck and shook her hands out, trying to get as relaxed as possible. If she could not do it for herself, then she would do it for Reno. He had a lot invested in her career, and she owed it to him.

Charlie motioned that she was ready to begin again, and Reno cued the music. For the first time that day, Charlie sang from her heart, not thinking about any of her problems.

"Searching through windows...Future unknown,
Testing the waters...You learn as you go.
Clinging to reason...succumbing to haste,
Mistakenly happy... it seems such a waste..."
Searching through windows...Hole in the wall,
Frightened of nothing...But afraid of it all.
Foregoing promise...Do as they say,
Compromising yourself in \every way.
Searching through windows...What do you see?
The exit to Eden...The abyss of Hades?
Picture of happy...bleeding the wound,

Internally broken...will it be over soon?."

Chapter 27

ʌ

It was early evening when the airplane taxied down the runway in Providence. Steve and an excited Christina sat in their seats impatiently, both eager to see Catherine.

Steve had finished his work in Mpumalanga a week early. He had hired two additional conservationists because from the moment he stepped on African soil, he could barely manage without his wife. Never before had he worked so diligently. Once the lions were in safe hands, he knew he could manage his job from the states.

Steve put his hand on Christina's arm when she tried to unbuckle before the plane had stopped.

"Wait until you see that seatbelt light turn off," he pointed to the safety light above.

Christina watched the light like a pot of water that never boils. When it finally signaled, she unbuckled and swiftly jumped to her feet, "Hurry, get your bag, daddy," she tugged on his arm.

"Alright, sweetie," he chuckled and he stood – as best he could in an airplane – to appease her.

In the terminal, as they watched everyone else's bags circle the baggage carousel, Steve wondered if Catherine would be at their house, or at Charlie's. He had come this far without calling and did not want to ruin the surprise now. He had never intended for it to be a surprise at all, but with the chaos in changing their flight and rushing between connections, he barely had time to tend to Christina, let alone call Catherine.

All the way home, his stomach fluttered with anticipation. He could not remember the last time they had spent any time apart, if ever. He had never gone abroad without her and decided he would not do it again. Being his own boss gave him some flexibility and he was going to utilize that power.

At the highway split, he debated where to go first: Charlie's house or their house. Since his house was the closest, he thought he would try it first. He had traveled so much, what would another fifteen miles be? Charlie's house was on the other side of Narragansett. One thing he liked about the new Providence airport was that it would only take ten minutes after getting the luggage before they would be in their car and on their way.

By the time he reached home, Christina had fallen fast asleep. Pulling into the driveway, his elation dropped when he saw that the house was dark. He suddenly wished he had called her to meet them. His heart skipped a beat when he saw that her car was in the driveway. He hoped she was home but shrugged it off, figuring that she probably dropped it off sometime during the week.

He glanced at the clock. It was ten after nine. Since Tina was sleeping, he decided he would tuck her into bed and then give Catherine a call. He hoped she was not asleep. He wanted nothing more than to hold his wife. It had been too long.

Steve walked into a dark house carrying a lethargic Christina, stepping over toys that were left on the bedroom floor. He knew he was home. He tucked his sleeping angel under the sheets and kissed her forehead. Steve quietly shut Christina's door and went into his own room. He turned on the light and began to undress. He tossed his shirt on the mirrored dresser when he saw movement on the bed. Startled, he jumped, feeling his adrenaline tingling all the way to his toes. He whirled around. As quickly as he did, he realized it was his wife buried beneath the blankets. Why was she in bed so early?

He went to the side of the bed, gently sat on the edge, and began stroking his wife's hair as she lay sleeping. When he touched her hair, he was taken aback by the heat of her forehead and realized Catherine was ill. He kissed her forehead. She was burning up with fever.

Catherine awoke at his kiss, "Steve?" She asked weakly.

"You're burning up," he felt her head again with the back of his hand.

"I'm cold. So cold."

"Honey...," Steve tucked the blankets snugly around her body, "How long have you been sick? Why didn't you call me and tell me?"

Catherine shrugged and licked her dry lips.

"Why isn't anyone here with you?"

Catherine shrugged again.

"This pisses me off. Where are your sisters?"

"They don't know I'm sick. This just happened. I must have caught a flu bug or something."

"Let me get you some water," Steve left the room and came back with a thermometer, a towel and a glass of water. He fluffed her pillows behind her and helped her sit up to drink. She took a couple of sips and then her body began to convulse and her face turned pale. Steve reached for the garbage pail just in time for Catherine to throw up in it. Steve put the wet towel on the back of her neck and rubbed her back until she was done vomiting. After a ten-minute vomiting spell, Steve decided she needed to be seen by a doctor.

"I'm taking you to the emergency room. Let me get Mrs. Callahan over here to watch Tina," Steve grabbed the telephone on the nightstand and dialed and covered the mouth piece, "Why didn't you call one of your sisters to come over here?"

Mrs. Callahan answered her phone before Catherine could answer, which spared her telling him the truth. She did not want to tell him they had had a falling out. She wanted to forget about her sisters and did not want to even see them. Her real family was home now.

Steve updated Mrs. Callahan, their neighbor and part-time nanny, of the situation, and after saying "thank you" twice, hung up the phone, "She said she'll be right over."

When he turned to Catherine, he saw she was sleeping. He bundled her up in the comforter and carried her down the stairs and into the car. Mrs. Callahan, wearing a pinkish floral bathrobe, met him in the middle of the street. Steve thanked her again.

As Steve raced to the hospital, Catherine floated in and out of consciousness. His anger brewed. She cared so much for her sisters and did everything for them. How could she care so much about them when they let her lay at home, sick and alone?

When the time was right, he was going to give them both a piece of his mind.

Chapter 28

∧

When Catherine awoke, she did not know where she was. The room was dark and it took her a moment to realize she was in a hospital. She followed the I.V. from her arm up to the pouch that held the fluids. She groaned aloud and tried pulling up onto her elbows, but decided against it when the fluid bag swayed back and forth.

How had she gotten to the hospital? Who had dialed 911? The last thing she remembered was being in her bed at home, cold and alone. She had dreamed that Steve had come home, but that had to be a dream.

A nurse walked into the room, flipping on a light, "Good, you're awake. We were getting worried about you."

Catherine had too many questions to figure which one to start with. She prioritized, "What happened?"

The nurse wrapped the Velcro from the blood pressure cuff around her arm and stuck a thermometer in her mouth. "I can see from your wet hair that your fever broke."

Catherine tried to ask again but almost choked on the thermometer when she saw Steve walk into the room. She squeezed her eyes shut and then opened them again, not believing what she was seeing. The nurse made notes on the clipboard and took off the blood pressure cuff. She pulled out the thermometer and jotted down the results and without saying a word, left the room.

Catherine was too numb to speak.

Steve went to her side and took her hand gently into his.

"My knight in shining armor!" She smiled up at him, "I thought it was a dream."

"We're home now."

"If I'm dreaming, don't wake me up."

"Shhhhh," he brushed her hair off her face, "Just rest. There's plenty of time to talk."

"But...," Catherine was interrupted by a knock on the door, and the doctor walked in.

"Hi, Dr. Edwards," Steve said turning toward him.

"Steve." The doctor nodded then turned his attention to Catherine, "So...how're we doing this morning?"

"Is it morning?"

Doctor Edwards elbowed Steve, "She's back to her normal self."

Catherine shrugged. She was not trying to be funny.

Steve laughed superficially, "Thanks for meeting us here, Dr. Edwards. You know how she won't see anyone else."

"Wish my wife was the same way," he laughed at his own joke and took her wrists into his hands, checking her pulse. Steve watchfully went to the chair by the window and sat.

"How long have you been sick?" Dr. Edwards asked Catherine.

"It just started yesterday morning. My throat was a little raw and...," Catherine coughed then swallowed, trying to wet the tickle at the back of her throat. She went into a coughing fit and Dr. Edwards handed her the glass of water that was sitting on the stand next to the bed. She sipped the water, gagging when she tried to hold back the cough, but finally the urge subsided. She apologized copiously.

"Bronchitis, right?" Steve asked, cutting right to the chase.

"Yes. She's dehydrated also," he flipped open his chart. "I'd like to run a couple of tests while she's here."

Confused, Steve asked, "Why would you need more tests if you know it's bronchitis?"

Catherine glanced at her husband. She noticed the growth of hair stubble thick on his face. His hair was disheveled, and his face showed creases of worry. At that moment, she was filled with an overabundance of emotion. It was refreshing to be around someone who cared about her, especially after the past week with her ungrateful sisters.

"Honey, let the doctor do his job."

"I don't get it," Steve said, standing.

Doctor Edwards intervened, "No need to be alarmed. I'd just like a little more information. She got awfully dehydrated and I just want to make sure everything's okay."

Steve regarded his wife and she gave him a quick smile.

"I don't think any of this is necessary. I just want to take her home."

"I've asked Dr. Burns, a neurologist, to stop by."

"A neurologist?" Steve interrupted uneasily, approaching them, eyeing the doctor who was now on the opposite side of the hospital bed. Catherine touched his arm lightly, following with a gentle patting.

"I understand your concern, Steve, but it's only precautionary. It'll only take a couple of hours. If you want to go home, the nursing staff can call you when she's ready to go home."

Steve looked down at his wife. "Let's go home now. We don't need any more tests. There's color back in your face and you look a hundred times better than before." She patted the spot on the bed next to her. He suspiciously sat down.

"Steve, just humor me, okay? I really don't mind," she blinked back tears.

"It's not... I don't..." Steve stopped when he saw tears welling up in his wife's eyes. He turned to the doctor. "Do what you have to do, but I'll stay while you run the tests."

"The nurse should be here soon to take some blood. I'll be by later this evening." The doctors disappeared through the door, leaving them both alone. Neither one spoke a word. That was the way they were. They had an implicit language of silence between one another. Steve began stroking her hair and Catherine closed her eyes, relishing the affection she had been deprived of.

Chapter 29

∧

Charlie's blue Mustang sped through downtown Providence, her tires squealing around every corner. The roof was down and the sun reflected off her long brown hair. Charlie did not care that her hair would be a gnarly mess and impossible to comb through. She was on a mission to find Ethan. In a hurry, it seemed that every traffic light turned red as she approached.

Ethan never played in the same place. When she called his house, his machine said he was at his day job, which meant (to those who knew him) he was playing on the street.

She turned onto Weybossett Street, and there he was, leaning against a brick wall, singing and playing his guitar. She pulled up in front, not caring that it was a no-parking zone. She got out, slamming the door forcefully. She flipped her sunglasses on top of her head to pull her hair off her face and walked right up to him, stepping in front of two young girls who were watching Ethan, totally enamored. Charlie placed her hands on her hips and stood directly in front of him, waiting for him to speak first.

On impulse, Ethan took a step to the side. Charlie had stepped into his personal zone, and he felt uncomfortable. By her reaction, he knew Iris must have told her the news. He knew she would be upset.

"What are you gonna play next?" the blond girl wearing tennis shorts and a tank top with no bra asked.

Charlie turned to the girls, "Could you please excuse us for a second?"

Disapprovingly, the girl turned to her friends and snickered. When she turned back to Charlie and saw that she was still glaring at them, the girls decided to leave. They walked halfway down the block then stopped. They whispered amongst each other.

"Why are you scaring away my crowd?" Ethan asked.

"What's this about you moving to San Francisco?" Charlie ignored his question and laid right into him.

Ethan did not answer. He looked away, unable to hide his guilt.

"Were you even going to tell me?"

"Of course I was going to tell you. I wouldn't leave you high and dry. I've been looking for a replacement. I didn't want to say anything 'til I found someone to take my place," Ethan said nervously.

Charlie stepped back. It surprised her that he admitted the truth about their plans.

"Deep down, I was hoping Iris was lying."

"I'm sorry."

Charlie put her hands over her face, "I don't get it. Things are just starting to happen with the band," she moved her hands back to her hips, "With us! Why do you want to leave now? It just doesn't make sense."

"Sure it does. Think about it, Charlie. This is your dream, not mine," he placed the guitar in the open case, laying it on top of the tips he had made for the day, "Don't get me wrong. I think you're talented, and I really like playing with you, but I don't want to miss out on something special for someone else's dream."

"You helped write these songs, for crying out loud!" Charlie yelled angrily. She forgot that she should not strain her voice.

"No, I helped *you* write those songs. They're yours."

Charlie rolled her eyes, "I thought that if we ever made it big, that you would be there through thick and thin. I really thought we were working toward the same goal."

"I never said I wanted to be famous. Everyone who knows me knows I just love music. Period."

"Apparently not everyone."

"Don't be hurt, Charlie. I think you knew. You just didn't want to hear the truth." Ethan looked her in the eyes, and Charlie looked away. Deep down, she knew the truth. She had always known. She just thought she could convince him once things started taking off. When she had met him, he did not have a home. He had wandered into her life, and she had supposed that she could just keep him there. Evidently, changing a nomad was like changing your heritage.

"Don't you at least want to finish the CD?" Charlie asked as she kicked away a pebble at the end of her shoe, unable to look him in the eye. She already knew the answer.

"I'm already on several songs. If we get to record more before Iris and I leave, then great. I bet your producer friend could even replace me with a better guitarist." Ethan tilted her chin to look at him. He felt guilty leaving her, especially since he could see how much she thought she needed him.

"Right now you think you need me, but I'm really not that good."

"Are you crazy? You're the best I've seen. You're awesome, Ethan. I don't understand. Why do you even do it if you don't think you're good?"

"Because I love music so much."

"That is exactly why I know you will regret this. I know you want this."

"The only thing I want right now is Iris. She's the one."

Charlie scoffed as she shook her head, "You don't even know her. Even she doesn't know what she wants."

"I don't agree. I think she knows a lot more than you give her credit for."

"Oh, now she's made me out to be the bad guy. And she's the poor little misunderstood artiste."

"It's not that way at all."

"Oh, yeah? How is it then?"

"It doesn't matter. I'm not going to fight with you. Face it, Charlie. We're moving to San Francisco with or without your consent."

"Sometimes you can be so bullheaded, Tom!" Charlie suddenly stopped. She held her breath, hoping Ethan had not caught her Freudian slip.

Ethan smiled mischievously, "I'm not even gonna touch that one."

Charlie flipped her head away from him, "That was an accident."

"Uh huh," Ethan said with sarcasm, "You said it."

"When are you leaving?" Charlie said redirecting the conversation.

"Next week."

Her body jolted from the shock, "I can't believe what my ears are hearing. How do you propose replacing yourself by next week?"

"I've already spoken with two different guys."

"You sure don't waste any time did you?"

Before he could answer a police car pulled up next to them and rolled down the window, "Whose car is that?"

Ethan pointed at Charlie.

"Move it or I'm writing you up."

"I'm leaving right now, Officer," Charlie hurried to her car. She stopped before she opened her door, addressing Ethan. "Don't worry about finding a replacement for me. The sooner the two of you leave the better."

As she drove away, Ethan stumbled back to the brick wall of the building behind him and slumped all the way down to the ground.

* * *

It took tremendous strength for Charlie not to put the pedal to the metal on the drive home. By the time she merged onto Interstate 95, the afternoon traffic was getting rush-hour thick.

Her mind raced. It would be impossible to replace Ethan so quickly. Iris was ruining her life with her selfishness. It seemed like Iris always got whatever she wanted, at any cost.

Charlie took the highway split onto Route 4 toward Narragansett. The traffic was still bumper to bumper. Charlie's head pounded from stress. Iris could give anybody a headache.

When she reached the street where her little white beach house resided, she decided not to stop. Iris was probably at her house and she did not have any idea what she would say if she saw her. Charlie wanted her house to herself. It would take much reserve to not go crazy on her sister if she saw her. Charlie could usually control her temper, but this time Iris had taken things to the next level.

Not slowing down, Charlie drove past her street and headed to the end of the street toward the dirt path that lead to the lookout over the ocean. After pulling off to the side of the road, onto the gravel turnout, she shut off the engine. The sound of the waves as they crashed against the rocks below was soothing.

Charlie dropped her head to the steering wheel, feeling defeated. How much more would she have to endure? She needed Ethan, especially now. She wrote the lyrics, and he wrote the music. They were a good team. Ethan was the last person she expected to lose from her band.

Charlie sat at the lookout point until the sun melted into the water and finally dipped below the horizon. She turned on the radio. Tina Turner's "What's Love Got To Do With It" was playing. She quickly switched stations, not stopping until she found a song without love in it, finally settling on a contemporary jazz station. No lyrics, just music; that's what she needed.

"There," she whispered aloud as she turned up the volume. Trying to blast out the world and all the unwanted thoughts that haunted her mind, Charlie cranked the music as loud as her speakers would allow.

Thirty minutes had passed before Charlie had left the solitude of the ocean cliff and pulled into her driveway. She looked up to the sky to say a quick prayer for strength to God before she got out. The amber sky was beginning to fade to dark gray. When she was done, she inspected her house. It looked empty and peaceful. She shut off the car and warily walked into the house.

She prayed that Iris would not be home. If she were, she decided she would call a cab and send her on her way. She could go stay with Catherine. Let them duel it out, because she was through with Iris. Done.

As soon as she opened the door, she knew the house was empty. It was dark inside, and the blinds had not been opened. Charlie dropped her keys onto the coffee table next to the front door, and the familiar clank resonated off the walls. She had not heard that hollow echo for such a long time. She was alone in her house, and it felt good. Without turning the lights on, she plopped down on the couch and sat in the dark for a long time.

* * *

She must have dozed off, because the next thing she knew, the room was pitch black. Charlie got up and went to turn on the lamp next to the television. She blindly reached for the switch and found it, but not before knocking something onto the floor.

Charlie crouched down to pick it up. It was a videocassette. She placed it back on the table from which she had knocked it off and went to her room to change her clothes, not giving the videocassette a second thought.

Undressing, Charlie opened her closet and took out an empty hanger. She hung the yellow suit she was wearing and reached for a long tee shirt, but changed her mind when she saw a big navy blue sweatshirt folded atop the middle shelf. She pulled it out and looked at it. It was Tom's sweatshirt; she had not returned it. He had worn it the last time they made love on the beach, about two weeks before the wedding. It was his decision to make that time the last time until they were officially husband and wife. He said it would make their wedding night extra special, and she had agreed. She longed for him, and her body ached for his touch. He had been the only man to drive her crazy, just from one kiss.

Charlie pulled the sweatshirt to her face to capture any lingering scent of Tom. She wrapped her arms around the sweater, making sure his scent could not escape. She inhaled deeply, and at once she became overwhelmed with anxiety. She missed him terribly.

Still holding the sweatshirt to her face, she glanced at the phone on her bed stand, and then forced her eyes to look away. She wondered what he was doing. Then the thought of him kissing another woman came back to her. He was probably with the girl she had seen him with at the club. She was probably nursing his wounds. Her face flashed red, and it took all her strength to dismiss the jealousy. She did not have a claim to him any longer. She slapped her own cheek, punishing herself for even thinking about him.

It did not stop her from smelling his sweatshirt. She pulled it to her face again. The memories of that night came back to her. She would never forget that night. Tom had brought red wine, brie, and fruit. They put candles in the sand, surrounding their blanket. The sky was star-filled, and the night was picture-perfect. Tom had always been a romantic at heart. She loved that about him. They had made love right on the beach. It was an ideal night; full moon above, crashing waves beside, and the oblivious world around.

The memory was too strong for her to stand, and her legs gave out on her. Falling to the floor, Charlie wept aloud and uncontrollably for the first time since her fateful wedding day. She wept for what she lost and what she would never have again. The sweat shirt, still nestled against her face, soaked up the flood of tears and drowned her sobs. Charlie curled into a ball on the pink fuzzy rug on the floor and let go completely.

Chapter 30

Λ

A few days later, Steve and Catherine sat holding hands in Dr. Edward's office. Catherine was still sick but feeling much better than before. The doctor sat behind his oversized oak desk, rummaging through Catherine's thick file. They both regarded each other as he flipped through the papers.

Catherine spoke first, "So have there been any new developments since my mother died?" Dr. Edward's eyes moved from hers to Steve's.

"Catherine?" Dr. Edwards asked uncertainly.

"Are there any developments?" Catherine spoke trying to sound convincing and strong but the burning sensation in the pit of her stomach made her feel weak on the inside. She knew what the doctor was going to say, long before he had run any tests. She had known for a long time. It was time to let Steve in on the news.

Steve blinked, completely shocked at the revelation. He could barely mutter her name, "Catherine..."

Catherine could feel her husband looking at her, but she could not turn her head. Instead, she focused on the doctor.

"I'm sorry, Catherine, I was hoping my suspicions were wrong." Dr. Edwards' eyes turned from Catherine to Steve, "Steve?" He waited for Steve to acknowledge that he was being spoken to and continued. "Catherine called me a month ago. She had been having some problems. I had hoped these tests would prove her suspicions wrong."

"Wait a minute. She has bronchitis. How does one go from bronchitis to Lou Gehrig's disease?"

"Steve. Catherine has genetic Amyotrophic Lateral Sclerosis. She inherited the genetic defect from her mother. We were able to access her mother's DNA through blood samples, and I'm afraid the tests came out positive."

"Look at her! She's fine!" Steve bellowed, suddenly angry. "I want a second opinion!"

"Steve, honey," Catherine said calmly placing her hand on Steve's shoulder, "I've suspected this for a while."

"I still want a second opinion."

"You should...but, you should prepare yourself." Explained Dr. Edwards. "Normally, the way the testing for ALS is done is through a process of elimination; however, we had access to Catherine's mother's DNA." He paused, and then spoke cautiously. "The results are accurate."

Catherine glanced at her husband and could see panic in his eyes. She too, was afraid, but she had had time to prepare herself with her suspicions. Steve was being hit with the knowledge for the first time. She could not imagine how he felt. She knew that he loved her, and she did not want to cause him unnecessary pain. She had prayed that she had multiple sclerosis or something else. Anything other than ALS. She knew she was going to die.

* * *

After the doctor's appointment, Catherine found solitude in the greenhouse at her home. She repotted an ivy plant that had over grown its container. She could not believe how rapidly it had outgrown its home and took pride in the fact that she had brought it to life. She wished she could do something like that to herself; her nervous system the roots, her blood the water, and the soil the vitamins she needed to grow a new body.

Steve walked into the greenhouse. He stood in the doorway, his hands in his pockets, lips pursed together tightly. After a moment, he walked over, picked up the garden hose, and began watering the hanging plants, misting the sensitive ferns gently. He kept turning his head to his wife. He wanted to talk to her but could not speak.

Peripherally, she caught his glimpses, but she waited for him to speak. It saddened her to see him so distraught. She wished there was something she could say or do to make him feel better. Worrying about him seemed to distract her from the fact that she was dying, and it was an odd sensation to feel relief in that. She had taken the news better than she thought she would. It probably had not hit her yet. Or maybe it was because she had already known the truth? It was the hidden reason she had been working so diligently at getting her sisters back together. All she wanted was for them to be a real family. They were going to need each other after she was gone. Catherine had always been the glue to hold them together. She feared that if she did not succeed in making them closer, they would lose each other all together. It was not what their mother would have wanted, and it was not what she wanted. Time was running out.

"You haven't even told me about the lions," she said, breaking the silence for simple conversation.

"Huh?" Steve wiped his brow and shut off the hose.

"The Cape Lions," she could see him struggling to focus.

"Oh, yeah." He set the hose down on the ground and stood by the plants. "Well, our suspicions may be right. The lion resembles the extinct Cape black-maned lion. The notes written from Frederick Courtney Selous back in 1908 supported those similarities. He believed that they were out there. It was the black mane that went all the way to their hindquarters. Remember Estelle Rossouw? She made it her mission to find the ancestors of his supposed lions. And after years of searching, it looks like she's found those endangered Cape Lions."

"How exciting! When will you know for sure?"

"She's one of the only people who has seen them...and honey, so have I. We know they exist," he came toward her and took her hand in his. "We're making contact with feline specialists all over the world. Before I left, I spoke with Peter Jackson, of the International Union of Conservation Organization. You know, the Cat Specialist Group in Switzerland. He's confirmed our thoughts. His opinion is valued."

"When will you be done with your notes? I'd like to read them."

"I haven't even started them."

Catherine dropped her eyes. She knew she was the reason he had fallen behind in his work.

"Don't worry. I have people doing the work."

Catherine smiled uncomfortably. "Do you think the species can be saved?"

"If it is the Cape Lion, we may be able to breed it with other black-maned lions. I don't want to get my hopes up. I mean, there could be a problem. Like when a horse and a donkey mate it could cause infertility. Then we'd be back to square one. We have a lot of work ahead of us."

As he continued talking about the Cape Lion discovery, Catherine felt an odd sense of euphoria. It was working. She was getting him to talk about something other than what was going on with her.

She walked to the wooden bench by the door and sat down. Steve followed, watching her intently. There was a momentary silence. Catherine thought quickly for something else to ask.

"Did Tina get any good pictures?"

"She got some really nice shots of a female playing with her cubs." Steve smiled at his wife.

Steve wiped his thumb lightly across her cheek, "You had a little dirt on your face." He pointed to the spot on his own face, mirroring the dirt on her face. She closed her eyes as he bent forward and kissed her forehead pressing his forehead to hers. She opened her eyes and saw that his eyes were closed. They stayed in that position for a long time.

"What are we going to do?" Steve whispered, not letting go of her.

Catherine pulled away so she could look into his eyes. His eyes were circled dark with worry; his facial growth resembled dirty sand.

"Honey, the doctor said I could have five years," her hand twitched, almost as if on cue, and she grabbed it with her other hand and rubbed it. She spoke while looking at her trembling hand. This time it was her own voice quivering with fear, "But I have a feeling that I've already used up a couple of them."

Steve's heart pounded rampidly, and he receded from his wife, "How can you say such things?"

Catherine shrugged, not sure how she could be so blunt, "I'm sorry. I shouldn't have said that." Catherine returned to her ivy plant. The conversation had become too deep, and she wanted to get back to simple.

"You're not going to be able to travel, are you?" Steve asked.

"We'll see."

"Well, I'm not going without you again. I'll just work from home. I'll send interns. They would love that."

"Don't go getting ahead of yourself over little ol' me. I will be fine. When things get bad, we can hire a nurse," Catherine advised, wondering how she would handle being cared for. It was she who always did the doting. Catherine picked up the little ivy plant she had pulled from its pot and picked up its new home, a brown ceramic pot. Her hand twitched and it fell crashing to the gravel floor. For a moment, Catherine stared at the mess she had created then turned away from it.

"I didn't like that pot anyway!" He said and they both laughed nervously. He bent over to pick up the mess just as Christina bounced in the greenhouse, her braided hair flipping up and down as she bopped, her pink dress covered with mud.

"It's time to eat! Mrs. Callahan made Beef Stroffenoff!" Christina ran to her father and began jumping up and down, which was his cue to pick her up.

"Looks like you've been making mud pies. Is that our dessert, sweetie?"

"No, daddy. Mrs. Callahan made us chocolate chip cookies for dessert."

"Oh, then I better get us washed up. We've all been playing in the dirt," Steve said offering a gentleman's arm to Catherine. She curled her arm around his and her husband escorted his family inside. Catherine glanced back at the broken planter.

"Come on. Let's go in. I'll clean this up later."

It was not like her to leave clutter behind. There were a lot of things she would have to get used to, and being taken care of was one of them. She told herself she would not allow the disease to run her life. Right after dinner, she would go back out and clean it up.

Chapter 31

∧

At the club on Saturday around five o'clock, Charlie organized the stage for her performance later. After setting up her microphone and adjusting her levels, Charlie stepped off the stage, leaving the guys in the band to set up the rest of the equipment. She went behind the bar and pulled out a box of microphone cables, then went back to the stage and handed it to Tony, the drummer.

Turning to hand the box to Greg, the bass player, Tony said, "I'm gonna go out to my car and catch a few winks before the show," he yawned deeply. "You guys think you can finish up?"

"Out all night again, Tony?" Greg, asked, turning to get the other guys involved as he started singing the Kinks song, "Lola – L-O-L-A..." They all join in.

"Up your ass, Greg. Why is it you're the only one who doesn't know I was with your wife?"

They all laughed. Greg did not like being the butt of the joke, and he flipped them all off for laughing.

"Okay, I'm gonna go home and get ready. I'll see you guys in a while." Charlie went to the table where she left her purse and put it on her shoulder. She fished her keys out of her pocket and turned to Tony and Greg.

"Where's Ethan?"

"He had to pick up his van from the mechanic. He had some work done to it. He should be here soon."

Charlie nodded and turned to leave. Before she could make it to the door, Catherine walked into the club. Charlie was surprised to see her. The last time they had spoken was during the big blowout at the house with Iris.

"Hey, what're you doing here?" Charlie asked anxiously, feeling the guilt swell like a tidal wave for not calling. "I meant to call you...I'm sorry...I guess I've just been a little...busy." She scrunched her nose because it was obvious she was lying.

"That's okay. Is Iris still around?"

"Yeah, but not for long."

"You gonna let her go?"

"Let her go?" Charlie asked. What kind of a question was that, she thought? She had no control over Iris. She had not even seen her in days. "What choice have I got?"

"I saw your car out front, and I wanted to talk to you."

Charlie suddenly felt the urge to get out of there. She felt another fight coming on with Catherine, and she just wanted to escape. Charlie readjusted her purse on her shoulder. "I was just going." She brushed past her sister. She could see the light through the door window; if only she could make it there.

"Hang on a second."

Charlie whirled around defensively. "I'm not gonna get into another row over Iris again. We just need to let her go and figure things out for herself."

"I didn't come about Iris..."

"Well, we're not gonna talk about me!"

"I'm not here to hound you either."

"Oh," Charlie stepped back. She had fully expected to hear another one of Catherine's lectures. "Well...," Charlie pointed to the bar, "I forgot something...," Charlie said, stalling. She went to the bar, saw Greg's black canvas bag lying on the counter, and picked it up. She dropped it off at the stage and unzipped it, appearing to be looking for something.

Catherine stood, waiting patiently with both arms crossed. Catherine could see that it was going to be impossible to hold her sister down for a real conversation, so she followed Charlie to the stage and sidled up closely.

"Charlie? Come on."

"Go ahead. I'm listening."

Catherine began to speak, "I just...well...ever since mom died, I made a commitment to take care of you guys." She cleared her throat and continued, "I've always tried to maintain some sense of family between us."

"What?" Charlie said, frustrated. She finally stopped rummaging and turned toward her sister, then shook her head, confused. "I'm sorry. I'm lost."

"I said that I've always tried to maintain some sense of family between us."

"That was your decision, Catherine. I don't remember Mom ever putting that kind of pressure on you."

Charlie glanced back at the bag, then to the stage. She wanted anything to take her away from another one of Catherine's relentless speeches.

"We are all we have."

"I know families that only see each other on holidays who get along better than we do."

"I know I haven't been a very good replacement for her, but I tried. Really I have."

Charlie froze. She could not believe her ears. Catherine actually believed that she was mom's replacement.

Catherine continued, "What happened the other day wasn't your fault. Iris can be...difficult. Don't start beating yourself up over what happened. Let's just hope she figures out what she really wants and...you know...lives her life."

Charlie growled under her breath and breathed deeply.

"Charlie..." She sighed. "Come on. Just hear me out."

"I've got to go to the bathroom. I'll be right back." Charlie shoved her purse at Catherine. "Hold this. I'll be right back." Then she darted off to the bathroom. When she reached the door, she turned, "Oh, I forgot to ask. Did Steve and Christina get back okay?"

Catherine nodded hugging the purse tightly.

"Good."

Charlie disappeared behind the door, leaving Catherine standing in the middle of the dance floor all by herself. After a moment of standing, she marched to the bathroom. She was not going to let Charlie get away that easily. She needed to tell her what was happening.

Even though Charlie was in the stall, Catherine continued the conversation precisely where she had left off. She had prepared what she was going to say over and over in her head, and she was going to tell Charlie even if she had to hold her down and sit on her.

"Charlie, I'm trying to talk to you."

"I'll be out in a sec."

When Catherine turned around, she caught her own reflection in the mirror. She looked directly into her own eyes for a moment and realized that she did not look like herself. Her eyes looked as if they had lived far beyond her forty years. When the toilet flushed, her attention turned to the opening bathroom stall door. Something came over Catherine. She yanked the door open, darted inside and pushed Charlie back inside the stall. She quickly bolted the stall door.

"What're you doing?!"

"I...I'm only forty years old. I'm just entering the prime of my life."

"And I'm twenty-seven and I've got to go get ready for tonight."

"Isn't that what they say...that women are at their prime at forty?"

"I don't know what you're talking about."

"Forty...that's when we're the most sexual and vital."

"Alright, I get where you're going. Yes! I agree! Forty is it!" Charlie tried to get past Catherine, but Catherine put up her hand. Charlie laughed at the ridiculousness of the situation.

"Catherine, you've gotta stop reading those stupid magazines while you're waiting in line at the supermarket. What the hell's gotten in to you?"

"Oh, Charlie..."

She stopped when she saw the sadness spill across her sister's face. Catherine sighed, exasperated.

"Did you and Steve have one of your secret fights that you think I don't know about?"

"It's not fair! It's just not fair!"

"Damn it, Catherine! I don't have all night! What are you going on about?!"

"I...I...I can't believe it's happening to me!" She pounded her fist to her own chest, "To me!"

"Let me out of here!" Charlie started to push past Catherine, but Catherine put her body in front of her, using it as a barricade.

As they struggled, Catherine leaned closely to Charlie's ear and whispered, "I have ALS!"

Charlie stopped. Frozen. She could not believe what she had just heard. She stepped back and just blinked, her stomach wretched, and she turned away from Catherine.

"I have it. I have Lou Gehrig's."

Charlie shook her head. "Why would you say something so stupid?"

"I'm gonna die like mom!" Catherine yelled.

The desperation in Catherine's voice alone proved to Charlie that she was telling the truth, but she did not want to hear or believe it. "Stop it! I mean it! It's not funny!"

"Charlie...I'm so afraid."

"We're all afraid!" Not wanting to believe that Catherine was speaking the truth, "Why do you think I didn't go through with the wedding? You think you have it? Well, so do I!"

"I'm not imagining this! It's real!" Catherine was overwhelmed with fear and started to shake uncontrollably. "I don't know what to do! I never thought I..." Tears were streaming down Catherine's face. "I'm not gonna see my baby grow up! My beautiful Tina...."

Charlie stood frozen unable to speak. It was all too much for her to endure.

"Why me?" Catherine cried, "Why me? I try so hard. I'm a good person. I'm a good wife. I try so hard!" Catherine grabbed hold of Charlie and hugged her. Melting down the front of Charlie, falling onto her knees, she began crying hysterically, "Help me, Charlie. Help me...oh, God...I'm gonna die just like mom."

Charlie was paralyzed, unable to do anything as her sister clung to her, bawling helplessly.

Suddenly she became calm, "I don't want to die in a hospital." She looked up at Charlie, dark mascara streaking down her face. She took Charlie's hand and held it tightly. "Promise me you won't let me die in hospital!"

Charlie tried to speak but could not find words. She opened her mouth, but all that came out was an indistinct sound. Her tongue was paralyzed.

"Charlie! Please tell me....,"

Catherine clung to her sister. She needed emotional support from her sister and was sobbing hysterically. All Charlie could give in return was her physical form. She stood in the middle of the cramped bathroom stall, unemotional, holding onto her own sanity with every breath.

"Tell me...how am going to tell Tina? Who's going to take care of her?"

It took every fragment of strength Charlie could muster to make herself budge from the unyielding position. She knew she should say something to Catherine, anything to try and make her feel better, but the words did not surface. Now her body was immobile and she was unable to do the right thing. Catherine was terrified and Charlie could not make her feel better.

Charlie pulled her lead-filled hands and put them on top of Catherine's head. She could not massage, or do anything. It was already a feat lifting her uncontrollably dead hands. Even though she knew she should bend down and wrap her arms around Catherine and hold her, she could not. What scared her was that she knew why she could not. She was afraid if she let herself go, her own sanity would be at stake. She was emotionally void, and it took all the courage she could muster not to run away. She wanted to be anywhere but there, listening to her sister's wails. It was too much. But she had to stay with her even though it did not feel natural.

Her hands were just sitting on top of Catherine's head, and there was nothing inside her to summon, nothing she could draw upon to make her sister feel better. Her fingers would not budge. A chill swept through her, and she did not know if the coolness came from within.

Charlie pretended that she was someplace else. It was easier that way. To break down now would do permanent damage. If that happened, she feared she may never recover.

A voice deep inside her spoke, maybe her mother, or perhaps the voice of her conscience, but whoever it was, she listened to it. The voice seemed to know what to do. Charlie closed her eyes and followed the voice instinctively. As if by magic, her hands began to caress, slowly, almost robotically, through Catherine's thick blond hair. It was all she could do and she hoped it was enough.

The two were in the bathroom for a long time, Catherine crying, Charlie consoling the only way she could. The echoing of Catherine's sobs began to fade, allowing Charlie to go a different place in her mind.

* * *

It took awhile for her to get Catherine situated in her car. Charlie feared she was too upset to drive, but Catherine assured her she would be fine. Catherine apologized repeatedly for putting so much so quickly on Charlie, but Charlie kept telling her that she was okay. The truth was that she was emotionally drained and did not know where she was going to get the energy for the evening of singing ahead of her. She did not even think that good old-fashioned caffeine would work. She knew that drinking beer between sets, her usual drink, would be unwise. When Catherine drove off, she glanced at her watch. There was barely time to go home to freshen up.

Deadened from the brain down, Charlie managed to make it to her own car. She put the key in the ignition but did not turn it. Numbly, she sat in the driver's seat going over what had just happened. Why did Catherine believe that she had it? Part of her wanted to believe this was some sort of stunt to get attention.

Charlie pulled the rearview mirror toward her and inspected her own reflection. She did not like what she saw staring back at her - dark haunted eyes, with deep circles; she looked far older than twenty-seven years. The more she looked into her own eyes, the more she thought she looked like her mother when she was sick. The reflection was not so much her mother's as was the sight of the haunted eyes that looked back at her.

Charlie started the engine and left the parking lot, not turning right, the path that lead toward her home, but going left instead. Unsure where she was going, she knew she needed to think. As she drove, the same question ran through her mind. Would she be next? The only reason she did not marry Tom was because she knew she would eventually get it too. She had some of the symptoms. Why had it never occurred to her that either one of her sisters could have it too? She had never noticed Catherine possessing those similarities. How could it be possible that one disease could strike one family so many times? Was fate really that cruel? Was Iris next?

A black cat flitted out into the middle of the road and caused Charlie to instinctively swerve out of its way. As she slammed on the brakes, the car slid back and forth but she regained control. It was in the moment afterward that she realized she was going to pass out.

She shook her head trying to blink away the blackness that was enveloping. Her life was shit and she was falling apart. Charlie sat for a moment waiting for the blackness to pass before she pulled back onto the road. As she drove, she began thinking about Steve. It was the first time she had even thought about him. She had questioned herself so many times about leaving Tom, but she now knew that her decision to cut him loose was probably the best thing she could have done for him. Steve loved his wife, and Charlie cringed at the thought of the sorrow he must be feeling. Steve and Catherine had a unique relationship. They were extremely close; true soul mates. She and Tom had that same unique connection. Her life did not have meaning without him. She was trying to focus on her music, and it helped her escape, but the music did not hold her at night when she could not sleep. The weight of her problems grew heavier and heavier. Now, more than ever, she wished she had Tom to lean on. But that was now the past and she had no regrets. She would just have to find a way to get through it all on her own. She thought of what her mother used to say to her when she was a kid: "This too shall pass." Charlie whispered it aloud but stopped when she realized the ridiculousness of that statement. There was too much to "pass." Everything was going wrong in her life. Everything.

It was not until Charlie pulled up to Dr. Edwards's office that she realized where she was going. Deep down, it was something she had wanted to do for a long time. Fearing the outcome, she had never taken the blood test. It was not until her mind was on overload that fate had led her to the doctor's office.

She pulled into an open spot and left the car idling. Did she really want to see Dr. Edwards? And why had she come now? Was it to confirm what Catherine had told her? Was Catherine capable of making up something of this magnitude just for attention? She knew Catherine was not lying. Saint Catherine never lied, cheated, or intentionally hurt anybody's feelings.

Charlie sat in her car, her thoughts running rampant in perfect sync with the humming engine. When she finally shut off the car, she was left only with the noise in her head. Why had her subconscious had lead her all the way to their family doctor's office? She supposed all she needed to do was get out of the car and walk inside. She would have to let fate take it from here.

With heavy legs, she made it into the waiting room. She penciled her name onto the waiting list and sat down next to a rack of outdated magazines. In the seat next to her sat an elderly man who was pale and coughing excessively. Every time he coughed, Charlie discreetly leaned the opposite direction. It would be her luck to catch a cold on top of everything thing else. She supposed it would be the icing on the cake. Finally, the nurse rescued her from Mr. Influenza and called her back to an examining room.

"Dr. Edwards will be with you in a moment," the nurse said after checking Charlie's vital signs. Once again, she was alone with her thoughts. She wished she had brought in one of the magazines from the waiting room. She glanced around the walls looking for something to read, anything to get her mind off of Catherine, her mother, Tom, Steve, and ALS.

Silence.

When would the doctor get here? After she had read and reread the informative medical posters all over the wall, she sat watching her foot swing back and forth, glancing up every fifteen seconds hoping that the doctor would come through the door.

Waiting.

She glanced at the clock and rolled her eyes when she realized that only three minutes had passed. Her stomach was tied into knots. She could not believe that she had come here. She hated doctor offices and the bad memories that she associated with them. Dr. Edwards had always been her doctor, and although she trusted him, she could not help fearing medical facilities. They reminded her of those terrible final days with her mother. The door handle turned and her stomach churned. Dr. Edwards entered, carrying Charlie's file.

"I've been expecting you," he said as he pulled up his chair next to the table.

"You have?" Charlie fidgeted, uncomfortably. "How could you possibly know that I was coming when I didn't know I was until now?

"To talk about Catherine. To find out if she really has Amyotrophic Lateral Sclerosis...," he paused. "Just like your mother had?" Charlie's eyes moved to the floor, "Just like you think you have?"

Charlie looked up at him, her eyes filled to the brim. She dared not blink and open the floodgates.

"It's okay, Charlie."

"Is it, Dr. Edwards? My mother died. My sister's dying. I haven't seen or heard from my father since I was a kid, and I'm all alone now. Every time I trip, or my arm falls asleep, I think, oh my God, I've got it."

The room fell silent. The doctor spoke in a calm, soothing voice. "So, why don't we test you then?"

Her eyes widened, fear unmistakably imprinted behind her brown eyes. She murmured faintly, "Because...I'm afraid."

Dr. Edwards put a reassuring hand on her shoulder. "You understand that there is no specific diagnostic test for ALS. Generally a series of tests including nerve conduction and electromyogram are performed that allow us to exclude other conditions, and to confirm disease progression. However, we have been able to confirm that Catherine had genetic ALS because we were able to get a hold your mother's DNA. The discovery of some of the gene mutations that cause genetic ALS is rather new, but quite accurate and painless. In essence, we'll simply see if you have the same mutation as your mother."

"I'm not sure it's what I want to do. I saw how cruel this disease was to my mother...," Charlie stopped for a moment, "...and will be to Catherine."

"I understand your fear. It's not an easy choice," he went back to his seat, "But, it is *your* choice."

Charlie looked intently at Dr. Edwards, "You think about it and I'll be right back. We can draw some blood today."

Charlie did not answer. Instead, she just nodded. The doctor excused himself from the room. She could not believe she was proceeding with this. Did she want to know? Was it selfish getting tested, knowing her sister was going to be needing her? She was not sure what forces brought her to his office, but she knew that something inside her was telling her to find out her destiny. She was afraid to find out, but the fear of living without the knowledge was nearly unbearable. If she did not do something soon, she would have to admit herself directly into the nearest mental institution. She was already damned near ready for a straight jacket.

Charlie stood and grabbed her purse. How could she be so selfish? Her concerns should be with her sister. She pulled open the office door at the same time Dr. Edwards was returning. He had a nurse with him. He could see that she was crying.

"Are you alright?" he asked, escorting her back inside the examining room.

Charlie shook her head, too ashamed to make eye contact with him. She knew that he could see through her. "I have to go. Catherine's going to need me."

"Have a seat, please," Dr. Edwards said guiding her back to the examining table. "I know you're afraid, but you need to know that I've been working with your sister for six months now."

Charlie blinked. "What? She knew for six months?"

"No. It took a while to locate your mother's DNA and then to find the mutation. Fortunately for you, it would be much simpler. We could draw some blood and have the results in about ten days."

Charlie stood, not wanting to hear how quickly she could find out if she was sentenced to an early death, "I can't do this. I should not be here thinking of myself. I should be with my sister...trying to make her last years better."

"Charlie, look at me," he delayed speaking until she finally looked him in the eyes. "Your sister told me about the wedding. She knows that you think you have it too, and you will be no help to your sister in this state. Listen to me, as your doctor; I'm telling you that for your own peace of mind, you should take this test."

Charlie stared at him with wide, frightened eyes.

Dr. Edwards did not wait for her to balk, "All you have to do is get some blood drawn. I've made arrangements with the same neurologist that's working with Catherine, Dr. Burns. They're expecting you at the hospital. It's an outpatient procedure. We'll send the samples to the ALS Research Center, where Catherine's DNA is on record. They can even code the results to protect your privacy."

Charlie's head nodded yes but her mind screamed no. Catherine had been concerned about her sister's welfare when really it was her own that was at stake.

"Dr. Edwards? If I do this, I need to do it today...right now before I change my mind."

The doctor picked up the telephone and dialed Dr. Burns. After a brief conversation, he hung up the phone, "You can go to the hospital right now. Dr. Burns is expecting you."

Like a puppet on a string, she stood and reluctantly staggered to the door. It weighed a thousand pounds as she pulled it open. Her feet seemed even heavier as she stepped through the doorway.

Dr. Edwards called out to her before she shut the door. "Charlie, it'll be alright. If you change your mind and decide that you don't want to know the results, they will be sent here to me. I'll put them in your file. Then when you're ready to know..."

Charlie turned back to him. "Thanks you, Dr. Edwards but I would like to have them sent to my house."

Dr. Edwards protested. "That's not what we do in genetic counseling. A doctor needs to help you deal with the results."

Charlie bit her bottom lip and shook her head. The way he said *deal with the results* made her think that he knew she had it too. "I'm not interested in counseling, doctor." Before he could protest any more, she shut the door.

Chapter 32

∧

Sunday afternoon, Charlie drove Iris to Catherine and Steve's house. Iris stared out the side window, chewing on her fingernails, her freckled face etched with worry. Charlie glanced occasionally at her sister, agonizing whether she had done the right thing telling her about Catherine's diagnosis. Maybe Catherine had wanted to tell herself. Iris had not taken the news very well. She ran off into the bathroom and latched the door shut. Charlie had wanted to knock on the door to see if she was all right, but she opted against it every time she raised her hand to knock. She could not shake the vision of Catherine in the bathroom stall at the club. It was then that she decided to let Iris deal with things the best way she could.

The fifteen-minute drive seemed to take eons, but they finally arrived, pulling in behind Catherine's van. The side of the driveway where Steve's Jeep was usually parked was empty. Charlie cursed inside her head. She had hoped he would be home. He was strong, and she needed his strength, but she also did not want it to be just the three of them.

Charlie knocked on the door and opened it without waiting for a response. She set her purse and keys on the table in the entrance and slipped her shoes off. Iris followed suit. They both went into the living room, walking on the soft off-white carpet. Catherine was sitting in a big overstuffed chair by the window, letting the sun filter on her face. The house was completely silent, which meant that Christina was probably with her father.

"Hi," Catherine said, her face brightening when she saw them. Charlie and Iris both returned uncomfortable hellos, and Iris plopped on the burgundy loveseat that was positioned directly across from the chair Catherine was sitting in. Charlie stood for a moment. The room was silent. Without saying a word, she went into the kitchen. Iris' eyes widened when being left alone with Catherine.

Catherine noticed Iris' discomfort, "How are you doing, Iris?"

"How're you doing?" Iris returned the question without answering.

"I feel better now. The antibiotics have pretty much cleared up my chest, but Dr. Edwards wants me to take it easy for a little while."

"Good." Iris bit at her thumbnail, but it was already raw to the quick. "Why are you just sitting here...I mean, it's so quiet. Turn on some music or something."

"I was praying," Catherine said quietly and turned back to look out the window.

"Oh."

"You shouldn't chew your nails," Catherine instructed.

Iris removed her hands and sat on them to stop her bad habit. "I only do it when I'm nervous."

"So when are you leaving for San Francisco?" Catherine asked softly, smiling as she spoke.

Iris wondered how she could smile considering what was happening to her. "I think we're going to stick around for a while." She wondered if Catherine knew that they were postponing their trip indefinitely because of Catherine's situation. She could not leave now. "Ethan decided...he wants to stick around 'til Charlie's CD is completed."

Iris shrugged and leaned forward, grabbing a home improvement magazine that was on the coffee table. Knowing she was not a good liar, Iris knew that Catherine could read her like a book. She figured it was best to blame it on Ethan and leave it at that.

"I thought your plans were definite."

Iris shrugged again and said without making eye contact, "He's the one with the wheels." Flipping through the magazine, she knew better than to make direct eye contact with her sister. Catherine would see right through her lies. Iris glanced nervously toward the kitchen entrance. She wished Charlie would come in and rescue her from the hole she was digging. As if a magic wish were being granted, Charlie walked into the living room carrying wineglasses and a bottle of wine. Iris laughed nervously, greatly relieved.

"It's okay if you have a little wine, isn't it?" Charlie set the tray on the coffee table, pushing the bouquet of fresh roses to the side. "These are pretty. Are they from your greenhouse?"

"No, from a florist."

"Oh," Charlie said, feeling dumb. As soon as she had asked, she saw the card sticking out of the vase. She recognized Steve's handwriting immediately and looked away before she could read what he had written in the card. She wasn't prepared to feel his pain. She had her own to deal with. "You said yes to the wine, right?"

"Sure, but I don't want you thinking that you have to start waiting on me."

"I'm not...," Charlie pulled the cork out of the bottle, grunting, and then continued, "...waiting on you." Charlie forced a smile as she poured wine into the glasses, handing the first to Catherine.

"So what'd they say? The doctors," Iris asked as she took her glass and started drinking.

"As far as they can tell, it's fairly advanced. But I could have as much as five years. And a couple of good ones before things get worse." Iris stood and began pacing. The room went silent as they all seemed to absorb what she had just said. "This is pretty shocking, huh? I know it was for Steve."

Charlie's head lifted at the mention of Steve's name. She could not help comparing Steve and Tom. She knew what was in store for his immediate future, and she felt so much pity for him. Charlie shook her head quickly, erasing her thoughts like clearing the slate of an Etch-a-Sketch, got up, and went to the window without pouring herself a glass.

"Does Tina know?" Iris asked.

"No. We thought we'd wait."

Iris stood to go into the kitchen but stopped suddenly. "I don't mean to...I can't...I don't know...I don't think I can do this again."

It was Charlie who answered from her position at the window, without looking away. "We don't have a choice, Iris."

"Hey you guys, it's okay. I don't know if I can do this either," Catherine said, her green eyes wide with fear.

Iris went to the coffee table and took one of the wineglasses and poured. Charlie had been so distracted, she had not poured anybody else a glass but Catherine.

Charlie, standing at the big front room picture window, looking out not seeing anything but what was in her mind, murmured, "It's starting to rain." Her voice was flat and emotionless. Charlie touched a raindrop on the window and traced its path as it fell and whispered to herself, "When it rains...it pours."

* * *

Driving back to her house, Charlie and Iris sat quietly, listening to the pouring rain pound on the vinyl top. The wipers were whipping full speed across the windshield in perfect rhythm to the drums of doom beating in their heads. The day was emotionally draining, and all Charlie wanted to do was put on some flannel pajamas, climb into bed, and go to sleep.

Charlie pulled into the driveway and shut off the car's lights. The only light was from the street lamp that vaguely illuminated the path from the car to the front door. Charlie sighed heavily and looked at Iris, who was just looking at the floor.

"Come on. Let's make a run for it."

Charlie scooped her purse up snuggly under her arm, got out quickly, and made a mad dash through the downpour. When Charlie reached the safe haven of her front door, and the shelter of the porch, she whirled around. She had expected Iris to be right at her heels, but Iris was still sitting in the car.

"Come on!" Charlie waved at her then went inside.

Iris sat in the car for a few minutes. Slowly she opened the door and got out. Not caring about the rain or her hair, or anything, she shut the door and stood by the car in the middle of the downpour. She looked upward, toward the dark sky and closed her eyes, feeling the wet, cold rain splatter on her face. She stood there for a long moment, in the middle of the rainstorm, getting drenched, not knowing why she was unable to make her legs walk to the house. Instead, she turned and walked down the driveway, away from the house. She did not know where she was going. All she knew was that she could not go inside the house.

Back at the house, Charlie ran upstairs to change out of her wet clothes, turning on every light switch that she passed until the house was brightly lit and she felt safe. After putting her flannel pajama pants on, she went to the kitchen to put on some water for hot chocolate.

"Iris?"

No answer.

Charlie went to the front room window and pressed her face closely to see out. She cupped her hands over her eyes to block out the inside light, wondering if Iris was still in the car. She knew that Iris had not taken the news about Catherine too well. Iris was probably feeling guilty about the fight they had had last week. She had to know that Catherine knew that she still loved her, even though the two fought constantly. When their mother was dying, Iris had partied and slept around with boys and even had gotten involved with drugs.

"Iris? Are you in here?" Charlie called out to the empty house. With no response, she opened the front door and peered outside, squinting to see through the darkness. The car was empty. Charlie started outside to look for her sister, but as she stepped out onto the porch, the teakettle whistled.

* * *

Ethan sat on his couch, beer in hand, watching the Boston Red Sox getting their butts kicked again.   The doorbell rang. Ethan went to the door and opened it, not taking his eye off the television set, for fear of missing a play. He hoped the Red Sox would make a comeback.

Ethan turned his eyes to the door quickly, back to the television and then his mind registered who was at the door. "Did you...," Ethan looked out the door, "...walk all this way? In the rain?"

Iris nodded.

Ethan saw that her eyes were swollen from crying. He opened his arms and took hold of her, guiding her inside.

"You're soaked to the bone," he grabbed the throw blanket from the back of his couch, the blanket he got in Tijuana when he was eighteen, and wrapped her up tightly. He set her on the couch.

"Wait right here," Ethan said as he bolted up the stairs to his bedroom. When he returned, he had an oversized sweatshirt and a pair of socks, "Put this on."

Iris went into the restroom and put the dry clothes on. She came out and stood in the archway between the kitchen and living room.

"Come here," Ethan said, patting the couch behind him. Iris stepped over the coffee table that was filled with a bag of chips, some garlic dip and two empty beer bottles.

"Can I have a beer?"

He got up and went to the kitchen, returning with two bottles of light beer.

"Do you mind if I just sit here for a bit?"

"Do what ever you want, baby," excitement from the television distracted Ethan for a moment. Ethan had missed a double play made by the A's. "I'm getting so pissed at this game." Ethan muted the television set and looked at Iris, who was wrapped in the blanket with her knees pulled to her chest. She looked so despondent, helpless and sad. He flicked off the television.

Chapter 33

$\wedge$

Charlie, wearing Tom's sweatshirt and sweatpants, walked alone along the beach, not appreciating the sunrise and the brilliant colors that danced on the water. The ocean was tumultuous from the previous night's storm. The clear sky bounced off the reflection in the water, making the waves sparkle an almost luminous blue.

She had not been able to sleep much, and she wished the morning's fresh air would take away the heavy feelings of dread she carried. All she could think about was Tom. She wanted him to hold her and take away all of her problems. Until the past week, she was unaware how much she had relied on him. Now, she only had herself to take care of, and she was not doing a good job.

Leona was sitting on the ledge of her back porch drinking coffee and reading the Providence Journal when she saw Charlie walking across the sand. She folded the paper neatly and set it on the white wicker stand, right next to her luke-warm coffee, and walked down to the beach.

"Hey, girlfriend," Leona said, kicking off her sandals. She wanted to feel the cold, wet sand squish between her toes.

Charlie whirled around, surprised to see Leona, "You're up early?"

"A new ritual I've started."

"Where have you been? I haven't seen you since we were at the recording studio almost a week ago."

"I've been...busy," Leona smiled mischievously.

"You went home with my producer that night, didn't you?" Charlie knew the answer before she asked the question; she just wanted to pry. "A twenty-year reunion?"

"Goes to show you never can tell," she nodded teasingly.

"You look satisfied."

"Reno is fun," she smirked, "Better than I remember. It's been quite invigorating."

"That's great," Charlie mumbled, trying to mask her lack of emotion.

Leona touched Charlie's arm and felt stiffness. "I'm sorry I haven't been around. I got a little carried away with the whole thing. You know how it is with a new relationship." She stopped walking and tugged at Charlie's arm. Charlie sighed, relinquishing the stiff outer shell she tried to hide behind.

Leona looked into her friend's eyes; she knew something was off. "How have you been? You look sad. You really miss him, don't you?"

"Catherine's got Lou Gehrig's!" Charlie blurted, without hesitation, as if she were a volcano erupting.

Leona was taken aback, "Oh, my God, Charlie!"

"They just found out."

Leona grabbed a hold of Charlie and hugged her tightly. She rocked her friend with the rhythm of the incoming waves, vowing aloud that she would be there for her.

Chapter 34

∧

Across the ocean in Japan, Tom sat with the group of associates for the business he sought. The place was a dinner and karaoke club. A group of young people dressed in business attire were singing very poorly, "*I Shot the Sheriff.*" It took all of Tom's strength not to cover his ears. They were trashing Eric Clapton's work and he wondered if he could ever hear that song in the same light again.

The waitress offered the table hot towels, starting with Tom. Instead of washing his hands, he placed it on his face and held it there. Bob, the marketing director and representative for the Japanese company, leaned over to Tom and whispered, "Uh, Tom, it's for your hands." They were becoming friends as well as business acquaintances.

"I know," Tom said through the towel, and he pulled it from his face. Everyone was looking at him but he shrugged it off.

"What's wrong with you?" Bob whispered, "You've been acting really strange since you got here. In fact, you've been acting very different since our last visit."

"My fiancée dumped me on our wedding day, a week before I got here."

"I see," he nodded, understanding Tom's behavior, "That's not cool."

"You're telling me," he said and then realized that he was talking to a potential client. He shifted in his seat, "I'll be alright."

"Listen...," Bob leaned in closely to make sure that nobody else could hear him, "I'm sorry for you, but...," he lowered his voice even more, "If you don't get your act together, these guys aren't going to deal. Nikko...," he pointed under the table to the man he was talking about, "He's superstitious. If he even feels like you have a negative aura the deal will be off. It's a competitive world. I don't have to tell you that. I like you and your company. My opinion does matter with these guys, but they play hardball."

Tom forced a smile and nodded toward the businessmen at the other end of the table, and turned to Bob, "I got it under control."

A beautiful Asian woman with long flowing black hair and bright red glossy lips approached Tom and handed him a microphone to sing. Tom shook his head. He did not want to sing, not tonight, not with these people. The men at the table goaded him until he reluctantly took the microphone. *"Love Shack"* from the B52's began playing and Bob gave Tom the "thumbs up" so Tom went to him and grabbed his arm, forcing him to join him on stage. All the men at the table were laughing and having a good time. They thought it humorous to see Tom struggling and singing off key. Tom grabbed two more men, one of them Nikko, who seemed to be enjoying Tom's humiliation the most. Tom decided if he was being to be forced to sing, he would take a few down with him.

* * *

At Reno's Recording Studio, Charlie sat on a tall stool, inside a small padded room, singing the lyrics of one of her songs into the microphone. She sang the song she had written for Tom. She remembered the day she had written it; she had been combing her hair. She was still naked from when they had made love, and she stood in front of the mirror grooming. He was staring at her, starry eyed and in love. She sang to his reflection in the bed, joking with him. The memory made her sad now. When she created the song, it had a different meaning, flirtatious and vain in a teasing way.   Now it was simply sad.

Charlie sang:

> *"I'm in your eyes...I'm in your hair...*
> *I'm in the mirror when you stand there and stare,*
> *I'm in the teeth of your triumph and smile...*
> *I'm gonna put you in my pocket for awhile..."*

As Charlie sang, Reno and Leona sat outside the booth in front of the controls listening to her voice over the sound system.

"She's got a good voice," Reno said as he turned a dial and punched a button. "I really don't have to adjust much. I know who I'm going to send this to when we're done. I've got a connection over at Sony. I think we've got something here."

"Too bad this sound is coming from a broken heart," Leona grimaced. She took pride in being responsible for bringing Charlie and Reno together. He had all the connections to help bring her success. She hoped this would help heal her broken heart.

"She sounds great, though.   Keep encouraging her to pour her emotions into her songs. This is going to be a great CD."

Chapter 35

∧

"There you are," Steve said as he walked into the greenhouse. "It's getting dark out...you can water the rest tomorrow."

"I was just out here thinking."

"You look exhausted. If it must be done tonight, then let me finish this." He tried to take the hose from her, but Catherine pulled back.

"Really, I enjoy this."

"When are you going to see Dr. Edwards again? You're not getting enough sleep."

"It's not that bad."

"You were up most of the night." He touched her arm. "I know, because I was, too."

Catherine tilted her head sideways and half-smiled. "I'll go on the couch if it happens again," she said apologetically.

"That's not what I meant. I'm just worried," he bent over and picked up a bag of potting soil and began filling in his footprint.

It was true. She had not been sleeping.

"I don't know what's wrong, Steve. I get sleepy. I fall asleep as soon as I hit the pillow. An hour later, I'm wide-awake, tossing and turning the rest of the night. It's almost like I'm feeling anxious or something. Or a better way to describe it is like when you're sick with the flu, and you can feel every muscle in your body aching and throbbing, only this is more irritating and it doesn't go away. I just want to take my fists and punch my legs – anything to take away this feeling."

"Maybe Dr. Edwards can suggest something to calm your nerves or maybe even prescribe something that can help you sleep." He stood again and stared deep into her eyes.

"I'll call him tomorrow."

"You're such a worrier. I think it's time for Catherine to take care of Catherine."

Chapter 36

∧

The same afternoon, at the club, Denny was tending bar. It was slow, which gave him plenty of time to flirt with a group of beautiful young vacationing women. Denny told the same corny jokes to all women, trying to enchant them with his charm. With the exception of a few regulars, the bar was empty.

"A horse walks into the bar and the bartender says, 'Why the long face?'" Since they laughed at his jokes, he bought them a round of shots.

Gina stood at the other end of the bar, growing green with jealousy. Every second that passed made her more furious. On the other hand, Denny was oblivious to the laser beam glares he was getting from her. Finally, unable to refrain her jealousy, Gina stormed off angrily to the restroom.

The side parking lot entrance door opened, and in walked Ethan and Iris. They sat at the bar as Denny, knowing his friend's drink of choice, greeted Ethan with an ale and Iris with a light beer. Denny took pride in remembering everyone's drink.

"I heard you're going to San Francisco! That's the coolest!" Denny said, throwing his hand in the air for Ethan to slap.

Ethan looked to Iris, and then back to Denny. "This is not a high-five situation."

Denny looked at his rejected hand and lowered his arm.

Iris looked at Ethan, who slipped his hand into hers and squeezed it for reassurance.

"What?" Denny asked, confused with the silence.

"We're still going...," Ethan left the sentence hanging.

"You two don't sound too excited."

"Well...You know what Charlie's been freaking about for so long?"

"Yeah?" Denny said, although it sounded more like a question.

"Iris just found out that Catherine has it."

"Holy shit!" Denny stepped back, astounded. "I can't believe this. It's ironic." He turned to Iris, "You and I were just talking about all this the other day." He shook his head in disbelief. "When did all this happen?"

This time it was Iris who spoke. "Apparently, she's had symptoms for a long time now, but she had not checked it out till...," Iris said, stopping in mid-sentence. She was suddenly unable to talk.

Ethan regarded Iris, "You okay?"

Iris nodded then took a drink of beer, trying to rebuke the tears that surfaced. She swallowed hard.

"She got pretty sick last week with bronchitis or pneumonia - I can't remember, but while she was in the hospital they figured it out."

Another regular walked in the door and motioned for a beer.

"Hold on, let me get this guy his beer."

When Denny moved away to tend to the customer, Ethan put his arm around Iris. She smiled hesitantly at him with her sad brown eyes.

Denny served the beer quickly and came back to his friends.

"Man, what a mind blower! How's Charlie? She must be really freakin'."

"She's kinda alone right now. I mean...I'm staying at Ethan's. Tom's gone. Leona's hanging with Charlie's record producer. Did you meet him?"

"I don't think I met him. Man, this really sucks. So what're you guys gonna do?"

"We're gonna see how things go over the next few weeks. Iris said Catherine felt pretty good the other day. If everything looks calm, we'll head out."

"You think I should get a hold of Tom?" Denny asked Iris. Before she could answer, a drunken man approached. As Denny dispensed the old man's beer, the door opened and a group of people walked into the bar and seated themselves at a table by the dance floor. Denny glanced around the bar, looking for Gina, but she was nowhere to be seen. The girls Denny had been flirting with beckoned Denny back.

Iris put her head on Ethan's shoulder as they watched Denny run around tending to the customers. It was better that way. Iris did not want to talk about it any more. She just wanted to sit quietly, knowing she was safe in Ethan's arms.

Chapter 37

∧

Bright and early Monday morning, Catherine and Steve sat in Dr. Edwards' office. They were the first patients waiting for him, and the nurse situated them in the doctor's office per his request.

Catherine fidgeted with her blouse, distracted with the button that kept popping undone. She forgot that the eyehole was too small the last time that she had worn the blouse and wished she had fixed it rather than put it off. Now she did not have a safety pin to do a quick fix like she did before. She just could not squeeze the button through the tiny hole.

Steve watched her growing more and more frustrated with each attempt. He reached to fix it, but Catherine stubbornly pushed his hand away. She was determined to fix it all on her own. After a few more unsuccessful attempts, Steve took charge and effortlessly put the button through the tiny hole.

"I would have gotten it eventually," Catherine said stubbornly as she fought back tears. She knew that this was a sign that things were going downhill quicker than she had anticipated. She'd been stumbling, getting more leg cramps, her muscles were twitching uncontrollably, and she seemed to be dropping things a lot more. Now this. She could not even button her own blouse.

Doctor Edwards walked into his office, and they both looked up at him from their seats.

"Hello, Catherine," the doctor nodded to Steve, "Steve."

"Hi," they both said in unison and looked at each other.

"Now, I want to caution you, Catherine. Dr. Burns is still attempting to determine the extent of your nerve degeneration and its rate of progression. We don't want to interfere with this. However, sleep deprivation is very debilitating." Dr. Edwards wrote out a prescription as he spoke, "So, I'm going to prescribe a mild sleeping pill, Ambien, in a very low dosage. It should help you sleep through the night."

Catherine nodded.

"I want you to practice the deep breathing exercises we discussed. But, most importantly, I want you to stop worrying. You can't make anything better by worrying. That seems to be the chief cause of your insomnia at this point."

Catherine looked to Steve as he nodded, agreeing with Dr. Edwards. For a brief moment, Catherine had a flash of irritation at Steve.

She felt like he was betraying her, but she knew he was just concerned for her. She felt like they were ganging up on her.

"Once Dr. Burns finishes his testing, we can talk about options and some experimental therapy. But I don't want you to get your hopes up. These things will help prolong, not cure."

Catherine's heart dropped. Even though she knew there was no a cure for ALS, she hoped for a miracle. Something other than the imminent alternative she was forced with. She had read about a drug called Myotrophin and others, but what she had really wanted to hear was that they had a wonder drug. Her family needed her so much, and she knew it would not be long before she would be showing debilitation. She was going to be completely worthless to all of them.

The doctor handed Steve the prescription for the Ambien and dietary information. He wanted her to eat green vegetables loaded with iron and vitamins. As they talked, Catherine sat in her seat silently. Dr. Edwards's phone rang, and he answered it. Steve waited patiently for the doctor to finish speaking. He had other questions, questions that Catherine would not ask for herself. Steve grabbed a pencil and jotted down notes.

Catherine stood up and walked to the door.

"Catherine?" Steve called out to her, putting the pencil back in the jar on Dr. Edward's desk.

Without answering, Catherine opened the door and disappeared behind it. Steve watched her walk out of the doctor's office in shock. She had never walked away from him, and he knew he could never fathom the fear she was dealing with. When Steve stood to follow, he dropped the papers that Dr. Edwards had given him all over the floor. Disregarding the mess he had made, he went after his wife.

* * *

Tom sat at the hotel desk checking his e-mail on his laptop. It was nine o'clock in Tokyo, and that meant it was early morning in Providence. He wished he were back home. He did not like being nine time zones away.

The deal with the agency was coming to a closing date quicker than he had anticipated, but he knew that it would still be another four to five days. He was getting better at focusing his energy where it should be, with his work. He found that if he kept food in his stomach, his mind stayed focused. It was when he went without food that his mind would go crazy. So he kept candy in his pocket and made sure he ate all of his meals.

A knock on the door brought the late-night supper he had ordered from room service. It was just a light dinner of sushi and miso soup, but it was enough to fill him for the evening. He did not like eating heavy at night like he used to. Once he hit thirty, his metabolism changed, and his body stored fat. If he did not watch what he ate, he would grow a spare tire, just like his father. He promised himself he would begin working out again when he got back to America. He had to get into a routine, a schedule so full that it would take up all of his free time. This way he would not waste needless time dwelling on his failed relationship.

He took a bite of tuna after dipping it the wasabi. He blew on the hot soup as he opened his mail. When he opened the last one, he was sad to find that it was not from Charlie, but an advertisement for a low-rate credit card.

Tom flipped shut the laptop lid. It was hopeless. Charlie was not going to write. Every day he had hoped for an email, a message, or something from her asking him to come home. He needed to face the cold hard fact that it was over between them, and there was absolutely nothing he could do about it. It was not wrong for him to hope that she wanted to take him back, but it was wrong for him to hang onto the hope. She had made it abundantly clear that she did not love him anymore and that she did not want him in her life. Although he did not understand it, he knew he had to accept the truth.

He was surprised at how hungry he was, and he ravished the remains of his dinner quickly. He then stripped down to his boxers, brushed his teeth, and turned on the television, hoping for an American television program – to no avail. Instead, he settled for an episode of *Baywatch* with voice over dubbed in Japanese. He grew disinterested in the program after fifteen minutes. Lip reading was harder than he thought. Boredom took him back to his laptop.

Although he knew he would not have an email from her, and he felt ashamed for even hoping, he signed back onto the internet connection and opened his mailbox again. It was empty, just as he expected. He shut down his computer, placed it back into his briefcase, and climbed into bed. He picked up the book he was reading, resuming where he had left off the previous night.

The room was silent except for the muffled noise from the city below. He was on the tenth floor, which had a brilliant view of the over-populated city. He sat in the stillness of his room, trying to read. Every so often he glanced at the telephone next to his bed, hoping it would ring.

After reading a full chapter, he set the book down and picked up the phone. He held it in his hand for a long moment, then set it down. He glanced at his watch on the nightstand and calculated the time difference back home. It was six in the morning in Rhode Island, and he wanted to call her.

He picked it up again, and this time he dialed a few numbers before replacing it back on the receiver. What would he say to her if he got her on the phone? All he needed was to hear her voice. Then he would know that she was safe. He lifted the phone again off the receiver and dialed the operator. But before the operator answered, he slammed the phone down hard. What was he thinking? Listen to her voice? He was losing his mind. Irritated, he grabbed the pillow next to him and threw it across the room, then shut off the light.

Chapter 38

∧

Catherine looked at herself in the bathroom mirror, barely recognizing the reflection. She looked tired and worn. She opened the drawer and applied some concealer to cover her dark circles. She looked different. Beyond the eyes there was something missing.

Catherine closed the drawer and reached for the prescription that Dr. Edwards had filled. She looked at the bottle intently. Sleep was becoming precious to her - and scarcer. She had taken one of the pills the night before but she still could not sleep. They were not the answer she had hoped for. Nothing was worse than lying awake tossing and turning. It was the worrying that made her afraid.

Catherine opened the bottle of Ambien and took out a pill. She read the bottle's prescription again, which instructed her to take one every night for sleeping discomfort. She looked at her watch. It was nine o'clock in the morning. It would be seven hours before Christina got home from school. Catherine wondered how Christina was doing in public school. Against her wishes, she let Steve enroll their daughter into public school. Deep down, she knew it was the right thing to do, and that was why she gave in to her husband. Steve insisted that it was only temporary, and a part of her supposed that he believed what he was saying. She missed the time she and her daughter shared with home schooling.

Maybe if she took a couple of the pills, she could get some rest. Then perhaps she would have energy later for her family. Catherine really wanted to spend some quality time with Christina, especially since she was away from her all day at school.

Catherine took another pill hoping for rest to come soon. She walked into Christina's bedroom which was in complete disarray. Her daughter had left her television on, which was playing Bugs Bunny and Friends. As Catherine made Tina's bed, she glanced at the television. The cartoon playing was one of her and Tina's favorites. It was the cartoon where Elmer Fudd was trying to get some sleep and Daffy Duck was trying to tell Elmer that the house was haunted. Catherine suddenly wished her daughter was there with her watching television. She sat on the bed, drawn into the program. She could definitely empathize with good ol' Elmer wanting his rest.

After the cartoon was over, and Elmer finally got his rest, Catherine shut off the television. It was her turn to go to sleep. As she climbed into bed, and pulled the blankets up to her chin, she could not help thinking, "West and wewaxation at wast!".

* * *

Denny pushed his heavy bike into the parking lot, maneuvering it into his allotted spot. He knew he was in trouble with Gina. He should have never stayed out all night. He looked at his watch. It was almost noon. He shook his head back and forth, suddenly disgusted with himself. She had been so mad at him when she got off her shift last night that she did not say good bye. That should have been his cue to come directly home from work and tell her he was sorry for flirting with those women. He knew what he was doing, but at the time, he could not stop himself. He figured that since he was already in trouble, he might as well have some fun before he went home to face the firing squad. His thinking was wrong, and he knew it. It was his problem, and he just could not seem to get it right. Every relationship ended the same and it was always his fault. He seemed to always make bad decisions, and they always ruined things, mostly because he was making decisions with other things in mind.

Denny kicked the stand out and rested his bike in its spot. He ran his hands through his hair and fixed his leather jacket. He didn't really do anything wrong, he told himself. Those women invited him to a party and he went. He worked hard all day and deserved to have a good time. Anyway, if he had gone home last night, he and Gina would have fought until dawn. He wasn't married. It's not like he had sex with her, even though it was she who threw herself at him. It was only kissing. He just could not resist. But now he was consumed with a heavy feeling. He knew that it was guilt, even though he had never experienced that feeling before, and he sure as hell did not know how to deal with it. The smart thing would have been to go directly home after work.

His apartment was along the sidewalk adjacent to the entrance of the apartment complex. Something instinctively told him to look up at the window of their apartment, which was on the third floor.

Suddenly, Denny's expression turned to horror. "You wouldn't!" Denny screamed as he ran toward the grassy area beneath his window. As he ran, he saw his beloved pinball machine teetering on the window ledge.

"Noooo!" Denny screamed! "Gina! Darling! Let me explain!"

"Kiss my ass, Denny!"

"No! Wait! Don't!"

The pinball machine moved a foot further out the window. Gravity finally took over, and the pinball machine came crashing down onto the front lawn. Denny covered his eyes before it hit the ground. He did not want to see his baby destroyed before his eyes.

It crashed loudly and pieces flew as far as the sidewalk across the lawn.

Denny stood paralyzed, not believing what had just happened. When he finally breathed, he looked up at the window again. Gina glowered down at him with a look of pure satisfaction.

"...But Gina...," Denny said barely above a whisper.

"I can't believe you did it to me. I thought we had something special."

"We do..."

Gina interrupted him, "Save it for someone else, because I ain't buyin' it."

"I didn't do anything..."

She flipped him off and slammed the window shut.

Denny sat down on the grass, in front of his dead pinball machine, and put his head in his hands.

* * *

Catherine, in her own bed now, slept soundly. The blankets were pulled up snugly around her face, and the room was dark.

In her dream, Catherine heard Christina's laughter and she smiled in her sleep. She dreamt about the time last summer when she and Christina were running through the sprinkler in the front yard. Christina laughed again loudly. It was so real it pulled her right out of her dream back to reality.

Catherine blinked for a moment, realizing that she had been dreaming. She looked toward the window when she became aware that the room was dark. Light peeked through the slits of the Venetian blinds, but she knew it was streetlight, not daylight. Disoriented, she quickly glanced at the clock. It was almost nine o'clock and she squinted to see if the light was on the p.m. Confused, she pulled the blankets back and sat up on the edge of the bed.

She felt tired, and all she wanted to do was go back to sleep. Even though she had slept through the entire day, she could not believe how deeply exhausted she was. The effects of the sleeping pills were still in her system, and she felt groggy. When she tried to stand, her vision was blurry, and she felt like she was going to pass out. She sat back down quickly. She waited for a moment, hoping the dizziness would pass. She squeezed her eyes shut and then opened them as she tried to lift her head. It felt like it weighed a thousand pounds.

Once again, she heard giggling from Christina. Only this time, she heard Steve shushing her.

"Tina, you must be quiet and let Mommy sleep."

"Sorry, daddy," Christina said softly from the other room. They were in his office across the hall.

Catherine managed to get to the doorway and was going to go in, but she stopped. She stood behind the partially opened door. She wanted to watch the two people she loved the most interacting in a very intimate moment.

Steve was sitting at his desk, and he had Christina sitting on his lap as they scrolled through pictures from their latest trip to Mpumalanga. Christina reached to her left as Steve helped guide the photo she was feeding into the scanner.

"Push the button, Tina." She did and the scanner's light peeked through the cracks as it copied the picture from the paper to the computer.

"Now watch the screen and it'll appear right before our eyes."

"There it is, Daddy!" Tina exclaimed, excitedly. "This is cool."

Steve punched keys on the laptop, "Okay, now we pull up Photoshop and...," he moved the mouse, "Viola!" Christina, her eyes wide with amazement, watched her father click away at the computer. "These are going to look great, Tina. What are you going to write about the lions?"

Christina thought for a second, and when she knew the answer her face brightened, "That the mama lion takes the cubs far away from their home and leaves them there. Then the cubs have to learn how to survive without their family."

Steve looked at Christina with fatherly concern. "That's a very interesting fact. Many animals are forced to leave..."

Christina interrupted, excitedly. "But not elephants. Elephants stay together in a family 'til they get old and die. That's what the Crocodile Hunter on television said."

Steve considered the innocence of her comments, "That makes sense."

"Don't the lion cubs get scared all by themselves?" Christina asked.

Catherine, still watching from behind the opened door, had to bite her bottom lip to keep it from quivering. She wanted to grab hold of her daughter and never let go.

"I'm sure they do, but that's just the way it happens. The mama teaches them..."

"What about wart hogs?" Christina was suddenly bored with the lions, "Those are my favorites. I love wart hogs. They're so ugly, they're cute," Christina giggled.

Steve chuckled aloud and tried to bite back his laughter. He did not want her to know that he was amused.

Catherine watched them for a while longer from the doorway. She smiled proudly, wishing Christina would never lose that innocence. She watched her daughter's array of facial expressions as she rambled on and on about wart hogs. She wanted to go in and share in the moment but did not want to ruin what they had going on between them. Christina was so innocent and Steve was so patient. How did she ever get so lucky? Even having her life cut short, she realized that she had more in the thirty-nine years than most people had in an entire lifetime. She had been worrying for Christina, and it wasn't until that moment of watching them in the doorway, that she knew that Steve would take good care of her. Christina would survive because of the kind and patient man that Steve was. Relief swept over her, and she felt the heavy burden she had been carrying on her shoulders lift, as if a balloon took it all away. She understood now, and it was an overwhelming feeling of release, that they could go on without her.

Catherine whispered to herself as she squeezed her eyes shut, "They will be fine."

Chapter 39

∧

The ocean was unusually calm, and the blue-gray expansive stretched all the way to the horizon. The colors melted into one another as far as the eye could see. Charlie sat with Leona on her back deck. Leona was going through some recent photos she had taken, while Charlie sat quietly thinking. Her mind's worry consumed her every thought. A crease across her brow accentuated her mood as her face furrowed from her thoughts.

"You're face is gonna get stuck that way if you don't quit."

"Huh?" Charlie asked, confused. When she caught on she replied, "Oh, I can't seem to make the hamsters in the wheel quit running through my brain."

Leona put her hand on Charlie's arm and patted it gently, "I've got some Valium in my cupboard. That would help."

"Maybe," Charlie said, looking deep into the ocean. She half hoped the ocean was wild and tumultuous just to match her mood, "I'll let you know."

The two sat in uninterrupted silence for a long while. It was Leona who broke the silence, "So you think it's gonna last?"

"What? Catherine's sickness?"

Leona gave Charlie startled look, "No. Iris and Ethan." She picked up a photo of the couple out of the spread and handed it to Charlie, "I like this one."

"It's cute," Charlie handed it back, "I don't know." Charlie picked up a stack of photos and flipped through them. "This one's a better shot. Iris' smile is open. She's cute when she laughs."

Leona agreed and put that picture aside in a separate stack. "Well, I hope it does," Leona took a sip of coffee and kicked her feet back as Charlie continued flipping through them.

"Oh, wait. Go back. I like that one," Leona said, leaning toward Charlie.

It was a picture of her on stage, "Hmmm," Charlie studied it briefly then put it at the bottom of the stack, obviously disagreeing with Leona. "They all kinda look the same to me." She glanced at Leona's slighted expression and quickly responded, "No offense."

Leona snatched the stack of photos from Charlie's hand, "Offense taken! You need an enema!"

Charlie tried to laugh it off, "Come on. It's not you. It's me. I'm just..."

"You're just what?" Leona was not going to let her get away with it.

"It's hard to explain."

"When are you going to call Tom?"

Charlie flinched. Leona was the last person she expected to bring up Tom. Leona knew that she was trying to forget about him. It shocked her that she had even asked.

"But...I...Leona?" Charlie was flustered. She had never had to explain herself to Leona and was not prepared to do so now.

Leona mocked her stuttering, "But I Leona what?"

"I can't deal with this right now. Catherine...," Charlie got up and walked to the railing that overlooked the ocean. "Why are you doing this to me?" She was having a hard time separating her work from her music, and her music from her personal life. Everything was caving in on her, and she felt like she was suffocating, "You're the one person I could count on to not harass me. You've never done it in the past, and I don't understand why you're doing it to me now."

Leona went to her and put her head on Charlie's shoulder, "Charlie? Catherine seems to be doing fine," she waited a moment, "I think you need to work on you."

"I don't know what's wrong with me. It's like a quiet panic, and sometimes I can't breathe. I feel like walking out into that ocean and...," Charlie stopped. She could not say the words. She had never said aloud what she had been thinking until now...and it did not sound good. She just did not think there was much more that she could endure. Ending it all would be the end of all the pressure that was bottled up inside.

Leona, her head still on her best friend's shoulder, intertwined her arm through Charlie's. She knew Charlie needed counseling, and she hoped she could say the right words.

"Trust me, Charlie. I know that feeling. We've all been there some time or another. I had a month affair with a famous rock star once," she flipped her hair back from her face and then rested her head back in the same spot, continuing, "I still can't say his name. He's still making music and still sexy as all get out, but he broke my heart and I never thought I'd get over him. Anyway, I shut down completely for six months and could not even get out of bed. Then, one day, a friend of mine got me into counseling and I survived."

"You think I'm depressed?"

Leona lifted her head off Charlie's shoulder and moved in front of her. Without saying a word, she nodded. Charlie cast her eyes downward, and Leona put her hand under Charlie's chin, lifting her face back to hers, "But that's not bad. Everyone gets a little depressed once in awhile. With all that's been going on in your life, it's understandable."

"So, I'm just a little crazy?" Charlie cracked a smile and shrugged halfheartedly.

"Listen, I get crazy every morning before I have my coffee."

A laugh escaped Charlie's mouth, "See. That wasn't so hard now was it?" Leona fake-punched her in the stomach playfully, "Hey, I got an idea. Let's really get crazy and go for a swim. The water looks so inviting."

"You are crazy. It's too cold."

"Come on. We can run for a while and get some body heat going, then we'll strip to the buff and dive in," Leona grabbed a beach towel hanging on the railing, "Don't think. Just do. Come on."

Charlie watched her friend dart off the back porch and down to the sand. Reluctantly, she followed. What else could she do? Tell Leona no?

* * *

Iris, wearing a light denim jean jacket and shorts, sat with Ethan in their usual booth at their favorite coffeehouse, drinking coffee and smoking cigarettes. The waitress walked by and refilled their cups as the two sat peacefully.

"Do you want to order?" Ethan asked as he watched the waitress leave. He took off the Providence Bruins sweatshirt, exposing a beer tee shirt underneath. He too, was wearing shorts, because it was already proving to be a hot summery morning.

Iris shrugged and snubbed out her cigarette, exhaling the smoke from her lungs. The cigarette suddenly did not taste good to her any longer. She contemplated quitting.

"Iris, will you talk to me please?" Ethan reached across the table and touched her face. She looked at him but did not speak, "You are holding in so much anger. It's eating away at you, and I don't like to see you like this."

Iris fixed her big, innocent brown eyes deep into Ethan's green ones. She looked innocent and younger than her twenty-three years. He snubbed out his cigarette and waited for her response.

Iris took a deep breath and began the conversation with Ethan exactly where she had left off in her mind, "It was hard and I made it harder...for everyone. That's what I did." She realized she had not made any sense to him from Ethan's blank expression. She explained, "When mom died."

Ethan nodded and chose his words carefully, "Well, it must have been pretty hard for you, too."

"My mom was dying, and I put her through hell," Iris paused a beat and then frowned, "And now...I don't really know what to do. I mean... I don't even like Catherine most of the time. I mean, I love her, but sometimes I don't like her."

Ethan nodded, wanting her to go on.

Embarrassed that she admitted feelings that she was not proud of, she flailed her arms expressively as she spoke, "You know what I mean, right? But I also feel really guilty."

Ethan shrugged, "You're being tough on yourself. Remember that guilt is a feeling that is manifested in your own mind."

Iris picked up her cigarettes and pulled one out, then changed her mind and put it back in the pack. Her fingers wanted to do something, so she picked up the napkin and began twisting it as she spoke.

"It's just...it's...it's too soon to go through something like that again. Never would be too soon, to tell you the truth...I feel really selfish...I wasn't much help...back then." Iris looked down, too ashamed to look at him, "I was a selfish brat."

"Iris," he said her name softly.

This time she could not look up. She was humiliated to admit aloud that she was a bad kid, especially to Ethan. She did not want him to know anything bad about her.

"Iris? Look at me." Iris looked up, her eyes filled to the brim with tears, "You were only a kid. I don't think anyone expected you to be more than a teenager."

She sniffled and rubbed her nose. He understood her. Nobody else in her life had ever wanted to take the time.

"All teenagers are hellions. What makes you think that your rebellion is different than anyone else's?"

Iris looked at him as if she had never considered this before. She had never told this secret to anybody. Of course, her sisters knew, but she had never said it aloud before. It was something she wanted to forget. She felt like her rebellion somehow aided in her mother's premature death. Ethan, on the other hand, made it sound like her behavior was normal, like it all made perfect sense. Iris sat up straight. What she was hearing from him was something she needed to hear a long time ago.

"You were supposed to be a brat. I sure as hell was."

"I didn't help my mom get sicker?"

"That's ridiculous. She had a degenerative disease, and you were a kid. Say it out loud."

Iris smirked at his attempt at therapy, "Okay. I get it."

"Say it, Iris. You need to realize that you were a kid who was losing her mother. You didn't know how to react. You did what it took to survive. And, I think you've done a great job with raising yourself. Now, say it," he started for her, "I was a kid." He repeated it again until Iris finally joined him in his chant.

"I was a kid," Iris whispered, holding back the damn of emotions welling up inside. She repeated it again, louder this time, "I was a kid." She looked around embarrassed and ducked in her seat when everyone around stopped to look in her direction.

Ethan chuckled.

"I'm auditioning for a part in a movie," Iris announced, and the couple in the next booth wished her good luck.

They both began to laugh, and Iris wiped away the tears that were streaming down her face.

* * *

Charlie, in a pink cotton nightgown, sat up in her bed. Something inside her awoke, and she suddenly had the urge to write music. She had not been motivated to write for so long that she almost did not recognize the sign.

Earlier that evening, a couple of friends from her office had called and wanted her to go to dinner with them. But inspiration won the toss-up, so she sat at the desk by the keyboard with pad and pencil in hand, working out the new song that was stuck in her head. Sometimes, when she ignored the idea of a new song, she would lose it. That was why it was so important for her to follow the revelation of inspiration immediately.

The music just seemed to flow out of her, and she began to hum the tune. She wrote the lyrics as she hummed, starting over again, until the words fit perfectly. When she started singing the tune, the lyrics poured out confidently.

"When it rains it pours..."
" it really pours...

She suddenly halted, twirled around in her seat and flipped the on switch to the keyboard. She began playing the corresponding chords. She started singing the lyrics again.

> *"When it rains...It really pours...*
> *When it rains... feel the downpour...*
> *Can't stand the rain.. Don't let it rain..*
> *On me no more..."*

Charlie did not want to forget this song like she had with many others. Inspired one moment, forgotten the next. This one she was proud of. She sang it again, this time with passion. Her eyes closed, she felt every word, praying the prayer with her voice.

The verses came to her, as if it were predestined to be her song.

> *"I don't understand...*
> *How you simply can...*
> *Just leave, just go away...*
> *My heart was in your hands...*
> *Please help me understand...*
> *Decisions that were made..."*

The telephone rang, but Charlie ignored it. After four rings, she realized the caller would not give up. She contemplated answering but hesitated, fearing a break would sever the moment of inspiration.

Fifth ring. Charlie ignored it and began playing the chords again. On the seventh ring, a thought occurred to her. Maybe it was Catherine. Charlie jumped up and ran to the telephone in the next room.

"Hello?" She answered, out of breath and sounded a little aggravated for being interrupted.

A hysterical voice, a man. He was crying.

"I can't understand you."

She waited, but the crying continued, "Who is this?" She was about to hang up when it suddenly occurred to her who was on the other end.

Chapter 40

∧

The wind blew Charlie's hair off her face, and she felt big splatters of raindrops as she ran out the back door through the sand to Leona's house. She scaled two steps at a time as she flew to reach the back door. Charlie pounded on her door. God, she hoped Leona was home. When she did not answer, Charlie wiggled the door handle.

"Leona!" Charlie yelled, pounding incessantly.

The door opened, and Leona finally answered. Her hair was wet and she had a thick, green terry cloth robe on. She did not have time to speak but she knew something was terribly wrong by the look on her face.

"Catherine...hospital...," Charlie was out of breath and could not finish.

"Let me throw on some clothes." Leona darted into the other room and quickly reappeared dressed in gray sweatpants. Leona reached for her keys from the hook by the front door and hurried out. As she shut the door, her arm brushed against Charlie's, and she could feel her friend shaking.

In the car, Leona backed out the driveway quickly and slammed the car into first gear, squealing the tires as she sped off down the street. Leona swept through town, using her flashers and horn as an excuse to run through every stop sign and light that came in between them and the hospital. If a cop flashed her over, she would make him follow her all the way to the hospital because she was not stopping.

"Iris," Charlie mumbled, numbly. "I've got to find Iris."

"Let's go to the hospital and we'll call Ethan's and see if she's there."

"I wish I had my cell phone with me. I forgot my purse and everything." Charlie said.

"That's understandable." Leona patted Charlie's leg, "What happened?"

"I don't know. Steve called and he was crying. I could only make out a few words, and hospital was one of them."

They both sat in silence as Leona drove like a madwoman the rest of the way to the hospital. When they arrived at the emergency room exit, Leona parked right behind an ambulance, cutting the engine off quickly.

An ambulance driver hollered at them, "Hey, you can't park here!"

Leona tossed him the keys and followed Charlie inside.

Charlie saw Steve first. He was sitting zombie-like in a chair in the hallway. He heard them rushing down the hallway, and he looked up.

"What happened? Is she alright?!" Charlie shrieked, not aware that she was yelling. Steve's face told her that something was terribly wrong.

His eyes were swollen, and his lips were pale and trembling.

"What's wrong?!" Charlie hollered when he did not answer. "Steve?"

Steve opened his mouth to speak, but nothing would come out.

"You're scaring me," Charlie said, her voice filled with panic. She looked up and down the hallway. "Where's the doctor?" She took a few steps down the hallway and then turned back around when she could not figure out which way to go.

Steve's voice quivered and he spoke above a whisper, "They couldn't revive her..."

Charlie stumbled as she turned toward him slowly. Had she heard him right? "What...?"

When he looked at her, she knew the truth.

Charlie started to swoon, and her legs were suddenly weak. Leona grabbed a hold of her before she could fall, "What happened? She was fine! She...said...she was fine!" Charlie fell at Steve's feet. "She said that she had two to five years. I don't understand..."

They held each other, crying and Leona leaned against the wall, helpless.

"She was having a hard time sleeping," Steve choked on his words. "The doctor gave her something to help her sleep...but it was a really mild sleeping aid."

Charlie looked crazed, "Oh my God! ALS affects the breathing muscles. How could the doctor prescribe something like that for her?"

"They don't know the cause of...,." Steve could not say the word, "...yet. I thought she was asleep when I got up this morning...but when I came to see what she wanted for breakfast...," Steve broke down. Charlie hugged him again.

Leona hesitated in going to them because she did not know what to say. She decided to let them both know that she was there if they needed her. She crept up behind them and gently placed her hands on both of their backs.

The automatic doors to the emergency room opened and Iris and Ethan burst through. Iris froze in her tracks when she saw the state that

Charlie and Steve were in. Leona stepped back a couple of steps, feeling more helpless than ever.

Iris looked from Charlie's face to Steve's face and then back to Charlie's, "Charlie?" Her heart dropped, and she knew. She threw her hands in front of her in hopes to stop the news that she did not want to hear, "No...no...no!"

Leona ran to Iris and wrapped her arms around her, and at first she accepted Leona's comforting care, but then she began to fight Leona.

Leona told Iris as she tried to take hold of her, "Iris...Catherine's dead."

"No! Oh, my God!" Iris screamed and began wailing like a child. Leona rocked her back and forth and Iris pushed away. "No! It's not fair!" She panicked, "Please say it's not true!" After she turned to Steve and saw him, she knew that Catherine was really dead. She ran to Ethan and buried her face in his chest. Ethan held her tightly as she cried into his shoulder.

Leona approached Ethan and Iris and put her arms around the both of them, cradling them. Leona motioned for Charlie to come to join them, but Charlie stopped and turned to Steve. Without saying anything, she grabbed his hand and pulled him up, guiding him to the group of friends and family holding each other in a tight circle.

Chapter 41

∧

Charlie sat on a park bench alone outside the hospital. Pink and orange rays streaked the sky through billowy clouds - an unusual sunrise, considering it was the sunsets that were celebrated in Rhode Island. The air was crisp, and Charlie shuddered beneath Tom's sweat shirt. She wished he were here. She needed him, but she knew that Catherine's death was the confirmation to her that he should not be here. She could not do *this* to him – she knew it for a fact.

The sliding door to the emergency room opened and Steve appeared. His eyes had dark circles and his face was covered with a shadowy beard. He had asked her to stay because he did not want to be alone. She understood that and would not have gone anyway. The doctors had told him to go home and get rest and to come back in the morning, but Steve did not want to leave Catherine alone, even in death.

Charlie, without any words spoken, stood and followed him inside and down the hall to a small office.

Inside, Steve and Charlie met Dr. Edwards and sat opposite him. They clasped hands for courage.

"The medical examiner can't make a final determination as to cause of death without an autopsy. Without an autopsy, the death certificate will state accidental. At this juncture, an autopsy is the only way we'll really know what happened. I think we should perform one so a determination can be made as to whether Catherine's death was accidental or...,"

"Or what?" Steve interrupted the doctor, his voice abrasive. He did not like what the doctor was insinuating.

"Steve," Charlie said gently as she turned to look at him. He unclasped her hand and Charlie tried to grab it again, but he brushed her hand away.

To Charlie, he said, "He doesn't know her...doesn't know that she wouldn't...wouldn't...," Steve put his head in his hands, "She just wouldn't."

"I'm very sorry to have to put you through this, Steve. However, without an autopsy it's difficult to know for certain if Catherine's respiratory system was more affected by ALS than we were aware."

Steve shot up, "It was an accident!" Steve slumped back into the chair. Charlie reached her hand back out for Steve, and this time he accepted it. He clasped his on top of hers, "We were supposed to grow old...," Steve bit his lip and it turned white; he licked his lips and continued, "...together...tool around in our Winnebago...dancing under the stars in our bathrobes. That was *our* plan."

Charlie had been trying to be strong for Steve, but she could not. She missed Catherine and could not control the stream of tears that were flooding. She felt so bad for him. He loved Catherine and now he was all alone. Just like she was all alone. Just like Tom would be if she had allowed herself to marry him.

"I'll give you two a moment to regroup." Dr. Edwards left the room and then turned back before leaving, "Steve, you can petition the Chief Medical Examiner to waive the autopsy, if you wish."

Charlie and the doctor made eye contact, but Steve did not turn around. He just nodded his head. Charlie looked at the doctor and nodded to him. The decision was made. No autopsy would be done. It was for the best. Her death would be ruled accidental on paper. Both Charlie and Steve knew it was an accident, but what if they did the autopsy and found out otherwise? Charlie knew that for everyone's sake - Iris, Christina, Steve and herself - that it would do more damage than good finding out anything else.

* * *

Ethan sat at the club while Denny bartended. It was noon and the place was dead, which gave them time to talk. Ethan told Denny about the prior evening's events, and Denny stood with his mouth agape, in total disbelief.

"Iris wanted to be alone and I need a beer...and a friend."

"I can't believe this! Damn!" Ethan said as he shook his head back and forth. "This is unbelievable!" Denny wiped down the brass bar taps. "I thought I had it bad! How are they doing?"

"I haven't seen Charlie since it happened, but Iris is pretty withdrawn. She wanted to be alone. She left with her sketchpad. I feel so bad for her. I imagine she's feeling guilty because she and Catherine didn't see eye to eye very often."

"God! I didn't even think about Steve." Denny put the Brasso and rag away and started wiping out ashtrays, "I thought I was going to have a heart attack when Gina tossed my pinball machine out the window, but I can't imagine what I'd do if Tom died so suddenly like that."

"That must've been a sight."

Denny's attention had drifted, "What?"

"Your pinball machine taking a dive."

"Yeah, it was pretty nasty."

"Is it salvageable?"

"Nope. Not even the pin balls."

Ethan took a swig of beer and swirled the remaining liquid at the bottom of the bottle as he watched. Denny slammed two shot glasses on the bar and reached for the bottle of tequila. He slid one to Ethan, and they both shot it back without a toast. There was no reason to celebrate. The liquor was for their mood only.

"Where's Iris now?" Denny asked as he wiped his mouth on his sleeve.

Ethan shrugged, "Sketching around the city, I suppose." A moment passed. "She's having a tough time dealing with it. She loved Catherine, even though they fought so much. Sometimes they'd try to get along, but they'd always end up fighting. And Iris thinks it's because of her."

"It takes two to fight. Maybe it was their thing – you know. Fighting. I had a girlfriend like that. She wasn't happy unless we were fighting. Guilt is a bitch."

"I thought you didn't know what that feeling was."

Denny poured another round. "I'm beginning to understand...and it sucks."

* * *

Steve and Charlie were going through Catherine's closet. They had several dresses laid out on the bed. The room was in disarray. The blankets were a mess, and clothing was strewn all over floor.

"Did she ever talk about whether she wanted to be buried or cremated?" Charlie asked Steve, suddenly uncomfortable with the question. She had never even thought about how she wanted to be disposed of after life. As organized as Catherine was, she probably had it all planned out.

"No. We didn't even have life insurance. We never talked about that kind of stuff," Steve said placing another dress on the bed. "I guess we never thought it could ever happen to us."

"We never talked about anything like that either. Catherine's focus was always on everyone else's happiness." Charlie thought she might have said something wrong, because Steve looked away, and added, "I don't mean that in a bad way. I mean...she never talked about what she wanted for herself, that's all."

"I know," Steve said, plopping down on the corner of the bed. "I know. That's what I loved about her, her generosity. She thought that if she kept everyone else going and together...that everything would be alright."

Charlie put an outfit into a small bag, "I think maybe that was her way of not being like our mother. My mother was never happy. At least not for a good part of her life. And it was a pervasive feeling. She was pretty self-absorbed that way," Charlie stopped for a moment, remembering. "It wasn't until a year before she came down with ALS and she met Del that her outlook changed. It was really sad. She finally found something... someone...who made her feel happy...and then she got sick." Charlie sat on the wicker chair next to the closet, "At least with Catherine, she was always happy. She really loved you."

Steve stared at the floor and Charlie watched him. She wanted to say the right thing to make him feel better. She did not like the words people used when a loved one died, *she's in a better place* or *at least she's not suffering anymore.* Those words weren't comforting to her, so she would not say them to him. She would rather not say anything at all, than say something generic and overused. Charlie went back to the closet and began flipping through the dresses again.

"Catherine is...was...a good person with a heart of gold," Charlie winced. Those weren't the words she was looking for. He already knew that about his wife. "She made a lot of decisions about how she was going to be after mom died." Charlie turned and pulled a black dress out of the closet. "I guess we all did whether we realized it or not...I don't think it worked very well. But it wasn't our fault. We did the best we could...under those circumstances. I think Catherine turned out the best. I mean, the least affected."

Charlie picked up the bag of Catherine's clothes for the funeral home and carefully folded the black dress. She decided on her own that it would be the dress she would wear.

Charlie touched Steve's shoulder, "I'm going to take these over to the funeral parlor now. Why don't you try to rest?"

Steve nodded absentmindedly. Out of the corner of her eye, she caught a glimpse of Christina standing in the doorway sucking her thumb.

Charlie set the bag back on the bed, "Come in, honey."

Christina turned and ran down the hall. Charlie went after her, jumping over any obstacle that came in between. Steve followed Charlie. Christina went into her room and slammed the door, and as Charlie extended her hand out to open the door, she heard the door lock click. Charlie wiggled the handle anyway.

"Christina, honey?" Charlie knocked lightly, "Unlock the door for me."

Silence.

"Christina?"

"Go away." Christina yelled from inside her room.

Steve stepped close to the door, "Open the door, Tina."

No answer.

After a long moment, the door lock clicked. Charlie and Steve looked at one another, and Steve stepped past Charlie to go inside, but Charlie pulled back on his arm.

"Let me talk to her."

"I think she needs me."

"I know she does, Steve, but let me try first. Okay?"

Steve nodded and stepped aside as Charlie cautiously walked into the room. At first glance, she could not see Christina. She lifted the blankets and looked under the bed and then in the closet, but she was in neither place. Christina was nowhere in sight. There was movement in the life size dollhouse in the corner and Charlie spotted her. She crouched down and peered through the door, feeling like Alice in Wonderland. She took a deep breath for courage and entered the dollhouse.

"You're too big," Christina said, frowning.

She overlooked Christina's comment and let herself inside the cramped quarters. It was a tight fit, but she was able to squeeze inside. "I can fit...see? Can I sit with you?"

Christina shrugged, and Charlie sat at the small table anyway. The table was set up for a tea party. They sat in silence and after a moment, Charlie picked up an empty teacup and pretended to drink from it. Christina's eyes widen with alarm, "No! That's Mommy's tea!"

Charlie quickly replaced the cup back on its saucer, "I'm sorry, sweetheart. Which one is mine?"

Christina did not answer her. Instead, she picked up the same teacup and lifted it to an invisible "Mommy."

"Be very careful, Mommy. It's still hot," Christina placed the teacup back in its saucer. Christina picked up a small plate from the center of the table and aimed it in the same direction. "Would you like some cookies, Mommy?" She held the plate with her arm outstretched toward the empty chair for a long moment.

Suddenly her face contorted and she screeched, "Mommy? Do you want some cookies?"

Unexpectedly, the plate dropped from her hand and clattered when it hit the table. Christina began wailing as she pushed all the cups and saucers off the table. Charlie got on her knees and took Christina in her arms.

"It's okay, baby. It's okay. Go ahead and cry."

"I want my Mommy!"

Charlie held Christina tightly. Her heart went out to this little girl who had lost her mother - a mother who was very good to her. Charlie knew how it felt to lose a mother. She could empathize with her and knew that life as Christina knew it would never be the same. She wished, more than anything, that she could bring Catherine back to her. She wished she could trade places with her sister. Charlie began to cry with her niece.

"I want my Mommy," Christina cried again. "It's not fair."

"I know, honey, me, too." Christina sobbed uncontrollably as Charlie rocked her back and forth and whispered, "And I want my Mommy, too."

Behind them, Steve peered in through the small entrance and shed silent tears.

Chapter 42

∧

A small group of people, all dressed in black, began to disperse from around a casket over an open grave. The afternoon sky was perfectly clear, and the air had an unusually cool breeze that deflected the heat.

Charlie stood between Steve and Leona. Christina held her father's hand and held a single red rose in the other. Iris clung to Ethan, and they stood next to Steve and Christina. Denny stood in the background, by the shady oak tree, mingling with the other people.

Steve nudged Christina, and she stepped forward to lay the rose on the casket. She delayed, hesitantly touched her mother's casket and quickly pulled her hand back as if she had burnt her fingers. Steve knelt down to her level and she melted into his embrace. He picked her up and she buried her little head into his chest.

Charlie watched Christina, identifying with what her niece was going through. It did not seem so long ago that she too was standing at her own mother's funeral. She was much older than Christina was when she lost her mother, but the sadness was the same. Her mother had given her a St. Christopher's cross. She had taken it off her neck and placed it in her mother's hand. The touch of her mother's hands was cold and lifeless. Charlie blinked away that memory. Now she was eight years old and was remembering the day her mother told her the secret about death. On that particular night, Charlie recalled waking up in the middle of the night. Her cat Smathers had died and she had been crying all night long. She and her mother had made a grave for him in the backyard, burying him in a shoebox in the flower garden. That whole night, she had tossed and turned, having nightmares about whether Smathers had gone to heaven. Those nightmares had turned to dreams about her own death and she woke up too frightened to go back to sleep.

She remembered being drenched with sweat, and terrified. She summoned the courage to go downstairs in the dark. She tiptoed down the stairs and climbed into her mother's bed.

"Who's sneaking in my bed?" her mother whispered groggily.

"It's me. Charlie."

"Come here," her mother turned around and pulled her daughter in tightly, "What's wrong?"

She told her mom about her nightmare and how she was afraid to die.

"Really?" her mother asked. "I'm not afraid to die."

Confused, Charlie asked, "You're not afraid to die?"

"Why no, sweetheart. I'm rather excited. Don't get me wrong, I love this life, but there is another life waiting that is far better than this one. Anyway, I've been constructing a list of questions that I want to ask God. I can't wait to meet him because I want to know the answers to all of life's mysteries. You see, when you die, you become privy to all this knowledge. And I want to know all the answers."

"What kind of questions, mommy?" Charlie asked.

Her mother gently put Charlie's long brown hair behind her ear and poked her nose. "Like...Why can birds fly and we can't? And... is there life on other planets...and why are boys so stinky?" Charlie laughed, and her mother tickled her, increasing her laughter.

That night, Charlie slept with her mother, and from that moment on, she had never been afraid of death again. Even when her mother died many years later, Charlie had a secret that her sisters did not know. She knew her mother was finally getting the answers. It was a secret they both shared and she never told anybody else. Now, Catherine and Mom were together.

"Let us pray," the pastor said, guiding Charlie's thoughts back to the present.

Charlie bowed her head to pray.

* * *

After the funeral, family, friends, and neighbors mingled quietly in the living room at Steve's house. The doorbell rang and Mrs. Callahan answered it, letting in additional guests all carrying potluck.

Charlie sat staring out the window, in the same chair that she had seen Catherine sitting from so many times. She watched the sky fill with dark gray clouds, clouds that were taking over the sky for an evening thunderstorm. As she stared out the window, using the scenery for the backdrop of her thoughts, staring at nothing in particular, she allowed the gray gloomy sky to feed her emotions.

Denny nuzzled up beside Charlie and it took him touching her knee for her to notice he was there. She flinched.

"Sorry. I didn't mean to scare you."

"I was somewhere else."

"You gonna eat?"

"Later." Charlie stood up and walked toward the door. She looked over her shoulder to Denny and asked, "Come outside with me, Denny."

"I do need some fresh air, but it looks like it's gonna rain."

"That's all right with me."

Outside, they went to the swing set and both sat down. Neither one spoke for a long time.

A slight breeze blew Charlie's hair out of her face. She closed her eyes and took in the coolness of the wind, "I love how New England gets these evening thunderstorms. This morning it was perfectly clear and tonight it will thunder and lightning, then tomorrow, it'll be beautiful again." Charlie tucked her flyaway hair behind her ears to keep it from tickling her face. "Denny? Can I ask you something?" Her eyes were still closed.

"What?"

"Why are you and Tom so different? With women, that is?"

"We're not that different."

Charlie opened her eyes and turned to look at him. "Denny, you are complete opposites. What I mean is, why can't you fall in love?"

"Sounds like you have the same problem."

"Oh, you're wrong. I do love."

"I don't get it."

She would not let him change the subject, "I don't get you. Take Gina, for instance. I've never seen you so smitten with any of those other women. I really thought she was going to be the one to tame you."

"Yeah, Gina was great. I thought she was the one too. But, well...,"

"Then why'd you blow it?"

"Because we were getting too close. Maybe it scared me. Anyway, I'm not right for her. She deserves better."

"That's such a cop out, and you know you don't believe that."

"I couldn't love her the way I should."

"There's nothing better than love, Denny. Whatever form it takes."

Denny opened his mouth to speak but was distracted when the back door opened. Steve's parents, both in their late sixties, walked out and sat on the porch swing together. They both watched as Steve's father put his arm around his wife and pulled her in closely, consoling her.

"I used to think old people were gross," Denny admitted and Charlie looked at him disapprovingly. "I'm sorry, that sounded mean," Denny apologized. "Getting old is something I used to think about a lot."

"I can't believe what I'm hearing."

"Ignore me. I'm just rambling. I should not be talking about me."

"What?"

"Nothing."

"Go on," she nudged Denny, "I want to hear."

Denny took in a deep breath. "Like I said, I used to...well, I was afraid to grow old. But, now I think when I get there, I'd like to have an old woman beside me," Denny stopped to think.

"And...,"

"And, all I was going to say is that's part of the reason I don't stay with a woman for very long because...this is going to sound stupid, but if I can't picture myself with her when we're old, I get out before anybody gets hurt."

"Denny, how can you know if you want to be with someone when you're older if you don't fall in love? That's the only way you will ever truly know."

"You make it sound so easy, but it's not."

"Sure it is. Just pick someone out, someone your own age, let's say Gina for example. It's simple. Make her happy. Don't go changing your mind. Work on a lasting relationship. The years go by and before you know it... but of course, you'd have to grow old too."

"Getting old. That's unavoidable."

"Is it?" Charlie thought of Catherine and her mother and her eyes welled with tears, and she looked away from Denny. She was trying to avoid being sad for a moment, but she supposed it was inevitable. As if on cue, Denny reached over and grabbed Charlie's hand and held it.

"See what I mean?" Charlie said, using her thumb to wipe away the tears. "You have such a good heart. You love your friends. Why can't you do that for a girlfriend?"

Denny shrugged. He could not answer her. He did not realize that he had a different relationship with his women friends than his girlfriends until she brought it up. But she was right.

"You are so different with them. I know the real you, Denny. I know what's inside you and what you're capable of. You know what else I see?"

"What's that?"

"I see a man who needs to get his own apartment - one with two bedrooms. One for sleeping, and the other for a pinball machine."

"Uh, you didn't hear? The pinball machine is gone. Gina hurled it out the window when I was out late...with...well, that's irrelevant now."

Charlie burst out laughing. She pictured the petite Gina hoisting the pinball machine up to the window and dropping it. The more she pictured the pinball machine falling, the more hysterical she got. Her laughter caught the attention of Steve's parents, and they frowned, disapprovingly.

Charlie fell out of the swing and onto the ground, holding her stomach. Denny, who was now laughing with her, dropped onto the ground too.

"Oh, man. I needed that. Thanks," Charlie sighed when the silliness had finally passed.

"I'm glad you find it so funny. I was just laughing at you laughing." Denny admitted.

"I like her, Denny, and I think that you do, too. You shouldn't let that one go." Charlie began to giggle again. "She's definitely got personality!"

"Ha ha. Funny," Denny said, as he stood and helped Charlie to her feet. "We better go in before they call the state mental hospital and check us both in." Denny turned to go inside, and Charlie brushed the grass off of his back.

"Do I have grass all over me?" She asked as she turned around.

Denny picked grass off her back and pulled strands from her hair. He turned her around, "Charlie, you know, I'm your friend, right?"

"Of course."

"I never give advice, you know that too, right?"

"What is it, Denman?"

"There needs to be closure with you and Tom. I care about you, but I love him and I can't stand to see him this way."

The first rain drop landed on Charlie's nose, and she wiped it away. She looked to the sky and saw a flash of lightning.

"Let's go inside," Charlie turned and headed for the porch. At the back door, she turned around and looked at Denny. He did not follow her, and after a moment, she went back to him.

"Denny, I hear you. But you will never understand why I did what I did. Contrary to what you believe, I did what I had to do for Tom. He'll get over this, and me. He'll find someone to grow old with. He deserves it. I love him that much to make sure he gets that."

* * *

Leona was in the kitchen helping Mrs. Callahan with a fresh coffee setup when Charlie stepped back into the house. She had just started a fresh pot. Charlie reached for a cup and pulled out the coffee pot, slipping her cup underneath to catch the fresh streaming coffee.

"Where's Iris?"

Leona nodded toward the back door, and Charlie turned to see Ethan and Iris sharing a cigarette. As she scanned the people, she noticed that everyone spoke quietly to one another. The house was eerily tranquil.

Steve entered through the hallway and reached for a coffee mug. He appeared exhausted, but through it all, he still managed to smile at his guests.

"Where's Tina?" Mrs. Callahan asked as she passed him a plate of croissants.

"She's fallen asleep," Steve told Mrs. Callahan as he waved off the offer, "My poor little angel. She cried a lot today."

"Would you like something else to eat?"

"No, thank you, Mrs. Callahan. I'm not very hungry."

Mrs. Callahan gently touched his arm, then walked toward the hallway.

Charlie set her cup in the sink. "Steve, I'm gonna go home, okay?"

"That's fine. Thanks for...everything."

Charlie gave him a hug and a kiss on the cheek. "Call me if you need anything. I'll be at home."

"Are you gonna be alright? I mean, do you think you should be alone? You could sleep with Tina."

"I'll be fine, thank you." Charlie reached for her purse. "Unless you need me here."

"Oh...no," Steve fumbled, suddenly feeling silly for not wanting to be alone, "I think Mrs. Callahan's going to be here early in the morning for Tina."

Charlie went to the back porch where Iris and Ethan were still sitting, to tell them she was going home.

"Are you sure you don't want me to stay with you?"

"Yes, I'm fine. I am looking forward to being alone." Charlie turned to Ethan, "Thanks for being here for her. She's lucky to have you."

On the way home, Charlie broke down. She cried long and hard in perfect tempo with the windshield wipers that swept away the rain. She had a feeling that she would lose it when she was alone. It was hard being strong in front of everyone, but she did it. It was her turn to mourn for Catherine. By the time she pulled into her driveway, her eyes were swollen and dry.

Charlie walked around the side of the house, not avoiding the puddles of rain, and entered through the sliding glass door in the back

Before entering, she turned her head upward to let the rain fall on her face. When the moment passed, she went inside.

She tossed her purse onto the table next to the door. The street light was shining through the window, giving enough light to navigate through the darkness. Walking into the kitchen, without turning on the lights, she stood in the archway that separated the two rooms. An unfamiliar feeling overcame her. It was as if she did not recognize her own home. It was the oddest sensation, and she could not shake it. Although she was not tired, she did not want to stay awake. Television was a waste of time to her, but since the only other alternative was to do nothing, she opted to watch it.

This day was ranked high on her list of the worst days of her life. In fact, the year had to be the worst year. Charlie slipped off her shoes and jacket and stood at the window. The moon shone through some clouds, and she could see the waves crashing up against the breakers. She remembered the wedding day fiasco, and how Catherine fell in the water with her bridesmaid dress on. Charlie smiled, recalling how it seemed so funny back then. She'd give anything to have the past few weeks to do over again. She would do things differently with that hindsight. She would have listened to Catherine more and would not have taken her for granted. Was that not how it always was? Wishing to go back and change the horrible acts from the past?

After a long moment, she turned and pulled her sweater off as she walked over to the TV. When she reached for the remote atop the TV, she noticed an unmarked videotape. Curious, she popped it into the VCR and hit the rewind button on the remote, then walked down the hallway to her room to change her clothes. She was back in front of the television moments later, comfortable in her pink cotton pajamas. She was holding a pair of socks in her hands and was about to put them on, when she froze in her tracks.

She could not believe what she was seeing. Her mother was on the screen. Charlie dropped the socks on the floor when her mother spoke. Her legs gave out on her. She sank to the floor.

From the television her mother's voice came back from the past.

Hello, Charlie.

Her mother smiled at the camera, then paused for a moment.

*I've made arrangements to have this
delivered to you on your wedding day*

On my behalf.

Her mother straightened on screen, obviously uncomfortable.

*I wanted you to know how much I love
you and how much I wish I could be
with you on your wedding day.*

Charlie stared at the television set, frozen.

*My wish was for you to see this before
your wedding, but I don't want to make
you sad.*

Charlie wanted to turn off the television, but she could not summon the strength. She did not want to see any more, but wild horses could not make her leave the room. Where did the tape come from? Had Catherine left it for her to see?

*I know I haven't been the best example
of happiness or courage, but I want
to encourage you...to take your love
and live it to the fullest. Don't be
afraid. Nobody knows what the next
moment will bring. Somehow we find
the courage to face whatever that is.
So don't waste your life living in fear.
Live, sweetheart. Give it all you've got.*

Charlie closed her eyes and bowed her head. The message from beyond was too hard to comprehend.

*Remember that you only live once, so
make every moment worth while. Be
the best that you can be and...*

(she paused a long moment)

Love with all your heart.

Charlie opened her eyes when she heard the last sentence. It was almost as if her mother had been watching her for the past two weeks and sent her a private message from Heaven. She knew that was impossible, but how could her mother know back when she made this tape that she would have a problem giving in to love? It was eerie, and her hair rose on its ends. Then the irony of it all occurred to her. What if she would have gotten the tape before the wedding?

> *Treasure every moment you have. Yesterday*
> *is history, and you can't ever change that. So*
> *live for tomorrow, because that is where the*
> *true mystery lies.*

Her mother got emotional. It must have hit her, the extent of her words, and how she would not be there to give this message to her daughter in person.

I love you, darlin'.

Charlie watched the screen until the picture turned to snow, then flipped off the television and sat in the darkness. She wanted to rewind the tape and watch it again, but she could not make her hands obey. After a moment, she wondered if the whole tape was an apparition. It seemed too unbelievable to be true.

Unexpectedly, there was a knock. Charlie looked at the front door. She was not expecting anybody, and she definitely did not feel like company. She chose to ignore the door.

A second knock made Charlie realize that it had not come from the front door, but the sliding glass door. She did not know who would come to the back door, but she decided to ignore it. She did not want to see anybody and wished that whoever was at the door would go away.

By the third knock, Charlie almost yelled for the interloper to go away. She did not have to answer the door. It was her house. Then a thought occurred to her. Maybe somebody was hurt on the beach and needed assistance. She flashed another image, thinking that it could be Iris.

Charlie felt for the socks she had dropped on the floor. She suddenly had the urge to put them on. She felt naked and exposed. Quickly, she put them on her feet and darted for the sliding glass door. When she saw who it was, she tried to stop, but the socks made her slide across the linoleum floor. Shock swept through her like a jolt of electricity. Her hand opened the door as her mind screamed in conflict.

She opened the sliding glass door and stepped outside.

"I was in Tokyo. I came back as soon as I heard," Tom announced defensively. He wanted to tell her that he had gone before she told him to leave.

Charlie nodded and looked to the ground. Of all the people she wanted to see at that very moment, it was Tom. Nevertheless, she was at a loss for words.

"I don't know what to say...," Tom reached for Charlie and wrapped his arms around her, "I'm so sorry, baby."

Charlie began to sob. It was as if Tom's touch broke the dam that was holding back all her emotions. Charlie cried hard. She cried for everything she had been holding inside for so long.

Finally Charlie pulled away. Her face was wet and she wiped her eyes with the sleeve of her sweatshirt, "I'm sorry. I'm sorry I hurt you," Charlie said as she buried her face back into his chest.

"Shhh. Don't."

"I thought I was sparing you.... but I was just scared."

"It's okay. It doesn't matter right now."

She pulled away from him, looked him right in the eye, "You were right, I am a coward."

"No, no. I was just angry. I understand where you were coming from now." He brushed hair from her face and wiped away the fresh tears. "I understand."

"I didn't want you to go through what I went through...with my mom...and now what Steve's going through. But it was me..." Charlie tried to stop crying, tried to regain control. "It hurts so much."

"I know," Tom held her and stroked her head as she broke down.

"And then when Catherine told me...I thought I was gonna go crazy. It was like my mother all over again." Charlie cried with abandon, unable to stop the flow of emotions once they had started.

Tom rocked her in his embrace. He let her speak. It had been the first time she had opened up to him in a long time, and he let her spill her emotions.

"I couldn't get the memories out of my mind! I kept seeing my mother's face in Catherine's...,"

Letting go briefly, Tom darted through the house and returned with the throw blanket from the couch, and wrapped it around Charlie. He did not know if she was shivering because she was cold, or if it was because she was upset. Charlie stopped for a moment and turned her face to his. She looked up at him. The tears had washed away any make up that had been there, making her appear younger than she was. Even though her brown eyes were red, they were also wide with an innocence he had never seen.

"Go on, Charlie," Tom urged, his voice sturdy.

"Catherine was so afraid of dying," suddenly Charlie got angry and pulled away from Tom. "Everybody thought Catherine was the one who took care of Mom...because she was older and so mothering...but she wasn't. She was too afraid...I took care of my mother...I was the only one."

Tom did not breathe. He did not know what to say, so he kept quiet.

Charlie's anger turned to sorrow, "I had to feed her...and bathe her...carry her...," Charlie wiped the wetness from her eyes. "...and change her...when she...," Charlie stopped talking, suddenly unable to speak. She gasped for air as if she were having an asthma attack. She put her hand to her face as she tried to stop crying, but the sobbing would not subside. Her body wretched with every child-like sob, and she gulped for breath in between each word.

Tom stepped forward and took her in his arms again and rocked Charlie as he rubbed her back, "It's okay...it's okay."

Charlie continued when she was finally able to speak without whimpering. It was as if she was in a confessional, and Tom was the priest. She let it all out, spilling her heart with everything.

"And then Iris...Iris was no help at all. She went wild...she...," Charlie pulled back. "They left me to deal with all of it by myself! They never helped! They never even came by to see her! Catherine used her new marriage and traveling as an excuse. And Iris, she was always drunk!"

Tom just stood there listening as Charlie vented. He had not known anything about her mother's death and was shocked to hear what she was saying. It was no wonder she was messed up. He had no idea what she had gone through.

"She'd...," Charlie frowned, "Iris...would disappear for days or weeks. And then she'd waltz in with some new guy! Mom would be worried sick about her! She worried about them! When I was the one trying to take care of everything! And then it kept getting worse and worse...I didn't have anyone to turn to...," Charlie started crying again, "And I didn't have anyone."

"It's okay, baby. I'm here now."

Charlie was suddenly angry again. Angry that life had taken Catherine too quickly. She had so many things that she wanted to say to her.

"Everyone thought Catherine was so loving and motherly but she wasn't always that way. She was selfish! She was self-centered and absorbed with her own life that her priorities were fucked up...and then later, she tried to replace mom because she felt guilty for not being around during mom's illness or before her death."

Tom did not know what he should do, so he let her continue. He supposed he would find the right words when they came to him.

"She did take mom's place. She was a miserable bitch who was afraid of everything."

"Don't, Charlie," Tom did not want her to say something that she could not take back.

"You don't know!" Charlie screamed, stepping back from Tom. Charlie was angry with Catherine for dying. Angry with Iris for leaving. Angry that her mother was dead. Angry at the way she turned out. She was angry at life in general. "Catherine was the coward! She could never deal with anything!"

"I know you're upset, Charlie, and her death is a shock, but don't defile her memory." He chose his words carefully, "I hate to say this, especially right now, but you haven't exactly been open either."

Charlie looked at him in disbelief.

Tom continued before she could interrupt. He figured he had nothing to lose and all to gain, so he chose to speak his mind. "None of you ever talked about what happened. You shut down. Iris kept looking for a way out, partying her way through life. Look at her! She doesn't even know from one week to the next where she's going to be. And Catherine...may she rest in peace...Catherine tried to make up for not being there so much so she tried to literally take your mother's place. You need to step outside your own shoes and see just how not dealing with your mother's death has affected the three of you. You're not the only one who's messed up and confused."

Charlie stared at Tom.

"You've been bottling it up for too long. It's time you started letting some of that out. Don't you feel better?"

"I've been so afraid...," Charlie whispered to him, "...for so long."

Tom hugged Charlie tightly, "You're gonna be all right. It's gonna take a while but you'll survive this. You're a fighter, Charlie Hunter."

A sudden gust of wind whipped away the beach blanket.

"Let's go inside," Tom said and he guided her toward the door.

* * *

Iris walked alone along Providence's empty streets at morning's first light, sketchpad under arm. Walking and thinking was what she did when she was unsure of the next step in life. She noticed how the clouds cast interesting shadows by the early rays of sunlight on the buildings and ground. She came to a bridge with a flowing stream that overlooked a park and could not ignore the brilliant colors of the sky cast against the rippling water. It was breathtaking and soothing. She took it all in, closing her eyes and breathing deeply, as if she could inhale the beauty. She suddenly felt inspired.

Iris looked around for a spot she could sketch from. Sitting on a bench, pulling her color charcoals from her back pack, her hand began to dart quickly across the paper, turning the blank sheet into another masterpiece.

As she sketched, tears streamed down her face. The tiny droplets splashed onto the paper. Iris dabbed and smeared them into the charcoal, literally pouring herself into the drawing. After hours of sketching, the streets were becoming filled with people. She finally finished the drawing, her cheeks tight from dry tears. She set the drawing against the park bench she had been sitting on and stepped back to look at what she had created.

The drawing was of the Waterplace Park Bridge. The river flowing below and the brilliant sky above, Iris somehow caught the amazing shadows perfectly. On the bridge, Catherine was looking down, wearing a white gown, like that of an angel. Her long hair was flowing around her face like a golden aura. In the picture, Catherine looked down into the water and she was smiling her familiar bright smile. She had her right hand out and waved. In the water below, the reflection was not Catherine's image, but Iris'.

Iris stared at the picture for a long time.

"Good-bye," Iris whispered, waving back to Catherine's image in her picture, "I'll miss you."

Catherine waved and smiled back at her.

* * *

Looking as if they had been up all night, Charlie and Tom walked together along the water's edge.

"I'm sure Mrs. Callahan will help out," Tom said, trying to reassure Charlie. "You know she's been Tina's babysitter for years."

The gentle wind blasted a gust, and Charlie grabbed her loose brown hair from flying into her face. "This is going to be so hard on Christina."

Charlie thought of the day in the dollhouse and cringed. She knew more than anybody how it felt to lose a mother. Tom, as if reading her thoughts, slipped his hand into hers. There was no other place she would rather be than safely with him. It had been the first time she had told anybody about her resentment for taking care of their mother when she was dying, and how she felt bitter toward her sisters for running away from their responsibility.

"Everything feels so surreal. I can't believe she's gone."

"Yeah. Me neither."

"And now that Iris is going to be so far away...it's weird. I mean, it's like we were never really close...especially not since Mom died, unless you want to call fighting close. But I feel a void. It's like this huge hole opened up in me and the wind's blowing right through."

"I guess a lot of us don't notice what we've got until it's not there anymore." Tom squeezed her hand, knowing she understood the full extent of what he just said. "California isn't that far away. We can always go visit them or they can come back here."

"I don't think Iris wants to be around here. I think it's still really painful for her to remember."

"She should start a new life...," Tom stopped and kissed her on the forehead, "Charlie...and so should we."

Charlie smiled at him, wanting nothing else in life but to be with Tom. She felt guilty for being happy. Was it wrong for her to feel like this?

They walked for a bit, not speaking, stepping away from the incoming tide. Her thoughts were consumed by Iris. "You know, I think Iris has changed a lot in the last few weeks. I think she's finally growing up."

"Maybe so."

Charlie did not know if she was trying to convince herself, or if what she was saying was the truth, "I'm not sure if it's Ethan's influence or everything that's happened, but she seems more...mature."

"He'll take care of her."

"You don't think he'll leave her stranded far away, do you?"

"I don't think so." Tom chuckled. "You're getting way ahead of yourself. Quit worrying about everything. Let things happen. If she ever needs to come back, we can help her. But, I don't think it'll ever come to that. Ethan's a good guy."

Charlie felt relieved, "Yeah...he is. Maybe this is a good thing. Her starting over, that is."

"Good girl!" Tom grabbed her arm, "Let's go take a nap." Tom said, smiling mischievously. Charlie wrapped her arm about his waist and hugged him, then unexpectedly took off running toward her house. Tom took off after her.

Chapter 43

∧

Iris and Charlie sat at the kitchen table with two steaming cups of coffee. An envelope sat on the table between them.

"Yeah, well, Father Jack was pretty surprised, too," Iris said, reaching for the sugar bowl and putting a couple of helpings into her coffee.

"I should go see him. I'm sure it would help resolve some issues."

Iris added, "Yeah, he said a lot of good stuff. He talked about how faith in God and life gets really shaken with death, especially if it's sudden."

Charlie looked at her sister with new eyes.

"I'm going to call him."

"And he's pretty funny, too."

As they sipped their coffee, Charlie contemplated the envelope in front of her. Iris would not take the money she had put in there, and she was worried about Iris and Ethan sleeping in his van. It could be weeks before they found an apartment. "Are you sure you won't take the money? Just 'til you get settled."

Iris shook her head.

"I just wish you two could stay in a hotel until you find a place." Charlie slid the envelope toward Iris. "I'd really feel much better if you took this."

"I've taken enough of your money. We'll be fine."

"Consider it a loan then. Please."

"Ethan has some money saved up, and we'll look for work as soon as we get there." Iris pushed the envelope back across the table to Charlie, "So don't start acting like Catherine." Speaking before thinking, Iris choked on her words and she quickly apologized, "It just came out."

Charlie chuckled. "Iris, you didn't say anything bad about Catherine. She was bossy. You would never get away without taking it if she were here."

Iris laughed, "You're right." She agreed, but did not take the envelope. "I miss her so much."

"I know," Charlie concurred, "It's so quiet."

"I know. She used to get so mad at me."

"And you at her."

"It's gonna take awhile getting used to this."

"Yeah," Charlie nodded. "She was always there for us. She loved you so much, you know."

"I know, and I threw it back at her all the time. I don't think I ever realized how much I loved her. I took her for granted, and now she's gone."

Charlie reached for Iris' hand.

"I keep expecting her to come in and wipe the table clean." A laugh escaped Iris's lips. Her eyes welled, and she grabbed a paper towel from the roll off the counter, "I've got all these mixed feelings. I'm really excited about going to San Francisco, but at the same time, I feel really sad about leaving you."

"I feel the same way. I'm excited for you, but I'm really going to miss you." Charlie got up to embrace her sister. Hugging was something that was unfamiliar to their family. If Catherine were alive, she would be so proud of them.

"I'm glad you and Tom are going for it again. I knew you and he were destined."

"Yeah?" Charlie asked as she pulled away from Iris. "I didn't think you cared."

"I just didn't know how to get involved. That was always Catherine's department. But now I'm going to butt in when I feel it is necessary, and I hope you would do the same for me."

Charlie reached her hand behind her and pulled the envelope out of her back pocket and placed it in Iris' palm, "Okay, you said it and now I'm insisting."

Iris stared at her sister, "Charlie, I don't want this...," Charlie closed Iris' fingers around the envelope.

"I'm not going to win this one, am I?" Iris smirked.

"Sorry," Charlie said, feeling proud that she had learned from Catherine on how to be persistent.

"It's only a loan. I'm repaying you with interest," Iris said as she folded the envelope and put it into her own pocket.

"Whatever!" Charlie smiled, relieved that they would have money for a hotel if they needed it.

"Charlie?"

"Yessssss," Charlie sang.

"Remember what mom said on the tape...live life to the fullest...give it all you've got? That's what we're doing, right?"

"I think so. Life's too short to do anything but live every day as if it was your last."

Chapter 44

∧

Early the next day, Charlie and Tom stood in the driveway with Ethan and Iris. Ethan's van was parked at the curb.

"I'm going to apply to San Francisco State for the spring semester as soon as we get there. I think my drawings have gotten better, so maybe I'll get accepted."

"A true artist, ever critical. Don't be so hard on yourself. You have a lot of talent, Iris."

Charlie hugged Iris. "I'm really proud of you, Iris." They looked into each other's eyes, and Charlie expressed sisterly love through the gaze. She was really proud of her little sister's sudden maturity. She was finally doing something with her life. Something she really wanted to do, and Charlie felt it was the right thing.

"We should probably head out," Ethan said. "I hate to do this, but you guys could drag this on forever."

They all turned their heads at the sound of an approaching car but returned their attention to each other when they saw that it was only the mailman. He gave a "*hello*" beep and waved after he filled the mailbox. They all waved back.

"Do you guys have snacks for the road?" Tom asked.

"Not yet. We can stop and load up before we hit the highway," Ethan answered.

"Ethan's right. Let's hurry this part up. I don't want to start crying again," Iris said, making an over-dramatic frowning face.

They all walked over to Ethan's van. Iris gave Charlie another hug and jumped inside the van.

Ethan gave Tom a hug. "It's been...real, Mr. Mahoney. Take good care of the Missus."

"You know I will," Tom said, looking over at Charlie. "I'll never let her get away again."

Ethan started to thank Charlie, "Thank you...It's been..."

Charlie interrupted him, "No, thank you, Ethan. You've been a good friend. I'm going to miss you." Charlie nodded toward her sister, "You take good care of the Missus."

Ethan laughed and wrapped his arms around her, giving her a big bear hug. Tom and Charlie stepped back as Ethan hopped into the van.

They waved as the van pulled away. Tom's and Charlie's arms were around each other as they stood at the curb watching the van disappear. Tom slid his arm out and stepped away to go inside, but stopped when Charlie did not follow. He reached forward and tugged on her arm.

"Come on. They're not coming back."

"One can always hope."

"They'll be all right. Trust me. Ethan will take care of her," Tom said as she crossed the front lawn back toward the house.

She was sad. At least she had Tom. She could not imagine going it alone. Charlie shuffled her feet, kicking a rock that was in the grass as she sluggishly walked to the mailbox, opened it, and pulled out the mail. She flipped through it: junk mail, Radio Shack advertisement, Victoria's Secret catalog, ALS/MDA Miami Research Center, Visa bill.

Charlie stopped and her heart skipped a beat.

There was heavy breathing and she realized that it was her own.

Charlie wavered, suddenly feeling like her knees would give out on her. She dropped all the other mail on the ground, holding only the envelope from the Miami ALS/MDA Research Center. She was too numb to open it up. All the fear from the past two weeks rushed through her in one lightning-bolt flash.

Dazedly, she crossed the yard toward Tom. When she looked up at him, he was holding the *For Sale* sign that used to be in her yard.

"So...," Tom said, grinning, "What do you say...back in the ground?"

Charlie looked from Tom to the envelope then back and forth again.

He sensed something was wrong.

"What is it?" He asked fearfully. He had seen that look on her face on their wedding day, and his stomached churned nervously.

Without saying a word, she turned the envelope toward him so he could read the return address. Tom blinked and looked deeply into her fear-filled eyes. He felt sick and could not imagine what she was feeling. In the past twenty-four hours, they had come so far, and he was afraid that the progress they had just made would all be in vain. He did not know what to say to her.

Charlie turned the envelope back to her and she looked at it for a long moment.

Tom tilted her chin toward him. "I love you."

Charlie forced a weak smile then returned her stare back at the envelope in her hand.

"You know what?" Charlie finally said. "I don't want to know!" Her mind raced wildly. She could not believe what she was saying. All she knew was that she did not want to live with that fear. What good could come from knowing? Catherine knew, and it did not help her. There was not a cure for ALS, and she could not imagine sitting and waiting to get sick. If she read the results, then the experience of what she had been through the past few weeks - Catherine's death, and the progress she had made in opening up, her mother's message from beyond - would all have been in vain. There was a reason her mother left the videotape. She needed to take her mother's advice. It was finally clear to her. Charlie looked up at Tom with sudden clarity.

Tom watched Charlie not knowing what to do. He was too afraid to say anything. This was her decision and her decision alone. He just stood there with the sign in his hand.

Charlie bit her lip then announced to him, "I don't want to know if I carry the gene. I mean, what difference does it make? It's not like I can prevent the onset by knowing."

Tom paused, waiting to see if she changed her mind before he answered, "Are you sure?"

"Yes," she held the envelope out to him, "What about you? Do you want to see the results? You have the right, you know."

Tom pushed her hand away, "No. I'm with you."

"I want to live and love one day at a time, just like everyone else." When Charlie said it, she was genuinely surprised at how much she truly believed what she was saying.

"That's my girl!" Tom said excitedly as he jammed the *For Sale* sign back into the ground.

Charlie jumped into his arms and they kissed. For the first time in her life, she made a decision she was proud of. It was not a hasty decision, nor vague. It felt good to do something that she believed in wholeheartedly. She was not a coward hiding behind her fears.

"Charlie Hunter is in control of her own destiny!" she announced to the world, her arms wide open and accepting.

Tom twirled her around, "That's right, baby! It's you and me against the world!"

Healthwise, the future was unclear. The only thing Charlie knew for certain was that, for the first time in her life, she did not want to know what was right around the corner. She wanted a normal life, the life her mother should have lived. If she learned from the mistakes of her mother and Catherine, she could be happy. She had Iris, and they were a family. Catherine's dedication had shown her how to accept loved ones with or without their faults. Charlie now understood Catherine's intention. She sacrificed her last few precious days on earth for her sisters, trying desperately to undo the wrong from her past. It was her way of apologizing for neglecting her responsibilities and leaving Charlie with all the duties in caring for their dying mother.

Charlie wanted to live and love fully. If she only had one year with Tom or lived to be a hundred and three, she knew one thing for sure. There was no other place she would rather be than in his arms.

Forever.

The Beginning

After Note For The Reader

This story's subplot, ALS (Amyotrophic Lateral Sclerosis but more commonly referred to as Lou Gehrig's disease) is based from my own experience with my mother and her diagnosis with this disease. My encounter with the disease and how it affected my life does not necessarily mean that every case will be the same. By no means am I apologizing for my story and how I told it, but I feel that it should be addressed. Even though the characters were fictional, the ALS storyline was based from my perception of how things really happened in my life. My mother, Christine Hahn, was a brave person who faced unknown certainty with unbelievable courage.

She was diagnosed with ALS in 1993. At that time, she was having a problem with her arms and feet falling asleep. Six months later, she passed away, completely crippled and unable to breath. The sad thing about ALS is that it cripples your body but leaves your mind a hundred percent effective. My grandfather and my mother were both diagnosed with the disease, which means that my mother's side of the family carries the familial type ALS. There is no cure for ALS so now you can probably imagine where Charlie's fear was derived from. When I remarried, it was after my mother had passed away and the question kept haunting me, *How could I marry again knowing that there is a chance I could have this disease?* Through my writing and Charlie's life lesson, I learned to face the fear and live life to the fullest. I am thirty-six years old and am finally achieving my goal. Better late than never!

Amyotrophic Lateral Sclerosis (ALS) is a progressive disease of the nervous system. The cause is not known and there is no cure, although progress is being made on both fronts. ALS is also known as Lou Gehrig's disease after the famous baseball player who died from it.

ALS attacks motor neurons, which are among the largest of all nerve cells in the brain and spinal cord. In ALS, motor neurons die and the muscles do not receive then messages. As a result, muscles weaken and they lose their ability to move. There is, however, no loss of sensory nerves, so people with ALS retain their sense of feeling, sight, hearing, smell, and taste.

Significant progress is being made in the study of ALS. Although there is still no cure, recent clinical trials have shown that some drugs may increase the survival time for people with ALS. Only through continued research can we hope for more treatments and a cure.

For More Information Contact:
The University of Miami, Kessenich Family MDA ALS Center
Medical Director, Walter G. Bradley, DM,FRCP
1150 NW 14th Street, Suite 700
Miami, FL 33136
www.miami-als.org
1-800-690-ALS1 (2571)
305-243-7400